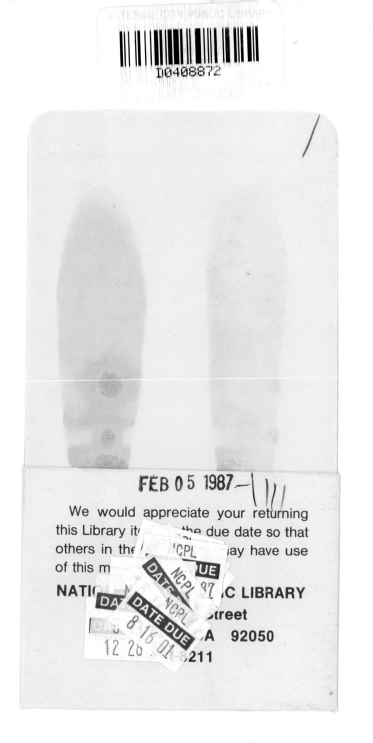

The Crossfire Killings

The Crossfire Killings

BILL KNOX

PUBLISHED FOR THE CRIME CLUB BY

DOUBLEDAY & COMPANY, INC.

GARDEN CITY, NEW YORK

1986

For Susan and John

All of the characters in this book
are fictitious, and any resemblance
to actual persons, living or dead,
is purely coincidental.

Library of Congress Catalog Card Number 86–2124
Library of Congress Cataloging-in-Publication Data

Knox, Bill, 1928–
The crossfire killings.

I. Title.
PR6061.N6C7   1986   823′.914
ISBN 0-385-23544-5

The Crossfire Killings

For practical reasons, some operational details in this story differ a little from those of the real-life Scottish Crime Squad's normal pattern. They prefer it that way.

B.K.
Glasgow, Scotland

PRELUDE

ZL 019   071732
FROM   DUTY OFFICER, HELENSBURGH
TO   DUTY OFFICER, CONTROL, DUMBARTON
           HQ CONTROL
           SUPT. LOCHGILPHEAD

<u>FOUND BODY.   LOCH LOMOND</u>
ABOUT 1330 HOURS TODAY TWO BACK-PACK HIKERS (1)
JAMES MOLLINS, BEAR AVE., GLASGOW, AGE 20,
UNEMPLOYED (2) SHEILA MARY HAZEL, FRIAR SQUARE,
CLYDEBANK, AGE 19, STUDENT, WERE WALKING ALONG
SHORE NEAR FEAN COVE WHEN THEY FOUND AFTER
DESCRIBED BODY AT FOOT OF ROCK FACE.
FEMALE, WHITE, 30–35 YRS., 5'5" MEDIUM BUILD, SHORT
BLACK HAIR, GREEN EYES.
WEARING—GREY SLACKS, GREEN SWEATER, WHITE
LACE-UP JOGGING SHOE ON LEFT FOOT, GREY SOCKS,
WHITE BRA, WHITE PANTS. YELLOW METAL RING,
SMALL BLUE STONE, NO INSCRIPTION, THIRD FINGER
RIGHT HAND.
WITNESSES REPORTED FIND TO POLICE, ARROCHAR, BY
TELEPHONE.
SGT. MACLEAN AND CONS. HARRISON MET WITNESSES
14.15, RETURNED TO LOCUS.
(PART ONE OF TWO-PART MESSAGE.)

ZL020   071735
FROM   DUTY OFFICER, HELENSBURGH
TO   DUTY OFFICER, CONTROL, DUMBARTON
         HQ CONTROL
         SUPT. LOCHGILPHEAD

FOUND BODY. LOCH LOMOND (PART TWO OF TWO-
PART MESSAGE)
ON EXAMINATION OF BODY, VARIOUS INJURIES AND
ABRASIONS INDICATED POSSIBLE FALL FROM ROCKS
ABOVE. TRACES OF BLOOD REMAINING DESPITE HEAVY
OVERNIGHT RAIN. CLOTHING WET WHERE EXPOSED,
DRY BENEATH BODY. SEARCH OF SURROUNDING AREA
REVEALED GREEN NYLON WATERPROOF ANORAK
JACKET, SIZE 14, NO MAKER TAB. SECOND SHOE JAMMED
IN ROCK ABOVE. POCKET CONTENTS SMALL SUM
MONEY (COINS), ONE CHOCOLATE BAR, PAPER TISSUES.
NO ID.
SEARCH CONDUCTED OF WIDER AREA WITHOUT
RESULT.
BODY REMOVED HELENSBURGH MORTUARY 15.40 HRS.
DR. J. FARRELL EXAMINED, REPORTED INJURIES
PERHAPS CONSISTENT WITH FALL BUT REQUESTS
PATHOLOGIST ATTENDS. DR. FARRELL OF OPINION
WOMAN DEAD BETWEEN FIVE AND EIGHT DAYS.
D.I. DONALDSON NOW CONTINUING INQUIRIES.
MESSAGE ENDS. AUTHORISING OFFICER SGT. BANKS.

ZL005   080910
FROM   DUTY OFFICER, HELENSBURGH
TO   DUTY OFFICER, CONTROL, DUMBARTON
         HQ CONTROL
         ALL SCOTTISH FORCES

UNIDENTIFIED FEMALE FOUND DEAD, LOCH LOMOND
REFERENCE ABOVE YESTERDAY, POST MORTEM

REPORTS DEATH DUE TO MULTIPLE INJURIES. FURTHER
FORENSIC TESTS UNDER WAY. ADDITIONAL
DESCRIPTION OF FEMALE AS FOLLOWS:
AGE APPROX. 37 YRS. HAS HAD APPENDIX OPERATION,
OLD FRACTURE RIGHT WRIST. MOLE INNER RIGHT
THIGH. DESCRIPTION OF TEETH: LOWER JAW, FOUR
INCISORS, BOTH CANINES PLUS RIGHT PRE MOLAR,
UPPER JAW, FOUR INCISORS LEFT CANINE FIRST MOLAR
RIGHT FIRST AND SECOND PRE MOLARS PLUS TWO
MOLARS. FILLINGS TO FOUR TEETH. NOW ESTIMATES
DEATH OCCURRED FIVE TO SIX DAYS BEFORE
DISCOVERY.
FINGERPRINTS OBTAINED AND FORWARDED WITH
DENTAL CHART TO HQ CONTROL, STRATHCLYDE.
REQUEST CHECK OF MISSING PERSONS LISTS FOR
POSSIBLE ID.
FURTHER ENQUIRIES CONTINUE, LOCH LOMOND AREA,
BUT NEGATIVE TO DATE. MESSAGE ENDS. AUTHORISING
OFFICER CHIEF INSP. HAY

SHQC 176   081544
FROM   STRATHPOL HQ (CHIEF SUPT GAVIN)
TO   GRAMPIAN POL HQ ABERDEEN (SUPT LAUDER)

CONFIRMING MY TELEPHONE MESSAGE. BODY OF
WOMAN FOUND LOCH LOMOND YESTERDAY
IDENTIFIED AS THAT OF DET. SERGEANT MARY
ELIZABETH DUTTON, STRATHCLYDE POLICE. ON
DETACHED DUTY SCOTTISH CRIME SQUAD. DET.
SERGEANT DUTTON DIED WHILE ON ANNUAL LEAVE.
PLEASE ADVISE AND EXPRESS ALL DEEPEST SYMPATHY
TO NEXT OF KIN, MOTHER, MRS. MARGARET MARY
DUTTON, DRYBANK FARM, NR. DYCE, ABZ. STRATHCLYDE
SENIOR OFFICER AND FORCE WELFARE OFFICER WILL
TRAVEL ABN FROM HERE LATER THIS PM. WILL

CONFIRM FINAL DETAILS. GRATEFUL IF YOU MEET AND
LIAISE.
MESSAGE ENDS.

Aberdeen Press and Journal, Thursday, May 9

DUTTON   Suddenly, the result of an accident, Mary Elizabeth,
Det. Sergeant, Strathclyde Police, beloved daughter of the late Chief
Inspector Henry John Dutton (retired), Grampian Police and Margaret
Mary Dutton, Drybank Farm, Dyce. Funeral arrangements later. No
flowers or letters please but grateful thanks to all friends and fellow
officers.

CHAPTER ONE

It was May, a sunny Tuesday afternoon, and the Glasgow skyline was a shimmer of concrete and glass punctuated at intervals by an older slate roof or a thin church spire. Even the Clyde, normally a lazy grey-blue ribbon of water, showed a glint of early summer as it flowed between the cranes and warehouses of the old, dying riverside dockland and the crisp, modern lines of the new waterfront developments which were taking their place.

The Strathclyde Police training centre was located in a parkland area about two miles south of the river, handily close to the M8 motorway. An unusual number of cars had driven through its gateway from mid-day onward because it was an important afternoon for the Dog Branch, the passing out display of a dozen dogs and their handlers, the end of a long programme of training and schooling.

Leaning against the white timber rail on one side of the display area, Detective Superintendent Colin Thane considered the group of dogs waiting at the start line for the next session. Their coats gleamed in the sunlight, the result of long hours of grooming. Some quivered with excitement, as if sensing this was no ordinary outing. One gave an impatient bark.

"You picked a good day," he told the lean, grey-haired chief inspector beside him.

"Not bad. I hope it's as good on Monday."

"Monday?" asked Thane.

"The May public holiday," said the chief inspector patiently. "I'm off duty, I'm going sea-fishing."

Thane indicated the dogs. "This bunch seem all right."

"They are." The man gave a pleased smile. "Damned clever devils, some of them. A couple of the new handlers aren't too bright."

Colin Thane grinned at the man. Chief Inspector Jim Preacher ran the Dog Branch with an awesome enthusiasm and dedication. Some people claimed he even barked in his sleep, and Preacher openly admitted he preferred most dogs to most people.

"You get top marks from me." Thane meant it. Already the dogs—all of them young, only one over two years old—had made an effortless job of tackling the training school's outdoor obstacle course. It was a series of ladders and walls, platforms and tunnels, plus a few extras that no cop in his right mind would have tackled. "Your usual standard."

"We try." Preacher was always wary of compliments. "I'll be happier once this next part is over."

Thane nodded. He had already exchanged greetings with most of the other visitors. They came from a scatter of forces and specialist law enforcement units, men and women from drug teams and bomb squads, from divisional units, and from a couple more who didn't like any label attached to what they did.

By the end of the week, all of the dogs they'd come to see would have begun active duty. That was part of the reason he was there, as joint deputy commander of the Scottish Crime Squad. But the rest of it amounted to a diplomatic mission.

An elite, low-profile and often undercover unit, the Scottish Crime Squad's operational base was a small huddle of anonymous buildings inside the Strathclyde training centre. That made the Dog Branch one of their next-door neighbours as well as part of the landlord's family. Even the best of neighbours could fall out, and the latest incident, a head-on shunt between a Dog Branch van and a Crime Squad car at the entrance gate, hadn't helped.

Now, on top of all that, some desk-bound Government expert with nothing better to do had decided the Crime Squad should make more use of dogs, should have at least one police dog on strength for an experimental period, with the aim of improved efficiency. The directors had stirred up delighted sarcasm from the Dog mob and acid derision from the Crime Squad's rank and file.

"Here we go." Preacher gave him a nudge. A young, black, deep-chested German Shepherd was being led forward by his handler, a young, freckle-faced constable in blue overalls. "You know the basics, Superintendent. This batch are all dual-purpose trained—general patrol duties and special searching, either explosives or drugs."

"This one?"

"This is Ringo—explosives trained."

The patch of scarred brown earth in front of them had been divided into a number of different sections, each about the size of a tennis court. Ringo's handler led him to one section then slipped the dog's leash and stood back.

"Go, Ringo," said Preacher as the sleek black animal set to work, nose close to the ground, working carefully. "Show them, lad."

Thane watched, fascinated. He'd often seen the dogs training, knew the way sniffing was played as a game in the early stages. First a young dog was encouraged to retrieve a scent-impregnated toy thrown like a stick, then gradually taken on from there. Once a dog was fully trained, new scents could be added to its repertoire as required—it knew what was wanted.

The black German Shepherd certainly did. It had finished quartering the area and was narrowing the hunt.

"Too damned nervous," muttered Preacher. He pointed towards the freckle-faced handler, who was watching tensely. "I mean him. Trust your dog—I keep telling him. Act twitchy and the animal knows it, feels the same way." Then, suddenly, he relaxed. "That's my boy—now sort it out."

Ringo was slowly inspecting one particular patch of ground. It looked no different from the rest, but the onlookers had seen a candlestub length of gelignite first wrapped in plastic then buried there, fifteen inches down. After that, a group of sergeant instructors and their personal dogs had marched several times over the whole section.

The dog stopped, glanced back at his handler, pawed the ground, and gave a short, sharp woof.

"Handler forward," ordered Preacher.

The freckle-faced constable almost tripped as he ran across. He marked the spot with a small, sharp stake then stood back as a sergeant instructor came over with a spade. The sergeant dug briefly, retrieved the plastic-wrapped explosive, and held it up while Thane joined in the hand-clapping praise. The constable dropped down, gave his big black dog an affectionate hug—and Thane could have sworn the dog grinned.

"At least they like each other," sighed Preacher. "Ach, maybe the dog can bring him on."

"How often do they fail?" asked Thane.

"Dogs, not often. Handlers, plenty of times." Preacher's lean face showed he felt that was the way things should be. "A dog doesn't get far on training unless it has the temperament, the dedication. Plenty of cops think they'd like to pose around with a dog, then get a fright when they discover the real work involved."

Another animal was already at the start line, a young Labrador bitch. Her handler was tall and lanky, an older man with a sleepy, lived-in face. Their test, in the next sector, was to locate a small quantity of cocaine wrapped in metal foil and buried the same fifteen inches down.

"This one is Goldie," said Preacher. "She's different—I'll guarantee it."

The Labrador bitch stopped as her leash was slipped. Sitting down, she gave herself a quick scratch, looked around, then yawned.

"Typical female." Preacher allowed himself a hint of amusement. "She's home and dry before she starts—but she'll prowl around a little, putting on an act, pretending things are difficult. That's why we teamed her with Jock Dawson—her handler. He works the same way."

Thane considered the lanky constable. The man's hands were in his overall pockets, and he seemed totally relaxed.

"He seems to know what he's doing."

"He does. He's been handling a long time—but he needs a new dog." Preacher gave his guest an odd, sideways glance. "What do you think of them?"

Thane waited. The Labrador bitch, her golden coat rippling as she moved, was making a leisurely circuit of her allocated sector. At the finish, she paused for another scratch. Then she ambled off again, stopped, and sat down. Without waiting for an order, the lanky constable made an equally leisurely way across. He felt in his pockets for his marker stake, couldn't find it, and dug the heel of one boot into the ground instead.

"It's there." Jim Preacher shrugged in resignation while the same sergeant instructor used his spade again and produced the foil-wrapped drug sample. He waited until the mixture of applause and laughter died down. "Well?"

"Pretty good," agreed Thane.

"Aye, I hoped you'd say that," said Preacher innocently. "You know this business about your bunch wanting a dog?"

"I know this business about being told we're getting one," corrected Thane. He sensed what was coming. "You mean—?"

"Goldie and Dawson." The Dog Branch chief inspector beamed.

"They're yours, Superintendent. Enjoy them—they can start tomorrow." He paused, a devil of mischief in his eyes. "I can't think of a pair I'd rather see going your way. Your people deserve the best, right?"

Thane drew a deep breath. He had a nasty feeling the Dog mob had just won another round, but there was nothing he could do about it.

"Tomorrow," he agreed. "And Chief Inspector—"

"Sir?" Preacher was still smiling.

"Damn you for a conniving villain."

Preacher managed to look hurt.

Colin Thane watched another couple of dogs go through their paces then left. It was a two-minute walk across the parkland to the Scottish Crime Squad's headquarters and it was too good an afternoon to feel annoyed about anything. Clear of the demonstration area, he lengthened his stride a little, felt the short grass springy under his feet, and began humming under his breath.

He was a tall, grey-eyed man in his early forties with thick dark hair, regular features and a muscular build. Wearing a lightweight Lovat tweed suit, a white shirt and a quietly patterned tie—a present from his daughter—his shoes were a pair of brown leather moccasins, old enough to be comfortable. Maybe he was a few pounds overweight.

The rest wasn't so obvious, spanning a police career which had begun as a beat cop in one of the toughest back-street sectors of Glasgow. Before his promotion to superintendent and immediate secondment to the Scottish Crime Squad, he'd been the youngest division C.I.D. chief in that city.

He'd got there the hard way. So far he'd survived.

The Crime Squad main building was a modern single-storey structure with discreet ground surveillance TV cameras and an anonymous parking lot. As he arrived, Thane thought about how to break the news about their new recruits to Jack Hart, the Squad commander.

Hart didn't like any kind of police dog. Once, a long time ago, a large, excited Doberman had mistaken him for an escaping thief. Hart, a section sergeant then, had needed five stitches in his leg and a course of anti-tetanus shots. His section had solemnly taken a collection and had sent the Doberman a gift-wrapped bone.

No, Hart wasn't going to be pleased.

He went in through the glass entrance doors into a brightly lit lobby.

The girl at the reception counter was a good-looking and happily married detective constable with two commendations for bravery. She had an office job because she was pregnant.

"Superintendent."

Usually she was the kind of girl who had a smile for everyone. But not this time. Her face was pale and she looked angry. "Commander Hart wants you, straight away."

"Something on?" He looked past her. The usual bank of TV monitor screens and VDU terminals were flickering; one of the Squad's several telex machines was quietly chattering. But there was no sign of Maggie Fyffe, who was Commander Hart's secretary and ran the outer office. "What's happening?"

"It's Mary Dutton. Maybe it wasn't an accident." The girl bit her lip. "I was at her funeral yesterday. We went through training school together."

Thane was taken totally by surprise. Before he could say anything, shoes clicked towards them over the terrazzo floor, and Maggie Fyffe appeared from the corridor that led to Jack Hart's office. Middle-aged, always smartly dressed, Maggie Fyffe was a cop's widow and usually kept her emotions tightly caged.

"Better go straight through," she advised. "Forget about the dogs."

He went along the corridor to the door marked "Commander" and pressed the button beside it. The green "enter" light spat an immediate answer and he went in, nodding to the two men already there then closing the door again.

Jack Hart, a sad-eyed man with a lined face and high cheekbones, was at his desk with a thin file of papers open in front of him. The man sitting opposite him was Tom Maxwell, the Squad's other deputy commander.

"You've heard?" asked Commander Hart.

"Mary Dutton." Thane settled in the vacant chair beside Maxwell.

"Detective Sergeant Dutton," said Hart. The sunlight was pouring in through the large, double-glazed window behind him, striking his desk at an angle, casting its shadow on the dark green carpeting, emphasising the lines on his face. "How well did you know her?"

Thane shook his head. "I worked with her on a couple of cases, that's all."

He waited. He got on well with both men even though he ranked junior in the trio. Though it was never mentioned, Maxwell had six months seniority as a superintendent. But for once he could sense a degree of tension between Hart and Maxwell, as if something had been cut short by his arrival.

"Tell him, Tom," ordered Hart.

"I had Mary working with me for almost a year—and I knew her father when he was alive." Maxwell spoke quietly. Grey-haired, medium height and medium build, Tom Maxwell could have been mistaken for a bank manager most of the time. But he walked with a limp, a permanent souvenir of a fall from a roof when he'd been chasing an armed bandit. "Eventually she wanted a change, so she switched to one of the under-cover surveillance teams—that was before you came."

"So you knew her fairly well," said Thane.

Maxwell shrugged. "I suppose. Better than most people here, though that's not saying a lot. She was a loner."

"She was also a damned good cop." Hart cut him short. "Colin, the funeral was yesterday, in Aberdeen. Tom was our official representative —you know that."

"A couple of car-loads of us went up. Then there were some Strath-clyde people and a few from the Aberdeen force—they still remember her father." Maxwell gave a slight grimace. "I stayed on afterwards, to talk with her mother, to make sure she could cope with any problems— the usual thing."

Thane nodded. He had had to do it twice in his career. He didn't want a third time.

"Tom—" Hart made it almost a plea, and drummed the fingers of one hand lightly on his desktop.

"He needs the background," said Maxwell. "Damn it, Jack, she was one of our own people."

The Squad commander frowned and a slight chill entered his voice. "I don't intend to forget it, Tom, believe me."

Thane stayed back from it. Mary Dutton . . . he could picture a snub-nosed face and that short black hair. She had been plump, and she had had a raucous laugh. But what else? It wasn't easy to really remember.

"I talked with her mother," said Maxwell. "She will be all right, she's made that way. There was someone else there, one of Mary's friends."

"Sheila Swann," murmured Commander Hart, glancing at the opened file. "Age thirty, single, lives and works in Glasgow, occupation social worker. Go on, Tom."

"I'm trying," said Maxwell. "Shelia Swann had just got back from a holiday in Spain. She started work again today." Pausing, he reached into his jacket and produced a colour postcard from an inside pocket. "This was waiting at her office—from Mary Dutton."

Thane took the postcard. The photograph was a tourist-style view of Loch Lomond—blue water and green hills with a patch of purple heather in the foreground.

"The girl telephoned me in her lunch-hour," explained Maxwell. "I went to see her, get this from her, then came straight back. Read it."

Thane turned to the other side of the card. The smudged cancellation mark across the stamp showed it had been posted in the village of Arrochar on May 12. He switched his attention to the bold, firm handwriting, read the words, stared, then read them again, more slowly. Now he knew why both Hart and Maxwell were on edge.

"Weather fine, enjoying it all, don't regret Peace Camp. But two old customers have showed—God knows why, they're not peaceful material. Moving on before they remember me. Hope you're Viva Espagna-ing okay, and behaving. Love Mary."

He set the postcard down on Hart's desk, mentally cursing the staccato style of all holiday cards.

"May 12—three days into her leave," said Hart. "The post mortem estimate of time of death is either May 12 or 13, they can't narrow it more."

Thane drew a deep breath. "This Peace Camp, and the 'two old customers'?"

It was Maxwell's turn. "We knew about the camp. It's in the hills above Arrochar—semi-permanent. Ban the Bomb, Meditate against the Military." He gave a shrug. "That was Mary's style. But what she did in her own time—"

"And the 'two old customers'?"

"Could be any pair of villains she ever dealt with," said Maxwell. "Her mother showed me a card she'd received, posted the same day, but it just said everything was fine."

Thane laid the postcard on top of the file on Hart's desk. A car started up somewhere outside and he could hear a telephone ringing in another office. He looked at Hart.

"What else?" There had to be more. He was certain of that much.

"Not a lot—yet. But try putting them together." Hart spoke slowly. The telephone in the background stopped ringing as he went on. "First, we know Mary left the Peace Camp that morning—on her own, the way she'd arrived, no explanations. She was carrying a back-pack, which hasn't been found. Second, according to Sheila Swann, her original plan had been to stay there a week."

"Then she falls down a rock face," said Maxwell bitterly. "Everyone says terrible, nobody really asks did she fall or was she pushed—and that includes me."

"All of us," Hart said. "I'll spell it out, Colin. It looked like an accident, so right from the start things were read that way—and I'm not blaming anyone. It happens, maybe people get careless or maybe they just want to hurry the whole business along, make it easier on relatives."

"But what about the post mortem?" Thane still felt bewildered.

The same telephone began ringing again. Thane wished someone would answer it; he wanted the file lying in front of the Squad commander, but he knew he would have to wait.

"I've got a copy of the report," Hart said. "Death due to multiple injuries, the apparent result of a fall, a vague mention they'd maybe run some further tests." He grimaced. "Well, now our pathologist friends aren't so happy. They're reviewing their initial report, preparing a new one."

"Have they said why?"

"No." The telephone had stopped ringing in the other office but there was a new sound from outside, the clatter of a tractor-drawn grass cutter. It came into sight, spouting a green haze of mown grass as it rattled past. Hart let the noise fade a little. "That's one of the first things you're going to have to find out."

Thane gave Tom Maxwell a sideways glance. The other man's normally placid face was stony and he muttered something under his breath.

"I've told you, Tom. I'm Squad commander, it's my decision." Hart shook his head with a degree of sympathy. "You're too damned close to it—family friend and the rest." He switched to Thane, seeking some kind of support. "You want the practical side? The Carran brothers go on trial in the High Court tomorrow. Do I go and tell the judge the main Crown witness is too busy to attend?"

There was no answer to that. The Carran brothers were twins, called themselves design consultants, and had used that as a cover for a vicious blackmail and extortion racket with a long trail of victims left broken and ruined. Two had committed suicide. It had taken months with the Carrans as a target operation before Tom Maxwell had been able to bring them in. It had been a major effort in committed time and man-power; there was no way it could be endangered.

"So." Commander Hart took their silence as enough. "Colin, put everything you can on hold, I'll reassign the rest." He pushed the file across the desk. "That's yours. Speak to Sheila Swann, try to nail down this post-mortem shambles—"

"Who's handling that end?" asked Thane warily.

"Now?" Hart allowed himself a wintery grin. "You could say God has moved in."

"MacMaster?" Thane winced. Professor Andrew MacMaster held the Regius chair of Forensic Medicine at Glasgow University, treated most of his professional colleagues with a benign contempt, and openly con-sidered the police a rabble of illiterate peasantry. But MacMaster, an elderly, dried-up stick of a figure, also possessed one of the finest medico-legal minds in the Western world. When he took over a case, when he found error, someone was likely to be nailed to a wall. "I suppose—"

"Yes. He's expecting you this afternoon."

Thane sighed. "How do we stand with Strathclyde?"

It mattered. Detective Sergeant Mary Dutton, still officially a Strath-clyde officer though posted to the Crime Squad, had died in Strathclyde police territory. Strathclyde officers had carried out the usual investiga-tions, identified her. By rights, she was their case.

But the Scottish Crime Squad position, as usual, was unique. Central Government funded, free of ties to any regional force, it worked inde-pendently, chose its own target cases, prowled where it wanted. As S.C.S. commander, Jack Hart could ignore regional boundaries and po-lice protocol—in most situations. He usually tried for some kind of diplo-matic understanding, then went ahead anyway.

"Their A.C.C. Crime knows we're going in." Hart spoke deliberately. "He doesn't like it, but I've patched up an agreement he can sell to his Chief Constable. For now, we own the operation. Later, depending on how things shape, if we're on a murder hunt, it becomes a joint opera-tion. But I don't want any kind of war with Strathclyde—particularly not on this one. Understood?"

They nodded, Maxwell still unhappy.

"Good." Hart settled back in his chair. "That's it—except for one thing, Colin. The man who ran the Strathclyde enquiry paperwork was your pal Phil Moss."

Thane winced. Detective Inspector Phil Moss was on Strathclyde's headquarters staff. But before that he'd been Thane's divisional C.I.D. partner for several years and was still a close friend.

"He needs his tail kicked," said Maxwell.

"Maybe—maybe not." Hart eyed Thane. "It's too early to say. I don't want anyone around here acting as judge and jury, either way."

He glanced at his watch, a sign the meeting was over. But as Thane and Maxwell rose to leave, he beckoned.

"Wait, Colin. Something separate."

Maxwell shrugged and left them. As the door slammed shut, Hart sighed and shook his head.

"Our Tom is anything but happy, and I'd feel the same way," he said wryly. Producing his cigarettes, he lit one. "Now—what about this damned dog business?"

Thane had almost forgotten. "One starts with us tomorrow."

"Great," said Hart sarcastically. "Some hairy, four-legged slavering thug of an animal, I suppose?"

"She's a Labrador bitch." Thane realised he sounded almost defensive. "I saw her working—she's good."

"Her, it—what difference?" Hart drew on his cigarette and considered Thane again, frowning. "I forgot. You're a card-carrying dog owner."

"Yes." Meaning a large comedian of an animal, a Boxer dog who answered to Clyde, and caused regular chaos in the Thane household.

"Nobody's perfect." Hart sucked his teeth for a moment. "All right, we'll sort out something for the brute once she gets here." The matter dropped from his mind. "Mary Dutton. Say something to the troops. They'll know by now, but make it official."

Thane nodded. As he turned to leave, the Mary Dutton file in one hand, he saw the Squad commander lift another folder from the carpeted floor. It was yellow in colour, much thicker, the S.C.S. budget requisition for the year ahead.

Jack Hart had been working on it for the last couple of weeks. Soon he'd have to battle the requisition through a committee of Government

ministers and civil service bureaucrats. Not everybody liked the Scottish
Crime Squad's existence; Hart would have to be ready for a hard sell job.

He had been ready to find Maxwell lurking outside, but there was no
sign of his opposite number and Maxwell's office door was closed.

Farther along, the main duty room was always busy in the late afternoon. It was a time when some of the day shift began drifting back,
when the first of the night teams began to appear. It usually meant noisy
gossip around the desks, telephone calls, a rapid pecking at typewriters as
reports were roughed out.

Thane went in. There were about a score of men and women in the
big, open-plan area, most of them standing around in small groups. Few
looked like police officers; some could have been candidates for a line-up
parade. But there was an oddly subdued air over everything, and the
room went silent as he was spotted.

Looking around, Thane saw the people he wanted. Francey Dunbar
was a detective sergeant, in his twenties, with a mop of jet black hair and
a thin straggle of moustache. As casually dressed as the rest, he was
sitting with his feet up on a desk and looked half-asleep. The other, a
tall, slim, red-haired girl wearing a man's plaid wool shirt over denim
trousers, had been talking to a bulky, unshaven sergeant more or less
affectionately known as the Animal. Her name was Sandra Craig, and
she was a detective constable.

Thane gave Dunbar and Sandra Craig a slight nod in the general
direction of his office. He knew the rest of the duty room were waiting.

"All right." He raised his voice. "You've heard about Mary Dutton.
We don't know anything for sure, we're going to find out. When we do,
you'll hear as soon as anyone." He paused. "Who was friendly with her
—I mean really friendly?"

The duty room stayed silent for a moment, he saw frowns and glances,
then a petite blonde girl with heavy makeup, a short leather skirt and a
skin-tight sweater raised a hand.

"Me, I suppose, sir. At least, we talked sometimes. But she didn't
communicate too much."

"Did she ever mention a Sheila Swann?"

The blonde girl nodded. She was a sergeant, she had a law degree, and
she had an evening rendezvous with a Dutch airline steward who was a
gold smuggler. The Animal would be near at hand as her minder.

"Were they close friends?" asked Thane.

"She never really mentioned anyone else."

Thane pursed his lips. The Dutch steward had led them a few places without realising it, and now he was due to be pulled in.

"What happens tonight with your Dutchman?"

"He's buying me dinner." The blonde girl shaped a smile. "We'll take him as soon as he pays the bill. Unless—"

"No, do it." They needed the Dutchman out of circulation. "But I may want some help later."

The blonde girl nodded.

Thane turned on his heel, left the duty room, and went back along the corridor to his office. Going in, he left the door open and dropped the Mary Dutton file on his desk.

The room was only about half the size of Commander Hart's office, but a lot better than anything he'd had in his old divisional days. Rank brought its varied privileges in the police scale of things, including the carpet on the floor. The view from the window was out across the Squad parking lot, with trees beyond that and a distant glimpse of traffic on the city centre-to-airport stretch of the motorway.

Thane watched the ant-sized vehicles for a moment, trying to think ahead, then faced round as he heard a light knock on the door. Francey Dunbar and Sandra Craig came in together, Sandra settling quietly into a spare chair, Dunbar heeling the door shut with a lazy minimum of effort then taking up his favourite position, leaning against Thane's big grey metal filing cabinet.

"Why us?" asked Dunbar without preliminaries. "She was Superintendent Maxwell's Girl Friday for long enough."

"That's your answer," Thane told him. "Think about it."

Dunbar gave a slight grimace. A frown showed on Sandra Craig's face.

"Are we off everything else, sir?" she asked. "Even the whisky hassle?"

"Which could go critical," mused Francey Dunbar.

It might. Three times in so many months a bulk tanker-truck load of malt whisky had been hi-jacked on its way south from the Highlands. The last truck driver had resisted and been savagely beaten. But Francey had picked up a whisper. They now knew who was buying, and the hi-jackers had to make another delivery soon from their hidden stock.

"Sorry, Francey." Thane shook his head.

"We could still keep an eye on it," said Sandra. "There's an equal chance it could tick over for a spell."

Francey Dunbar nodded and stuffed his hands into his pockets in a way that made the heavy silver ID bracelet on his right wrist clink. The name tab was blank, but his blood group was on the underside—both necessary precautions on his personal list.

Sandra Craig and Francey stuck together when it mattered, despite their other differences.

Francey Dunbar could be awkward, even stubborn when he felt inclined. Some thought him a troublemaker, but he'd just been re-elected as the Squad's delegate to the Police Federation. He had an off-duty devotion to a beloved red B.M.W. motor cycle and any girl he could persuade to mount on its pillion. But he also had some surprisingly thoughtful outlooks on life.

Thane still remembered the way he'd been warned about Francey Dunbar. But Dunbar was still the kind of sergeant he wanted. Most of the time, anyway.

Dunbar cleared his throat, a warning on its own. "Somebody botched things up—or that's how it looks," he said dryly. "He won't be too popular."

"He?" Thane raised an eyebrow.

"Phil Moss." Dunbar shrugged. "Except it doesn't seem his style."

"Shut up, Francey," said Sandra Craig wearily. "You'd cause a war in —in—"

"In a peace camp?" suggested Thane without rancour. "That's one start point, this Peace Camp. You take it, Francey."

"Our expert," said Sandra. Dunbar flirted with a range of meditation classes and the occasional contemplation session. "He'll be on home ground."

She was a very different package from Thane's thin-faced sergeant, whose moustache now framed a grin. Sandra Craig had looks and persuasiveness which took her anywhere. In the Squad, she accepted whatever came along and was one of their best pursuit drivers. But she also had the extra edge in being able to handle some situations where a man would have floundered. If she appeared some mornings looking like death and still wearing the previous night's makeup, only Francey dared comment. The biggest mystery of all was the way she could eat anytime, anywhere, yet keep a figure any model would have envied.

Thane had her next on his mental list.

"How much do you know about Mary Dutton?"

"Not a lot." Her mood became instantly serious. "Nobody did, sir—it was the way you heard in the duty room. But people liked her."

"Start asking."

"People like Linda?" She meant the blonde sergeant.

Thane nodded. "Linda, anyone."

"Men," said Francey. "This woman Swann might know."

"Don't push her," warned Thane. "Not yet. Then we've another headache, the biggest and maybe the most important." He took Mary Dutton's postcard from the file, gave it to Francey Dunbar, and waited until he and Sandra both read it. " 'Two old customers—not peaceful material.' All right, Criminal Records can do a computer scan and other checks, give us some kind of list of cases she was directly involved in, names, convictions. But it won't be complete—we need the rest, as much as we can get."

They knew what he meant; their faces showed they knew the size of the task he was handing them. Any detective, any cop, could come in contact with several hundred thieves and crooks and general villains in the course of a working career. They were a police officer's stock in trade, to be known and remembered even if there was never an actual arrest, a charge or a conviction.

"We may need help," warned Dunbar.

"You'll get it," promised Thane. "What about her desk, Sandra? Has it been cleared?"

"No. Not yet—I don't think so." She looked puzzled then understood. "Her notebooks. If we get hold of them—"

"Presuming they're for real," said Dunbar. But he nodded. "We might get lucky."

Police notebooks were supposed to be written up daily—every call, every incident, every name. But it didn't always happen that way. A forgetful or idle cop could end up with a panic writing session near the end of a month, screaming for help in the process. But notebooks mattered. They could be demanded in court, months or even years later, which was one of the reasons why every page had a printed number so that nothing could disappear or be altered.

"Find them," ordered Thane. "Force the desk if you can't get a key."

"A bent paperclip is usually good enough," said Sandra. She glanced pointedly at Thane's desk. "You're talking about duty room furniture, sir."

"Just do it," said Thane. "I'll be out for a spell."

Dunbar raised an eyebrow. "Phil Moss?"

"Professor MacMaster first, on the post mortem. Then D.I. Moss—I'll give him your regards," said Thane. He indicated the Mary Dutton file in front of him. "I'll leave this. Read through it, both of you. But remember, we're not sure of anything—not yet."

He waited until they'd left him. There was a pack of cigarettes in his top drawer, just as there was another pack in his car and another at home. But he'd almost stopped smoking. He pushed temptation aside, sat down, and opened the file. There were photographs of Mary Dutton's body, photographs of where she'd been found, a couple of sketch maps, then the thin collection of paperwork that had gathered to date.

Two of the photostat copies of Strathclyde Headquarters documentation carried Phil Moss's scrawled signature. Maybe he should call, tell Phil what was getting under way. . . . He started to reach for the telephone then changed his mind. Phil Moss would know by now, and he'd rather do any talking with his former second-in-command face to face.

Whatever way it shaped.

Thane skimmed through the file again, used a pencil to underline a few places and names, then shoved the papers aside and glanced at his watch. MacMaster was waiting; it was anybody's guess how the tyrannical old despot would play the situation.

He got up, took a deep breath, and went out to his car.

Traffic was light on the motorway route into the city, most vehicles heading in the opposite direction, trying to beat the evening rush-hour. Over the Kingston Bridge, Thane exited to join the Clydeside Expressway, stayed with it along the river, then turned off through some tenement streets towards Glasgow University.

They were busy streets, and his car, a dark blue Ford from the Squad pool, crawled along with the traffic flow. A half-eaten meat pie was lying on a paper bag on the passenger seat and he sighed. Sandra had been out with him that morning, and as usual, she had needed something to keep her going.

He rehearsed a growl for later, half-listening to a message murmuring from the low-band radio. It was for another car, well out of town, and

Thane shrugged then kept a casual eye on the busy pavements. He was in Byres Road, the main shopping street for the University area, ethnic restaurants and liquor stores, boutiques and book shops. Students in jeans mixed with pensioners carrying shopping bags. A group of teenagers, probably unemployed as so many were, watched the flickering screens in a TV dealer's window.

Suddenly, for no real reason, he thought of Sandra again. Supposing it had been Sandra who had died, not Mary Dutton—

His mouth tightened. He knew how Tom Maxwell must be feeling.

A moment later, he took a right turn into the start of the broad scatter of old and new buildings that made up Glasgow University. Originally built on a hill, sprawling out from there in all directions, the University campus had swallowed up several small streets in the process. The Department of Forensic Medicine was located in one of them, a shabby stone terrace of one-time private houses.

A big, black old-fashioned Daimler limousine was parked close by in a No Waiting zone. But Professor Andrew MacMaster always showed a total contempt for minor incidentals, and no traffic warden had ever found enough courage to put a ticket on the Daimler.

Thane parked behind it and went into the Department building. The interior had been repainted since he'd last been there; the walls were now a bright cream gloss, but nothing else seemed to have changed. He exchanged a nod with the uniformed doorman and went up the stairway, with its beautifully polished woodwork, to MacMaster's private territory.

The Regius professor's secretary, a cheerful, fair-haired woman in her thirties, looked up from her typewriter and gave him a friendly smile.

"You're expected, Superintendent." She paused, glancing at the door behind her, and Thane could hear a low murmur of voices. "He has a student with him, but they're almost finished."

As if on cue, the door suddenly opened. The young, pale-faced medical student who backed out closed it quickly again, gave Thane a despairing glance, shook his head, then hurried away.

"Next," murmured MacMaster's secretary. She gave Thane a fractional wink. "He hasn't had a good day."

"Don't expect me to help," warned Thane.

He tapped on the door, opened it, and went in. Professor Andrew MacMaster, a tall, gaunt, bony figure with a thin, beak-nosed face and a slight tonsure of grey hair, was standing beside his desk.

"Thane. Well, at least you're not another student." MacMaster, wearing a dark suit with a University tie, a blue shirt and a stiff white collar, gave a sniff which was meant to be a welcome. He needed new dentures. They clacked as he spoke. "You saw the young gentleman who just left? I had to suggest to him that while he may have some kind of future, it is unlikely to be in the medical profession."

"That bad?" Thane grinned despite himself.

"Humanity may owe me a debt." MacMaster waved him into a chair and settled into the one waiting behind his desk. The way he sat, it might have been a witness box. "I'd rather forget it. Let's discuss your problem."

"I thought it belonged here," said Thane.

"Perhaps." MacMaster scowled. His long, thin fingers fanned down on his desk with an angry slap. "Someone made an error—I'll agree on that much. But the situation can—has been retrieved."

Thane nodded and sat silent for a moment, looking around the room. It was plainly furnished, the most striking feature a yellowed human skull in a glass case sitting on a shelf by the window. Students were told it was a souvenir of a long-ago murder case. In fact, MacMaster had bought it second-hand when he was still at medical school. There was a framed case of antique surgical instruments on one wall; an electronic microscope sat on a table.

He turned back to the shrewd, gimlet eyes waiting, watching across the desk.

"What went wrong?" he asked bluntly.

"Wrong?" MacMaster didn't like the word.

"The first autopsy report on Mary Dutton said 'accidental death.' Now you're drafting a new one."

"Correction." MacMaster snapped the word. "The initial post-mortem report—initial—said that certain injuries were present. The initial opinion was that they could be consistent with a fall."

"With an accidental fall," said Thane. "I can read, Professor."

"I always presumed the possibility." MacMaster scowled. "I told you, the situation has been retrieved."

Thane nodded. "What situation?"

The elderly expert gave him a glare honed on the souls of decades of lesser members of the medical profession. Then MacMaster seemed to make up his mind.

"Very well." He folded his arms. "The pathologist concerned is young, competent, but had had a long day. He made a fundamental error. He had a body brought in after a reported fall down a rock face, he looked for what he expected."

"And he stopped there?"

"He regrets it now," said MacMaster. "The rest of that aspect is a professional matter."

Thane could spare some sympathy for the pathologist concerned. The medical profession did its dirty washing behind tightly closed doors and could be ruthless.

"How did it surface?" he asked quietly.

"A Laboratory report. Apparently he didn't wait for it then didn't bother to read it."

MacMaster seemed to feel that was enough of an explanation. But Thane guessed someone had talked, complained. For a moment he felt the skull in the glass case was watching him, agreeing.

"What about now?"

"If you mean are we saying please, can we have our body back—no." MacMaster was mildly amused, on firmer ground again. "The actual autopsy was competent enough. The usual pathology specimens were retained as a matter of routine, and they tell everything we need." He paused and gave a condescending smile. "Would you—ah—like a preview?"

Thane nodded. Rising, MacMaster led the way across to the microscope on the table. He fiddled with switches and focus for a moment, then stood back.

"Can I set a scene for you, Superintendent? I'll keep it suitably simple, police style."

"I know you will," said Thane dryly.

"Good." MacMaster seemed mildly amused. "We're presented with the body of a healthy young female—only an approximate time of death, because she'd been lying in the open. Unidentified at that time. We have abundant, conclusive medical evidence as to cause of death—a fractured skull, consequent brain damage." He used a bony finger like a pointer on his own body. "Then other injuries, of course. Here—a shattered femur. Then the right shoulder, broken. Damage to the lower vertebrae, about here, and to the rib cage. All accompanied by the inevitable cuts, abrasions and contusions. Our reasonable conclusion?"

Thane sighed, playing his part. "That she'd fallen down that rock face."

"But I distrust reasonable conclusions," said MacMaster. "I can show you why. Use the microscope, Thane—the little wheel on your left adjusts the focus."

Thane bent over the twin eyepieces. The back-lit slide beneath them was hazy and he gave the focus knob a fingertip adjustment. The image firmed into a purple-stained abstract pattern of small, tightly packed streaks and whorls.

"It could be rather nasty wallpaper," said MacMaster. "In fact, that's a cross-section of bruised muscle tissue from the young woman." There was a soft click, suddenly there were two images side by side under the eyepieces. "Now I've added a similar cross-section of tissue, from another bruise. Different?"

It was very different. There were only a few of the purple streaks on the new slide and they were smaller, thinner, with most areas totally clear.

Thane looked up. "Simply?"

"Simply." MacMaster didn't smile. "When there is deep-seated bruising during life or at the moment of death you have what's termed the extravasation of blood and infiltration of the muscle tissue by corpuscles —blood in circulation leaks in, Thane. That's your first slide."

"And the other?"

"Bruising can occur after death. But genuine infiltration is only possible while the heart is still beating. Many of her bruises were ante mortem, others were post mortem."

Thane stared at him. "You're saying she was dead before she went over?"

MacMaster nodded. "For some little time. Perhaps an hour or two— though that's only my humble opinion. Do you want the rest, or would you rather wait for the formal report?"

"I want it now." Thane moistened his lips. "All of it."

"All right." MacMaster moved a few paces back towards his desk, stopped beside the skull in the glass box, and it might have been his sole audience. "A fall is a violent impact, when a body hits something. But turn that round, Thane—I'd expect much the same basic pattern of injuries if she'd been hit by a vehicle travelling at speed, hit and thrown, her head smashed against a kerb or roadside rock." He shrugged.

"Throwing her body over that drop was a reasonably clever idea, I suppose—just not quite clever enough."

"Proof?" Thane knew from past, bitter experience that MacMaster wouldn't have gone so far without more.

"We had her clothing. Most of it had been washed clean by rain. But I sent it across to Strathclyde police laboratory—they're rather more in tune with the basic and technical." It was said dryly, against a background of feuding. "They telephoned me about half an hour ago, I thought I'd tell you first before I advised Commander Hart. They found minute traces of roadside grit. They also identified some flecks of vehicle paint—they're trying for a computer match on possible origin." He paused, eyeing Thane with a detached professional interest. "Commander Hart did mention his—ah—background concern when we spoke earlier."

"So what's your educated conclusion, Professor?" asked Thane with sarcasm.

"That there's every likelihood your woman sergeant was murdered."

Then taken from where it happened, taken to the top of that rock face, and dumped like a sack of garbage. Thane felt a cold wave of anger flooding through him.

"Couldn't you have started with that?" he demanded.

"I could. But I believe in logical sequence," said MacMaster. "Come to one of my pathology lectures, Thane. I lay considerable stress on logical sequence." He sighed, came over slowly, and surprised Thane by laying a bony hand lightly on his arm. "It can be a protection, man—emotionally as well as professionally."

He saw Thane to the door. Behind him, the skull in the glass case seemed to say its own goodbye.

CHAPTER TWO

All Scots have long memories—particularly for disasters and defeats when, of course, it was never their fault that things went wrong.

Well over a thousand years ago part of the west of Scotland was a kingdom called Strathclyde. Strathclyde joined Norway in a war against the English, lost, and the name was wiped from the map.

In the 1970's it was decided that Scotland's local government needed re-organisation. With a few strokes of a pen on a map the entire west of Scotland, from the land of Rabbie Burns on the Ayrshire coast to remote Highland crofts in the mountains of the north, from Lanarkshire mining villages to Gaelic-speaking islands off the coast, was compulsorily amalgamated into one region.

The centre of the new region was the city of Glasgow. The region was and is an administrative nightmare and a politicians' benefit. But the planners revived memories of the old kingdom and called it Strathclyde.

Strathclyde Police Headquarters is a large chunk of red brick and tinted glass, several stories high and with about the same number of underground car park levels. It covers an entire block in the heart of the business sector of Glasgow and a high proportion of the staff shuffle administrative paperwork.

Detective Inspector Phil Moss had become one of them, and hated it. As liaison officer to the assistant chief constable (Crime), he had a tiny office to himself in the carpeted corridor known as The Promised Land, where only the force's top executives and their personal staff were located. Ordinary cops usually only visited The Promised Land to be disciplined into the ground or promoted.

It was 5 P.M.—go home time, and the building was emptying when Colin Thane arrived. He found Phil Moss sitting at his desk, a small, thin, bleak-eyed figure he had seldom seen look more miserable.

"I know why you're here. I heard from my boss." Moss pointed towards the spare chair across from him, tight against a filing cabinet in the only space available. He grimaced as Thane settled. "I suppose I'm glad it's you, though I'm not even sure of that. It's a mess, right?"

Thane nodded. Phil Moss hadn't really changed from their Divisional days. A wiry, untidy bachelor in his late fifties, with thinning, mousy hair, he still looked, as usual, as if he'd slept in his clothes and had forgotten to shave. He'd been a minor legend out on the streets, an abrasive, acid-tongued cop ready to tackle anything twice his own size. Despite their differences, he and Thane had become friends and had stayed that way.

"What did MacMaster say?" asked Moss.

Thane raised a surprised eyebrow.

"Francey Dunbar phoned." Moss shrugged. "Said to tell you he's set up a meeting at the Swann woman's house for eight." He pushed a slip of paper across his desk. "Here's the address. So—MacMaster?"

"Mary Dutton was killed somewhere else," said Thane simply. "Probably run down by a car."

Moss swore under his breath, then ran a hand slowly across his forehead, his eyes almost closed.

"You know I wrote her off as an accident?"

"Everybody did," reminded Thane. "Till now."

"But I'm the cop who should have sensed something wrong—and I didn't. I just processed the paperwork, let it go." Moss drew a deep breath. "Apologies, Sergeant Dutton—whatever good that does."

"Did you know her?" asked Thane.

"No." Almost without pausing, Moss opened a small wooden box on his desk and flicked a white indigestion tablet into his mouth. He didn't really need them now; he'd lost a cherished stomach ulcer to a surgeon's knife more than a year earlier, the main reason for his transfer to Headquarters staff. But the tablets remained a defence in times of crisis. "Did you?"

"Not in any real way. But she had a good record."

"I read it." Moss sucked the tablet. "We identified her body through a fingerprint check—did you know that?"

Thane nodded. It had been an item in Commander Hart's folder. All police officers had their fingerprints kept on file, for a variety of reasons —usually so that their prints could be eliminated in a scene of crime situation.

"I could use some help, Phil," he said quietly.

"From me?" Moss drew a deep breath. "Thanks. I don't want to be shut out of this one—not now. I feel bad enough. What kind of help?"

"Names. Every known criminal she maybe brushed against before she was posted to my mob. Any other background you can get."

"The postcard." Moss understood, nodded, but was disappointed. "You'll get your list. What else?"

"The local sergeant who got to her body first. I want him there, at Loch Lomond, 10 A.M. tomorrow. If he knows this so-called Peace Camp at Glen Torbat, that's a bonus." Thane knew what Moss wanted to hear, but shook his head. "Sorry, Phil. I can't use you any other way—not yet. We've got to nibble at the edges."

Moss sucked on for a moment, his lined face miserable again.

"I may try some nibbling of my own," he warned. "If I come up with anything, you'll hear."

"Do that." It might cause them both problems, but Thane couldn't say no. He got to his feet and held out his hand. "Thanks, Phil."

They shook hands, and Moss managed a wisp of a grin.

Thane left him, then used the elevator at the end of The Promised Lane corridor to go up to the police laboratory floor. Matt Amos, the bearded assistant director, was on leave but his deputy, a tubby Irishman who grew roses as a hobby, grimaced as soon as Thane entered.

"If it's those paint fragments, we're still working on them," he protested. "You want priority, everyone wants priority—we're doing our best."

"When is your best?" Thane looked past him at the white-coated technicians still working at the equipment ranged around the laboratory area. "I need anything I can get."

"You know the largest piece we've got?" The Irishman thumbed indignantly over his shoulder. "It's about a quarter the size of a pea, we're layering it on spectographic analysis, then—"

"I know." Thane considered him thoughtfully. "How's the rose growing coming on?"

"All right." He met a suspicious frown. "Why?"

"You've got to keep feeding them, right?" Thane offered his bait. "I know a sergeant in the Mounted Branch who could maybe get you a load of horse manure—if you're interested."

"I'm interested." The Irishman swore softly. "All right, Superintendent. At the latest, tomorrow morning first thing. I'll stay on it myself."

One of the laboratory offices was empty. Thane went in and used the telephone there to call the Scottish Crime Squad. He spoke to Commander Hart first, told him what Professor MacMaster had said, then gave Hart a quick rundown on the rest.

Hart listened in almost total silence. Then a noise like a sigh came over the line.

"Stay with it, if you have to lean on anyone then do it. For now, we'll keep the whole thing under wraps—headlines wouldn't help. I'll decide how much to tell her mother." Hart was thinking as he spoke. "But go carefully in one area. Be sure of your facts if this peace camp seems directly involved."

"Howls about civil rights?" suggested Thane.

"I mean you've a murder on your plate. Don't let any political clown of either kind make it more difficult," snapped Hart. "I have to deal with them, I know what I'm talking about."

There was little more to say. Thane got back to the Squad switchboard, was told Francey Dunbar was out, and left a message for his sergeant to meet him outside Sheila Swann's house at eight.

"Anywhere he can contact you till then, sir?" asked the operator.

"At home," said Thane. "But I don't recommend it."

He hung up as the operator gave a sympathetic chuckle.

A few grey clouds had drifted in from somewhere and there was a hint of rain in the air by the time Colin Thane parked his car outside his house. It was in a quiet suburban street of small bungalows, each more or less alike, each with a tiny patch of garden front and rear. His garden had more weeds than most, and the state of the grass reminded him it was a couple of weeks since he'd last hauled his rusting lawn mower out of the garage.

He glanced at his wrist-watch. It was six-thirty. In Scotland, in spring, the northern daylight hours lengthened rapidly. Sunset wouldn't be until around eight. In another half-hour or so most of the families around would have finished their evening meal, TV sets would be switched off, and most husbands would be booted out to dig or cut or plant something. They lived regular lives and just now and again he envied them.

The usual barking began inside the house as he walked up to the porch. When the front door opened, an avalanche of Boxer dog overwhelmed him for a moment then, duty done, Clyde trotted off again.

"Welcome back to the zoo." Mary Thane grinned at him from the doorway, kissed him on the lips, then gave a gesture of mock despair. "That damn animal thinks it runs this place."

"He does." Thane closed the door and followed his wife in. The muffled sound of heavy rock music was coming from upstairs, but that was usual. "Who's home?"

"Both of them—but they've eaten, they're going out." Mary looked at him. She was a cop's wife; she had an instinct. "What about you?"

"I can eat first."

"Damn." She said it softly. "Tell me about it?"

He did, while they ate together in the kitchen. She had made a beef stew flavoured with a package sauce. It wasn't one of his favourites, but the two upstairs, Tommy and Kate, both in their early teens, liked it. The cheesecake that followed was a different matter. Thane had two helpings and to hell with the calories.

He talked while they ate and Mary Thane was a good listener. Telling her about Sergeant Mary Dutton, able to do it at his own pace, Thane found it helped put the little he'd got into perspective and she let him leave it there.

"Poor girl—and poor Phil." She got up as they finished, brought over the coffee pot from the stove, laid it on the table, then went out of the room for a moment. When she came back, she laid a glass of whisky in front of him. "Medicine."

"What about you?"

"Later."

He took a sip of whisky while she poured the coffee.

He was lucky, and he knew it. Thane now had to think to be sure how many years they'd been married, found it hard to believe when he did. A slim, attractive, dark-haired woman, Mary Thane still took the same dress size as when they'd married—her favourite claim was they were still the same dresses.

"How was your day?" he asked over the rim of the glass.

"So—so." It had been one of the three days a week she worked as a part-time medical receptionist at a local surgery. Their money problems had eased since his last promotion, but the work interested her. "There's some kind of stomach bug going the rounds—that kept us busy with appointments." She grimaced. "Jean Balfour was in. Remember her?"

He didn't, but he gave a vague nod.

"Her car was stolen yesterday. She got it back, but they took her handbag. She lost her cheque book and her credit cards."

"There's a lot of it." Every day's crime report sheets proved that. Give a thief a blank cheque book or some plastic money, presume he had the sense to know how to use them, and he could have brief prosperity.

"But she knows you're a cop. I had her jumping up and down wanting to know why the police don't do something about it."

People usually did. He grinned a little.

"Catch them, flog them, hang them?"

"For starters." She came over and laid a hand on his shoulder. "When do you have to go out?"

"Soon." He reckoned he had another half hour.

"Finish your coffee and take your drink through to the living room," she suggested. "I'll clear up here."

The rock music was still filtering from upstairs as he went through to the living room. It was comfortable, simply furnished, and had a broad bay window looking out across the garden. The sky had cleared. A neighbour across the street was busy clipping at rose bushes. Thane turned away, took another sip at his whisky, then heard feet clattering down the stairs at the same time as he realised the music had stopped.

"Hello." Tommy grinned in at him from the doorway. His son had dark hair, a thin build, and early teenage pimples. "How's the law?"

"Surviving." Thane thumbed in the direction of the garden. "But it could use some help. There's a thing called a rake in the garage."

"Maybe tomorrow," Tommy's grin took on a wary edge. "I'm on my way out, Dad. Tomorrow, okay?"

He vanished. A moment later the front door opened then banged shut again. Thane swore to himself and settled in a chair. He was trying to decide whether he'd energy enough to get up again and switch on the TV set when he realised someone else had come in.

"Dad—"

He turned and smiled. Kate was younger than Tommy, at the chubby stage, but was going to be very like her mother in a few years' time.

"Can I talk to you?" Kate carefully closed the door and came over, her face unusually serious.

"Got a problem?" asked Thane. "What have you been up to this time?"

"Nothing." She hesitated then shoved her hands into the pockets of her denim jeans. "But I've this friend at school—I said I'd ask you."

"About what?" Thane frowned a little.

"She needs to talk to someone—"

"A police someone?"

"Yes. But not you, not anyone she knows."

Thane beckoned her nearer, had her sit on the arm of his chair.

"I've had people tell me that 'a friend' has a problem and mean something else," he said gently.

Kate shook her head firmly. "I know about it, but I'm not involved. Honest, Dad. The other thing is, she—well she wouldn't want to talk to a man."

Thane stared at her. "Kate, if it's serious, if you're in any way involved—"

"I'm not." She could be stubborn, something else she had inherited from her mother. "I said I'd ask. Can you fix it tomorrow?"

"I'll get you a name and a telephone number." He pursed his lips. "A policewoman—your friend can call her. But—"

"Thanks." She gave him a quick smile and a kiss on the cheek. "Don't tell mum. Please."

She had gone before he could argue, and he heard her going out a few minutes later.

He hadn't made any promise. He told Mary before he left. If something was going on, they both had to know.

Mary Dutton's social worker friend lived in Tardale Street, on the western edge of Thane's former Millside Division territory. It meant a half-hour drive across the city, through the early evening rash of neon signs at bars and cinemas, the busy pavements around disco halls and amusement arcades. It was warm and bright, and he noticed a scatter of navymen in uniform among the crowds. A flotilla of NATO ships were in the Clyde; that always meant crews on shore leave with money to burn—but they weren't his problem.

He reached Millside, drove past one familiar landmark after another, then finally turned into Tardale Street. It was beyond the slum tenement area, two long rows of small red brick terrace houses with cars parked tightly along its length. Thane squeezed the Ford into a vacant slot, got out, started walking, and a car door opened ahead. Francey Dunbar emerged from a small black M.G. coupe, one of the Crime Squad's latest acquisitions, and greeted him with a nod as he arrived.

"Her place is number 26." Dunbar indicated a few doors farther along. "She sounded reasonable enough when I spoke on the phone."

"Let's keep her that way," said Thane dryly. His thin-faced young sergeant wore a leather jacket over an open-necked sports shirt, and dark trousers. He could have blended into any street corner scene. But this was different. "Next time it's like tonight, wear a tie."

"Next time," promised Dunbar, unabashed. He followed Thane along the street. "Sandra found Mary Dutton's notebooks. She's working on them."

"Tonight?"

"Her idea," shrugged Dunbar. "Uh—think we'll get anything more out of Professor MacMaster?"

"Maybe. There's a laboratory angle." Thane left it at that. "What about background on this peace camp place?"

"We had it wrong—or I did." Dunbar grimaced, checking door numbers. "I spoke to some people involved that way. They put me right."

"Meaning?" Thane noticed a curtain flicker across the street. Someone was watching them. Most streets had someone like that.

"It's commercial—log cabins in the forest, forget the outside world, but pay your bill before you leave. I'd call it a mental health farm—no TV, no radios, newspapers banned. The only phone is in the manager's office and you don't get to use it."

"Who goes there?"

"Anybody. They get group parties, stray business executives who want to have a nervous breakdown, the lot."

"Including one female cop." Thane sucked his lips. "Did you check with Special Branch?"

"Them?" Dunbar snorted. Special Branch handled political extremists and similar worries. They'd run a check on him once because of his friends; he'd found out about it and had never forgiven them. "No."

"Do it," ordered Thane. They had to be sure.

They reached number 26. It had a plain, street-level door like the other houses around. A shaded light showed behind its window. Thane glanced at the brass nameplate which said "S. Swann" then rang the doorbell. It chimed somewhere inside then, seconds later, the door opened.

"Police?" asked the woman who looked out at them.

"Yes. Detective Superintendent Thane." Thane showed his warrant card.

"Come in." She closed the door again once they were inside. "To your left—there's nowhere else to go."

They went through an archway from the tiny lobby and found themselves in a compact, tastefully furnished living room. A TV set flickered in one corner but the sound had been killed. The light they'd seen from outside was a standard lamp with a Chinese paper shade.

"Sit down." Sheila Swann gestured them both towards a couch, dragged a stool over for herself as they settled, and noticed the way Francey Dunbar was looking around. "There's this, then a kitchen at the back." She pointed to a narrow circular stairway. "Bedroom and bathroom up there. You're the Sergeant Dunbar who telephoned?"

"Yes." Dunbar glanced around again. "I've been thinking of buying a place like this."

"But that isn't why you came." A woman in her mid-thirties with a plump face and build, mousy-fair hair, and intelligent eyes, she wore a long hand-knitted wool waistcoat over a sleeveless white shirt-blouse and green track-suit trousers. Her holiday in Spain had left her with a deep tan, partly spoiled by a peeling nose. She turned to Thane. "Mary's postcard, isn't it?"

"Yes."

"And there's more?"

He nodded. "It looks that way."

"I see." Her hands were clasped over her knees. The knuckles whitened a little but she showed no other sign of emotion. "What did happen to her?"

"We don't know yet—not for certain." The half-truth wasn't difficult. "Some new facts have turned up."

"The kind you won't tell me." Sheila Swann pursed her lips. "I understand. Most of my social work clients are in some kind of tangle with the police or the law, it's just different when it becomes personal." She saw Francey Dunbar had quietly produced his notebook and a pencil. "What do you want to know?"

"Background, mainly," said Thane. "How long had you known Mary Dutton?"

"Four, maybe five years." The mousy-haired woman spoke calmly, quietly. "It was at a party, we were both feeling miserable, we got talking —we had something in common. I'd just divorced my husband, a man she'd expected to marry had just written from Canada to say he'd found someone else and wasn't coming back. We became friends after that— close friends." She pursed her lips again. "For a time, we even thought of putting our money together and sharing a house. But we weren't sure it would work."

"What about this holiday? You went to Spain, she went to the Peace Camp—"

"Yes." Sheila Swann instinctively rubbed the peeling skin on her nose. She gave a slight smile. "Originally we planned to be together, to go to the Glen Torbat Peace Camp. Mary tried it during the winter, liked it, wanted to go back."

"But you went to Spain instead."

"I—yes."

"Why?" asked Francey Dunbar without looking up from his notebook.

"You could say I had a better offer." Sheila Swann took a deep breath. "There's a man—someone I like, but that's all. I—" She broke off unhappily. "How do you think I feel now, Superintendent? If I'd been with her—"

"Maybe you'd both be dead," said Thane.

She stared at him, then swallowed.

"You mean that?"

He nodded. "What about Mary and men? Was there anyone?"

"Special?" Sheila Swann shook her head firmly. "She was like me. The occasional ship passed in the night—maybe docked for a weekend. Nothing more." She saw his doubt. "I'm sure of it. We didn't have many secrets." Suddenly, she got to her feet. "I brought back a bottle of duty-free gin. Would either of you—?"

They shook their heads. She crossed the room, opened a cupboard to disclose a small, built-in bar, and busied herself for a moment. Then she came back nursing a filled cut-glass tumbler and sat on the stool again.

"What did she tell you about the Peace Camp?" asked Thane.

"Enough to make it sound different." Sheila Swann raised the glass to her lips, and sipped. "Forget your troubles, Shangri-la in the Highlands —the way I felt at the time, Glen Torbat seemed a good idea."

"How about the people she'd met?"

"Some weird, some ordinary, but Mary said nobody got in your way. One bunch spent all their time trying to decide what day the world would end."

"Do you remember any name she mentioned?"

Sheila Swann nodded. "A man named Peter Crossley. She talked a lot about him."

"He's the manager," said Francey Dunbar.

"If you know it, why ask?" For the first time, there was an edge of irritation in the woman's voice. Then she shrugged. "I'm sorry. That wasn't necessary, was it?"

"We're nearly finished." Thane paused for a moment, sensing the first cracks in the tight control Sheila Swann had so far kept on her emotions. "Did Mary talk much about her job, about being a police officer?"

"Do you talk about it, Superintendent?" She took a long swallow from the glass. It left her lips moist. "We gossiped sometimes—privately. Things that happened to me, things that happened to her. But it stopped there. If people found out what she did for a living, fine. But she didn't exactly advertise it."

Thane heard Francey Dunbar give a grunt of agreement. He felt the same way as his sergeant. Strangers could freeze when they discovered they were talking to a cop, even if it wasn't the total Black Death reaction that greeted an introduction to a tax inspector.

"She'd talk cases, she'd mention names." Thane didn't wait for an answer. "Did she ever say she was scared of anyone?"

"No." Sheila Swann suddenly had tears in her eyes. "I don't think she was genuinely afraid of anyone, Superintendent. But these 'two old customers' in her postcard—it looks like she should have been, doesn't it?"

Thane glanced at Francey Dunbar, nodded, and Dunbar closed his notebook.

She went with them to the door, then touched Thane's arm just before he left.

"I want to know what happens, Superintendent. Can you—?"

"When there's anything positive," he promised.

She nodded her thanks, they went out, and the door closed.

Dunbar stayed unusually silent until they'd walked back to where he'd left his car. Then, leaning against it, he grimaced.

"Didn't get us much, did it, sir?"

"It helped." Thane felt he now knew a lot more about Detective

Sergeant Mary Dutton. The more he knew, the more it might matter. "Peter Crossley—anything on him?"

Dunbar shook his head. "I checked. There's nothing on file."

"Ask again when you talk to Special Branch." That was one item off his list. "Are you going back to base?"

"Yes." Dunbar gave a slightly crooked grin. "I thought I'd see how Sandra was making out, maybe push some raw meat into her cage—she'll be hungry by now."

"Tell her we're heading out of town in the morning, as soon as we're organised. She's included. If anything does turn up, call me at home before you leave." There was one thing left. Thane looked down at his feet for a moment. He had promised Kate a name, but his daughter knew Sandra and might not want her involved. "Did Linda Belmont nail her gold-smuggling Dutchman?"

"Yes. She got back before I left." Dunbar laughed. "The Dutchman tried to run for it and bounced off the Animal. He's locked up, very unhappy—and talking."

"Right." Thane made up his mind. The blonde detective sergeant looked young and could relate to anyone. "If she's there, tell her. If she's not, do me a favour and make sure she gets a message. She'll get a phone call tomorrow sometime—one of Kate's friends at school. Ask her to do me a favour, take it from there."

Dunbar reacted as if stung.

"If your Kate's part of it, what's wrong with me?" he demanded, his thin moustache bristling. "I get along with her—despite her father. She's a nice kid."

"But she's not involved—not directly," soothed Thane. "Anyway, you're disqualified—sex discrimination, teenage style. The girl who'll make the call won't talk to a man."

Dunbar still frowned. "There's Sandra—"

"No."

"All right," agreed Dunbar reluctantly. "What's it all about?"

"I'm damned if I know," admitted Thane. "But tell Linda I want to find out, so forget any schoolgirl promises."

"I'll tell her." Dunbar opened his car door then delivered a final protest. "But I still don't like it, Sandra won't like it—"

Thane closed the car door on him as he got in. By the time he'd

walked on to where he'd left the Ford, his sergeant's black M.G. had
snarled away from the kerb. Francey Dunbar wasn't pleased.

The evening was still bright, the sun just touching down on the horizon, dusk at least half an hour away. A bunch of young children ran past,
shouting and whooping, and a large ginger cat made a fast jump on to a
windowsill to avoid being trampled.

Thane decided he'd have done the same. Chuckling, he started the
Ford, turned it in the street, and began his return journey.

Colin Thane used a backstreet route for his journey back from Millside into the city. It would save a little time in terms of what he wanted
to do next but the other reason was sheer curiosity, to see how much real
change there had been.

A few of the worst slums had been demolished, leaving patches of
waste ground. A derelict football ground had become a housing development with a medical centre and community hall. But there was still
plenty of the rest, old warehouses and drab tenements where the Ford
crunched over broken glass and flattened empty, rolling beer cans. Here
and there a thin, pale face watched suspiciously from a doorway or a
drunk staggered homeward. There were the same, familiar street-corner
groups ready for anything to break their boredom. A young couple hurried past, pushing a pram which sagged under the weight of a gleaming
new washing machine.

There was a T junction ahead, with an advertising billboard which
shouted the city administration's slogan "Glasgow's Miles Better."
Someone had used an aerosol paint spray to cover it with a single crude
obscenity. Thane reached the billboard, turned left, and saw a police car
stopped ahead in a street otherwise empty of life. Blue roof light still
flashing, doors lying open, no sign of its crew, the car had been pulled in
at the entrance to a narrow lane.

Instinct took over. Thane gave the Ford more accelerator, reached the
police car, and pulled in behind it. As he stopped, two men and a thin,
red-haired woman erupted from the lane with the police car's crew of
two in close pursuit. One constable took the nearest of the men in a
flying tackle and brought him down; the other grabbed at the woman
then doubled up in agony as she kicked him in the groin. By the time
Thane had tumbled out of his car she had turned her attention to the

constable struggling with the man he'd brought down, doing her best to kick his head in.

The patrol car crew could look after themselves; the second man was across the street and running for another lane. Thane sprinted after the thick-set fleeing figure, followed him into the alleyway, dodging round broken crates and abandoned rubbish. There was a dead end ahead, a brick wall. The man glanced back, still running, then took a flying leap, grabbed for the top of the wall, only got his fingertips to it, and crashed down again.

Scrambling up, Thane's quarry grabbed a heavy length of timber and swung it like a club, snarling. Dodging clear, Thane took two steps backward, saw the man's broad, unshaven face clearly for the first time, and almost grinned.

"Still at it, Tank?" he asked almost mildly.

The length of timber froze in mid-swing, and the man stared, his unshaven face registered a mix of surprise and disbelief.

"Christ," he said bitterly. "What the hell are you doin' around here, Thane?"

"Passing through." Thane looked pointedly at the timber batten.

"Aye, sorry." The timber batten was thrown aside, and the man eyed him warily. Tank Mallard was a ned—Glasgow's label for any size of layabout hoodlum. He had gained his nickname over years of street brawling where the only real rule was someone had to win. But they knew each other; Mallard wasn't a complete fool. He forced a smile. "Didn't know it was you. No divvy in thumpin' boss cops, is there?"

"None," agreed Thane. He kept his eyes on Mallard but thumbed back the way they'd come. "Was that Maisie I saw?"

Tank Mallard forced what was meant to be a smile, and nodded. His red-haired sister Maisie had a history almost as long as his own.

"Maisie—the bampot wi' her is new around here. New since your time, Mr. Thane." He forced the smile wider. "How are you gettin' on wi' that Crime Squad mob, eh? Heavy stuff?"

"Sometimes." Thane beckoned. Sadly, totally subdued, Tank Mallard walked ahead of him out of the alleyway.

Another patrol car had arrived; a C.I.D. car was just drawing up. The other man who had been with Mallard was lying on the pavement, handcuffed, being sat on by one of the constables. Maisie was pinned against a wall, scowling.

Thane and his prisoner crossed the street towards them. As a startled constable took hold of Tank Mallard, one of the men emerging from the C.I.D. car gave a delighted grin and hurried over.

"Free-lancing, sir?" he asked cheerfully.

"Just visiting," said Thane. The C.I.D. man was young, his name was Beech, and every cop in Millside Division had been invited to the party he'd held the night he became the father of twins. He'd also been a constant, luckless thorn in Thane's side. "How are things?"

"I made sergeant last month." Beech beamed at him. "Promotion—someone, somewhere, likes me."

"Congratulations," said Thane. Someone, somewhere, must, but he couldn't think why. He glanced towards the prisoners, being loaded into the two patrol cars. "What was that all about?"

"A sailor off a Danish corvette—the usual, sir." Beech shrugged. "He met up with Maisie over a few drinks, she offered him some home comforts, Tank and his pal were the reception committee. Someone saw it going on and called in."

"How's the sailor?"

"Sore head, split lip, sore ribs, no wallet—at least, until we can see what Maisie has hidden away. But that's for a policewoman—if it was me, I'd wear rubber gloves." A thought struck him. "What about Mallard, sir? I mean, in the lane—assaulting a police officer, resisting arrest, anything like that?"

"No." What had happened was common enough; Thane wasn't looking for complications. He took a deep breath and looked around.

"Brings back memories?" asked Beech, interested.

"People and places," said Thane softly.

A lot of people, a lot of places—cops and criminals, all the real people in between. He'd always have a soft spot for Millside.

"Things have been quiet lately," said Beech. "Not like when you were here, sir."

Thane hoped he knew what he meant.

It was two hours later, dark and raining, before Thane finished. He had spent the time visiting half a dozen men and women in the city, a strange assortment from a former doctor who had written the wrong prescription once too often, to a sweet-faced, grey-haired old lady named

Brenda who could value a stolen diamond ring at a glance then sell it later for three times what she'd paid.

They had one thing in common. Very little happened they didn't hear about. Now and again, each for reasons of their own, they would make a phone call and pass it on. None of them made him particularly welcome, but they listened to what he wanted. None of them could help, none had heard as much as a whisper about the Peace Camp or about Mary Dutton apart from the brief press reports of her death.

If they had heard, they would have told him. In different ways, each of them owed Thane that much and more. Any time he wanted, he could leak a few facts to some of their friends which would have made life permanently painful.

But if they did hear, they would call him. He had to leave it at that.

Tommy and Kate were both upstairs in their rooms, in bed, when he arrived home. Mary had some supper ready and was watching a late-night TV soap opera. She switched it off and shook her head before Thane could ask.

"No, she hasn't said anything—and I didn't ask."

Thane went upstairs. When he looked into Tommy's room, it was in darkness and he was asleep. But a crack of light showed under Kate's door. He knocked quietly and went in. She was lying pretending to read, but he could see she'd been waiting for him.

"Give this to your friend." He laid a slip of paper on her bedside table. He'd written Linda Belmont's name and the Crime Squad telephone number on it. "She's a detective sergeant, she's the kind your friend can talk with—about anything." He looked at his daughter. "There's still nothing you think I should know about?"

She shook her head then, unexpectedly, reached up and hugged him.

"What's that for?" he asked.

"Worrying." Kate wrinkled her nose at him. "Thanks, Dad. But it isn't me—I just know about it."

He felt happier as he went back down. Mary looked at him, relaxed, and the TV set came to life again.

Next morning the sky was still grey and the air felt damp. Thane rose early, ate a quick breakfast once he'd shaved and dressed, and was on his way before Mary wakened Tommy and Kate.

By 8 A.M. he was at his desk at the Scottish Crime Squad. The early shift teams were still arriving and there was no sign of Sandra or Francey Dunbar, but they'd been busy the previous night. Sergeant Mary Dutton's black bound notebooks lay in two neat, string-tied bundles on top of his filing cabinet. Three typed pages of names were on his desk with a note in Dunbar's sprawling handwriting pinned to the top sheet.

"Nothing that shouts anything special" was his sergeant's disappointed comment.

Thane looked them over and felt the same way. Mary Dutton had come across the usual cross-section of thieves and villains, but the few likeliest candidates were without exception serving prison terms.

Another list of names, a teleprinter message from Phil Moss at Strathclyde Headquarters, waited beside them. He went through it slowly, with the same sense of frustration. The Strathclyde list was older; at least half a dozen of the criminals listed were dead, some were small-time offenders, and none gave him any real cause to pause and ponder.

He heard a knock and the door opening, but didn't look up, ticking off the last few names.

"Some days start that way. The trouble is, they usually get worse." Maggie Fyfe, her usual immaculate self, laid an envelope in front of him. "I'm supposed to be the boss's secretary, not general dogsbody—that just arrived for you, by dispatch rider."

"Thanks." Thane took the envelope, saw the Strathclyde Headquarters stamp, and sucked his teeth. "This might be better."

"Don't count on it," warned Maggie Fyfe, already leaving.

He opened the envelope, glanced at the contents, and almost called her back to tell her she was wrong. The mad Irish rose-grower at the police laboratory had done it!

The report was headed "Paint Fragments. Microspectronphotometric Analysis." Then came a column of figures and readings, but after that a plain language translation of what it was all about.

The laboratory team had taken the tiny flecks of vehicle paint recovered from Mary Dutton's clothing, most just large enough for the human eye to detect. Each fleck and its layers of paint, from basic primer coat outward, had been checked. All corresponded to the same pattern, the same source, with a double check in the form of chemical composition analysis.

"Paint fragments, from this common source, consist of a primer red-brown, undercoat light grey, undercoat black, outer paint colour mid-grey with an additional outer paint coat of metallic blue. This paint pattern, combined with chemical composition, identifies on computer match only with a Toyota make vehicle between two and three years old. Additional outer colour of metallic blue paint added by respray in U.K. after import from Japan. Toyota import statistics indicate vehicle most likely small pick-up truck or light van. A limited number of Toyota station wagons were also produced with this paint pattern."

Underneath it all, written in thick black felt pen, was the additional message "When can I have my horse manure?"

Thane chuckled. As far as he was concerned, the Irishman had just earned himself a lifetime supply. He verified a copy had been sent to Professor MacMaster at the University's forensic medicine department, then took the report through to the duty room.

It was still coming to life with dayshift people. Sandra Craig hadn't arrived and there was no sign of Sergeant Linda Belmont, the other person he'd hoped to see. But Francey Dunbar was there, zipping himself out of a set of motorcycling leathers, his red crash helmet propped beside him while he talked to a balding, stockily built detective. Thane went over to them, passing the duty room notice board, where someone had pinned up the hand-printed advice SLEEP SAFE TONIGHT. TAKE A COP TO BED.

"Sandra phoned, sir," said Dunbar before he could ask. "She's on her way." He indicated his companion. "I've told Joe what's on."

The man nodded. His name was Joe Felix, he was in his late thirties, and he wore a once expensive, now shapeless, tweed jacket with leather patches at the elbows. The third member of Thane's regular team, he was one of the Squad's electronics and surveillance experts. For almost a month, most of his energies had been devoted to the whisky hi-jack case.

"I've done a hand-over to one of Superintendent Maxwell's people, sir." He shaped a grimace. "Just when things were getting interesting. Anything special you want from me on this one?"

"Not yet." Thane shook his head. Felix's special talents covered everything from sophisticated bugging to a profitable sideline in repairing anything electrical. "But we've got this."

He handed Dunbar the laboratory report. His sergeant read it with Felix looking over his shoulder.

"Run it through the computer?" suggested Felix.

"If it wasn't stolen before it was resprayed," said Dunbar. Under the leathers he had a grey roll-neck sweater and corduroy trousers. He was wearing what looked like army surplus paratroop boots. "But it's worth a try."

Thane nodded. "That's yours, Joe—and names, a small army of them. You handle this end today. We'll work Loch Lomond and the Peace Camp at Glen Torbat."

"Thanks," said Felix. "I like getting the fun jobs."

"Francey." Thane switched back to Dunbar again. "Did you talk to Special Branch?"

"You don't talk to them, you squeeze things out of them," complained Dunbar. "They admit they know the Peace Camp set-up, but they're not particularly interested—they reckon it's harmless."

"And Crossley, the manager?"

"Nothing political they know about. He's just earning a living. The place is owned by a private company—they tried for charitable status for tax purposes a few years back but were turned down."

It was enough for the moment. Thane took another glance around.

"If it's Linda you're looking for, I talked to her," said Dunbar. "She says she'll play the phone call by ear."

"What phone call?" asked Joe Felix.

"Someone with a problem." Thane left it there, glad to see Sandra Craig arriving. Dressed in denims, a white shirt and an Icelandic wool jacket, a leather handbag like a small haversack slung over one shoulder, hair and makeup immaculate, she spoiled the whole effect by grinning from ear to ear.

"We're ready to leave," said Thane. "What's so funny?"

"Funny, sir?" The grin remained. "Nothing. But there's someone waiting for you in the parking lot."

"Now?" He swore under his breath, but let her lead the way.

An old, rusting Land-Rover was in the parking space usually reserved for Commander Hart. It was grey, with an enclosed panel body, and a ventilator had been fitted in the roof. A tall, lanky figure wearing a brown suit, a cloth cap pulled down over his eyes, was draped against the driver's door. There was a dog snoozing under the vehicle's rear axle— and Thane remembered why.

"Good morning, sir." The man made a slow-motion business of straightening and beamed. The dog didn't move.

"Good morning." Thane drew a deep breath. "Constable—"

"Dawson, sir. Jock Dawson—reporting for temporary duty." Dawson paused, snapped his fingers, and his Labrador bitch emerged into the open. "This is Goldie. She had a hard day yesterday."

"I was there." Thane glanced round. Francey and Sandra's faces showed innocent interest. Joe Felix was grinning, a few yards back. "What were you told about joining us?"

"Just it was plain-clothes duty." Dawson gave an amiable shrug. "Never really been out o' uniform before, but it's fine by me—and Goldie's a plain-clothes kind of dog."

"Good." Thane considered the dog-handler carefully, remembering the warnings he'd been given. "Where did you get the Land-Rover?"

"It's my own." Dawson smiled. "Not much sense in bringing one of the Dog Branch vans with police signs over it. I'll charge you mileage."

"Do that." The Labrador was sitting watching him. Thane felt as if he was talking to them both. "If you're ready to start, we could maybe use you right now."

"We're ready, sir." Dawson's angular face crinkled in a grin.

"I was afraid of that," muttered Francey Dunbar. Sandra dug him sharply with an elbow and he winced. "I mean, it's not giving him—them—time to settle in."

"We'll manage." Dawson eyed him suspiciously. The dog curled an edge of lip, showing pure white teeth. "Do your people get along wi' dogs, Superintendent?"

"Yes." Sandra came forward as she spoke and rubbed Goldie's golden fur behind one ear. "She's a beauty, Jock."

Frowning, Francey Dunbar took a couple of steps nearer. Then he stopped as an odd noise came from inside the Land-Rover.

"What the hell's that?" he asked.

"Well—" the lanky dog-handler hesitated and looked embarrassed.

The noise came again, caused by something big and heavy.

"What is it?" demanded Dunbar.

For a moment something that could have been a malicious glint showed in Dawson's eyes, then had gone.

"Take a look if you want, Sergeant," he said casually.

Dunbar hesitated.

"Go ahead, Sergeant," said Thane. "You asked."

Dunbar went to the Land-Rover, jerked open the handle of the rear door, and swung it back. There was a low, rumbling growl, like menacing thunder, and Dunbar sprang back as if stung.

"Easy, Sergeant," murmured Dawson. "Nothing to worry about."

They joined Dunbar. Inside the Land-Rover, fur bristling, eyes glaring, a black giant of a German Shepherd looked out at them. Dawson made a soft noise and the dog relaxed, gave a soft answering whine, and came out in a single jump. Tail wagging, it ambled over to join the Labrador.

"Like to explain?" asked Thane.

"My other dog, sir." Dawson shifted his feet and eyed Thane. "Rajah —he's over age, paid off now as far as police work is concerned, so now I've got Goldie instead. But they let me keep him, the way it's usually done."

Thane nodded. He'd heard how police dogs were retired at around ten years old, how their handlers usually kept them as family pets. But this great monster of an animal, with just a faint trace of grey around the muzzle, looked anything but geriatric.

"He'd get bored at home, sir—damn all to do all day." Pausing hopefully, Dawson glanced in Dunbar's direction. "He's no trouble. Not once he knows people."

"All right, bring him along. We're going out, probably for most of the day, starting at Loch Lomond." A small devil nudged at Thane's mind. "Francey—"

"Sir?" Dunbar glared at him, as if sensing what was coming.

"Forget your car. Ride with Dawson, explain things."

"I'll try," said Dunbar balefully. He watched as Dawson got both dogs into the back of the Land-Rover, then drew a deep breath. "Why me with the mobile zoo?"

"You blend in," said Sandra Craig sweetly. "Stay with it, Francey— you could get to like it."

Thane stepped between them.

"You'll ride with me." A thought struck him and he beckoned Joe Felix, annoyed he hadn't done anything about it before. "Joe, there's a note in the file that somebody took a look at Mary Dutton's apartment —routine style. Maybe we should do it again. Add it to your list."

"Sir." Felix nodded.

Felix stood with his hands in his pockets, watching the Ford then the Land-Rover draw away and head down towards the road. When they'd gone, he turned and walked back into the Crime Squad building.

It could be a long day. He'd have a cup of coffee before he started.

CHAPTER THREE

Framed by mountains and studded with wooded islands, Loch Lomond is twenty-four miles long, five miles wide, and Scotland's most beautiful tourist attraction.

It is also less than an hour's travel from the grime of working Glasgow, and the blue Ford and the grey Land-Rover reached its southern edge before 10 A.M. By then, the overcast sky was clearing. Bright sunlight turned the placid surface of the loch to a sparkling blue, and picked out the few small patches of snow still lingering among the mountain peaks.

The lochside road was narrow, winding, and busy with tourist traffic and local vehicles. Buses were mixed with trucks and cars, there were back-pack hikers and motor cyclists, sheep grazed blithely at unfenced verges. The few camp sites were filled with tents and trailer caravans.

The two police vehicles settled into the traffic flow, accepting the pace. Someone had thought he could do better. They passed a car crumpled against a rock, an ambulance taking aboard the injured driver and passenger.

"It's no good, sir." Sandra Craig had been muttering to herself in the passenger seat, puzzling over a map. She scowled at the way Thane sat relaxed behind the wheel. "We need a better map, large-scale. There's no road marked where we're supposed to be going."

"Don't worry," soothed Thane. "We'll have a trusty native guide."

"We'll need him." She wasn't finished. "This Fean Cove is out in the middle of nothing. How did the people who dumped Mary's body know how to get there?"

The same thought had been in Colin Thane's mind. The main road, the only real road along Loch Lomond, hugged the west shore. Fean Cove was located round the northeast wide of the loch, was part national forest reservation, partly privately owned, seldom penetrated by outsiders.

"Maybe they'd a better map," he suggested.

He glanced in his rear view mirror. The Land-Rover was still there, a tour bus close on its tail. He wondered how Francey was treating Jock Dawson. Squad teams didn't always take kindly to newcomers—Thane had experienced that for himself. But he had a feeling that Jock Dawson could look after himself.

"The whole set-up smells wrong." Sandra Craig folded the map and tucked it away, still scowling. They were travelling almost at the water's edge. On the other side, a steep hill was a mass of rhododendrons in full red bloom, splashed with yellow broom and dark purple heather. "If Mary did trip over a couple of city villains, what the hell were they doing out here?"

It was the best question of all, and Thane didn't have any kind of answers.

The road wound on; the traffic stayed heavy. At last they reached the north end of the loch, where the main road swung to the left. But there was a small side road, one Thane had been waiting on, which led off to the right. They took it, the Ford bouncing over potholes and scattering gravel, the Land-Rover close behind.

They covered the next two miles without meeting another vehicle, the landscape a mixture of rough moorland, scrub, and trees, Loch Lomond temporarily lost from sight. Then Thane slowed the Ford as he saw a police car stopped ahead. Two men were standing beside it. Stopping behind the police car, Thane wound down his window as the men came over.

"Sergeant MacLean, sir." The younger of the pair, thick-set, moon-faced, was in uniform. He saluted then indicated his companion, who was in civilian clothes. "Sid Harrison is local special constable. He was with me the day the body was found."

"Thanks for turning out, Mr. Harrison," said Thane.

Special constables were part-time volunteers. Harrison, wearing an oilskin shooting jacket over a wool shirt and ancient serge trousers, gave him a nod but seemed more interested in Sandra Craig.

"Want me to lead the way, sir?" asked MacLean.

"That's the general idea," said Thane.

"Sir." MacLean turned away, beckoning to Harrison.

"Wait," said Sandra Craig. "Does the road get any worse than this?"

"Worse?" MacLean gave a surprised blink. "This is the best of it."

She groaned and sank back.

MacLean's car set off and they followed. The road petered out and became a track, a creaking plank bridge took them over a foaming stream, and beyond it they plunged into a forestry plantation. A large dog fox stared at them then dived for cover among the close-packed trees. The foliage overhead almost shut out the daylight.

They came out into the open on a lip of high, barren ground which gave a panoramic view down Loch Lomond. MacLean's car coasted to a halt, the two Crime Squad vehicles pulled in, and Thane was first out.

The air was still, yet noisy with the whine of insects. Thane walked across to the edge of the lip, looked down, and his mouth tightened. Below him was a ninety foot fall of broken rock, loose scree and straggling vegetation. At the bottom, Fean Cove was a narrow curve of grey shingle edging the lapping water.

It was a harsh, wild scene. Beyond it, the rest of Loch Lomond was spread like a panorama. Across to the west he recognised the high peaks of Ben Vane and Ben Vorlich. On his side of the loch the dominating bulk of Ben Lomond, highest of them all, gave Thane the rest of his bearings.

"Aye, it's like a painting. But nobody in his right mind would trust it to stay that way," said a dry voice at his elbow. Harrison, the special constable, had joined him. Hands stuffed in his pockets, the man gave a grunt. "Those mountains breed rain squalls and worse, any time of year. A man could be out in a boat on that water in flat calm one minute, wondering what the hell had hit him the next."

"Do you live around here?" asked Thane.

Harrison nodded.

"Forestry worker?"

"No, electricity—I'm a maintenance linesman. My wife helps out the budget doing bed and breakfast for tourists."

Thane glanced round. Jock Dawson was letting his dogs out of the Land-Rover with Francey staying clear. Sandra was talking with Sergeant MacLean.

"What did MacLean tell you, Mr. Harrison?" he asked.

"Not a lot. Alan MacLean never does unless it suits him." Harrison chuckled and kicked idly at a pebble. The pebble flew over the edge and tumbled down the rocks. "He's the kind who probably has sergeant's stripes on his nightshirt. But it looks like you think the woman was murdered, right?"

Thane nodded. "Were you surprised?"

"Hard to say." The man's leathery face became serious. "Ach, a few things seemed wrong. Like the way we heard she'd had a back-pack yet never found it—and we looked, believe me. MacLean thought maybe she'd set up camp somewhere." He shrugged. "Is that why you brought the dogs?"

"Partly." Thane picked up another of the pebbles, threw it, and watched until there was a small splash in the water below. "There can't be many people who know how to get to Fean Cove."

"Damn few. We prefer it that way." Harrison considered Thane thoughtfully. "Why?"

"Maybe she arrived here dead."

"Killed somewhere else?" Harrison seemed puzzled. "It doesn't make much sense, does it?"

"Why not?"

"If I had to get rid of a body, I'd dump it straight in the water." The man chewed his lips, frowning. "You've places around here where the bottom is six hundred feet down. We've had people drown, we've known where they went in, we've known we'd never recover the body." Another thought struck him. "Any chance this was deliberate, that she was meant to be found?"

It was Thane's turn to swear under his breath. Harrison's notion fitted, could be one more indication of what they were up against. Reported missing, Detective Sergeant Mary Dutton would have become the reason for a massive, continuing police search. Could her killers have thought that through, cold-bloodedly decided they wanted her found, found in a way that everything pointed to an accident?

If they had, it was a gamble that had nearly come off.

"Now here's someone whose nose is itching," muttered Harrison.

Sergeant MacLean was striding towards them, an anxious smile on his face. Leaving Harrison, Thane met the Strathclyde sergeant halfway.

"Was he annoying you?" MacLean glared in Harrison's direction with the air of a man who felt he'd been left out of things. "I'm sorry, Superintendent—"

"He helped," said Thane. "Now it's your turn. I read your report,

Sergeant—typed, double spacing, no spelling errors. Now just tell me about it, your own words."

"But—" MacLean's round face went red. He suddenly wished that damned body had turned up on someone else's patch—any kind of senior officer could mean trouble and this tall, dark-haired man from the city, outwardly so easy-going, could be a prime example.

"From the beginning, Sergeant," encouraged Thane. "It won't hurt."

"Sir." MacLean swallowed and tried—awkwardly at first. He was stationed at Arrochar village, a few miles beyond the hills to the west, and his territory included a slice of Loch Lomond. Including picking up Sid Harrison, it had taken him about forty minutes to travel from Arrochar to the cottage where the two young holidaymakers who had found the body had managed to locate a telephone.

After that, going to Fean Cove and confirming there was a body, reporting back by radio, taking all the other routine steps required, he seemed to have done everything by the book.

"Any doubts in your mind about the two who found her?" asked Thane.

"None, sir." MacLean shook his head.

"That back-pack is still missing," mused Thane.

"They didn't take it." MacLean almost scowled. "I know the boy is unemployed, bound to be short of money, but—"

"Don't bother, Sergeant," said Thane softly. "Being out of work isn't a crime in my book."

The real crime was the way it kept happening, the way a constantly growing army of unemployed youngsters were being left stranded on welfare benefits. Wasted talents, wasted lives—even the thought generated its own anger.

"They're straight, sir. They'd had one hell of a fright." MacLean hesitated. "Anyway, I—uh—dropped in on them at their camp site later, once we knew a bit more. Just to make sure."

"You didn't put that in your report," said Thane. He paused, brushing a hovering fly away from his face. "You were told the basis of why we're here?"

MacLean nodded. "Detective Inspector Moss phoned from Headquarters. He said I was to keep my mouth shut till you arrived."

"That sounds like him." Thane smiled to himself. "Have there been any complaints of a prowler in your territory, any reports of people being scared or attacked—maybe around the camp sites?"

"Not this year." MacLean felt on surer ground. "We had a problem last summer—two girls attacked, one raped. But we picked up an army deserter, living rough. He admitted the lot, got a seven-year sentence, an' hanged himself in his cell after a month."

It was another blind alley, but he'd had to make sure. Nodding, Thane led the way back towards the cars then stopped again. He watched Dawson's dogs for a moment. Off the leash, they were exploring around the edge of the trees.

"Sergeant, how much do you know about the Peace Camp?"

"The place at Glen Torbat?" MacLean shrugged. "We've never had any trouble from them, sir. Plenty of weird stories, but none that were our business." He scratched his chin with a thumbnail. "I went out an' had a talk with them after we knew Sergeant Dutton had been there. It was the first time I'd been near Glen Torbat in months—it's right on the edge of our territory."

Thane thought of the map in his car. Glen Torbat was about a dozen miles away to the northwest, not far in straight-line terms, but buried in the hills.

"Suppose Mary Dutton had wanted to walk from Glen Torbat to Fean Cove. Could she have used any kind of short-cut route through the hills?"

"No chance, sir."

"You're sure?" Francey Dunbar had joined them. "I'd reckon she was fairly tough."

"And I'd reckon she'd be mad to even try it," growled MacLean, not welcoming doubt. "That's rough country, some of it rock-climbing stuff. I wouldn't try it without a mountain rescue team as back-up." He shook his head. "No, she'd have to stick to the roads most of the way. Maybe that's what happened. Maybe she tried to hitch a lift with the wrong people—it could happen."

"But why bring her here?" asked Thane. Everything kept coming back to that.

"Don't ask me, sir." MacLean gave Dunbar a glance which said, sergeant to sergeant, that was for better paid brains to decide. "But less than a dozen folk use this track regularly and they're mostly forestry workers."

"Now tell us they all drive metallic blue Toyotas," said Dunbar.

MacLean blinked. "You know about that pair of con men?"

Thane and Dunbar stared at him.

"Sergeant, you've lost us," said Thane softly. "What the hell are you talking about?"

"The credit cards thing—" MacLean paused.

"The credit cards thing." Thane drew a deep breath. "We had a laboratory report just before we came here, Sergeant. Mary Dutton was hit by a metallic blue Toyota. You say you know about one?"

"Yes, sir." MacLean's round face was desperately unhappy. "There's a full crime report on it, dated about two weeks back. Two men hit an hotel and a couple of shops at Arrochar village with phoney credit cards. Then one of them cashed a forged cheque at the local bank. They had a blue Toyota."

"You're sure?" demanded Francey Dunbar.

"We've two witnesses, one remembered the registration number." MacLean shrugged. "Fake plates—P.N.C. says the number belongs to a mobile crane in Manchester."

The Police National Computer didn't make mistakes in that area. But two weeks back meant several days before Mary Dutton's death. Thane sucked his lips.

"How much was the take?"

"Nothing heavy, sir. About fifty pounds, in cash, under two hundred from the shops."

The usual "stay small" pattern—the mark of experienced plastic operators, avoiding the risk of a verification call to a credit authorisation centre.

"No word of them being back again?"

MacLean shook his head.

But that meant nothing. Thane looked around.

"Where's Harrison gone?"

Francey Dunbar pointed: the special constable was just visible among the trees, standing with his back to them, the reason obvious.

"He can stay here with Dawson. I'll take the Peace Camp with Sandra." She was in the Ford's passenger seat again, eating a sandwich. "You take Arrochar—ride there with Sergeant MacLean, dig out everything they've got. You know what to do after that." He saw MacLean was still worried. "Nobody's fault, Sergeant. Don't look so sick about it."

Leaving them, he went over to the Land-Rover. Jock Dawson was leaning against the rear door, a cigarette dangling from his mouth. The big black German Shepherd sat at his feet; the Labrador bitch wasn't far away.

"Great place for dogs, boss." Dawson greeted him with a grin then took the cigarette from his mouth. "I'll bet there's half a million rabbits within spitting distance."

"I've a job for you, Jock." Thane met the German Shepherd's suspicious gaze and made a soothing noise. The dog bared its teeth. "I'm leaving you here. This area was searched, I want it done again."

"Properly," said Dawson. "Rajah and Goldie could use some exercise. What are we looking for?"

"Whatever you find."

"That kind." Dawson gave an understanding grunt. "What about afterwards?"

"Unless you hear differently, head for Arrochar—Francey will be there."

"Just one thing, boss—while I've the chance." Dawson snapped his fingers and the German Shepherd stood up, tail wagging. A soft whistle and the Labrador came trotting in. "How does Sergeant Dunbar really feel about dogs? He seems a wee bit unhappy."

"Francey always seems unhappy. That's the way he's made," said Thane wearily. "Get on with it."

The two cars left Fean Cove a minute later, heading back through the trees, MacLean in the lead again. Thane had pushed Sandra into the Ford's driving seat and she handled the car one-handed while she started on a second sandwich from the brown paper bag she'd brought along.

"Help yourself, sir," she said. "There's ham on wholemeal, or the others are pickles and mousetrap cheese—"

"Later." Thane tried to study their map while the car bottomed and swayed. He glanced up and winced. Any closer to the car ahead and it was as if they would have been touching metal. "For God's sake, Sandra, are you trying to give MacLean a coronary?"

"Me sir?" Her voice was innocent.

"You."

"There's no problem." The gap between the two cars didn't alter by a millimetre. Sandra Craig took another bite from her sandwich and chewed for a moment. "I heard MacLean say he doesn't trust women drivers. Why disappoint him?" She grinned and eased back a little.

Exactly as before, they saw no other vehicle on the entire journey round the head of the loch from east to west. Then, at last, they reached the main road again and were suddenly back to heavy traffic.

A few miles down, they reached the turn-off for Arrochar and took it. Within moments, both cars were down to a crawl as part of a slow-moving queue of traffic behind a massive, lumbering Royal Navy articulated truck. The truck, cargo sheathed in canvas, was guarded by two scout cars filled with Royal Marines.

Thane gave in and helped himself to one of Sandra Craig's sandwiches. It was cheese and pickle, and he eyed the naval presence ahead with a wry attempt at patience while he ate.

Arrochar was on Loch Long, one of the Atlantic sea arms of the Firth of Clyde. The distance across from the land-locked Loch Lomond was only about three miles, through a wooded gap between the hills. About a thousand years back, a Viking fleet had sailed up Loch Long from the sea, had dragged their longships by sheer muscle-power that three-mile distance over rocks and anything else in the way, and had launched them again in Loch Lomond. From there, they had ravaged their way through a whole series of unsuspecting, prosperous inland villages.

Things had certainly changed. That Royal Navy truck ahead had to be on its way to one of the NATO naval bases scattered around the Clyde estuary. Arrochar had an experimental torpedo test range, the U.S. Navy had a nuclear submarine base at Holy Loch, and the British had their Polaris base at Faslane. A vast new Trident complex was being established at Coulport—and there was all the rest, from underground command bunkers and ammunition stores to fuel depots and strange, totally classified structures.

Enough to spark a dour local joke that the Russians probably knew every sheep in the area by its first name and had an SS 20 rocket targeted on every last one of them. The Peace Camp at Glen Torbat was on the fringe of strange company, whatever its reasons for existence.

"Sir." Sandra Craig broke an unusually long silence. "Tell me to mind my own business if you want, but this problem you've got, Kate's friend —you know what I mean." She gave him a cautious, sideways glance. "If you need any extra help—"

"You'll hear." He cursed Francey Dunbar for talking too much. "Keeping you out was deliberate."

"Do-it-yourself psychology for parents?" She grinned. "Well, Kate's all right. At her age—"

"You couldn't be much worse than now," growled Thane. He felt a moment's guilt that he'd almost forgotten the matter. "Leave it."

She nodded meekly.

They parted company with MacLean's car at Arrochar, a very ordinary little village on the edge of the grey water of its sea-loch. MacLean's car headed into the village, and they kept on, heading north, past the torpedo range. Then they struck inland on a minor, single-track road which climbed through heather and moorland. A bearded tramp tried to thumb a lift then gave an obscene gesture when they didn't slow. Farther on, they disturbed a huddle of black rooks feeding on something small and brown and bloodied, flattened into the tarmac.

The hills grew higher; the air became colder. A small herd of deer watched them from a slope. Then they topped a final rise and saw Glen Torbat below.

Narrow and wooded, sheltered by two hog-back hills, it was a total contrast to the surrounding wilderness. As the Ford coasted down towards its gash, Thane caught a glimpse of a scatter of log cabins round a large stone-built mansion house. He had been keeping a check on their mileage. The twelve-mile straight-line distance from Fean Cove was just over thirty in terms of road travel.

Two crumbling pillars, each topped by a stone eagle, marked the entrance to a long driveway, and a large wooden sign to one side said "The Peace Camp" in letters a foot high. He nodded, and the car crunched over loose gravel as they drove in towards the house and the cluster of cabins.

Some of the cabins were big; some were small; all were of the same basic shingle and timber design with stove-pipe chimneys. A dozen men and women in saffron-coloured robes were playing football outside one cabin. Near the mansion, another group in track suits marched behind a woman waving a clanging handbell.

"Francey would love this," said Sandra Craig.

Thane didn't answer, intent on the house ahead.

Old enough to have seen better days, it was grey with a black slate roof. Moss clung to much of the stonework and where there was wood it needed a new coat of paint. But someone had put in a lot of work pruning a bank of roses outside the main door. The place had character of a kind, pride mixed with a hint of poverty.

Half a dozen cars and a white mini-bus were in a parking area outside the house. None of the cars was a Toyota—that would have been too easy.

They drew in, stopped, and got out. There was a tang of woodsmoke in the air, and as they climbed steps up to the front porch, Thane caught a glimpse of a donkey grazing in a paddock. The main door, heavy dark oak studded with ironwork, was open and they went into a large, square-shaped hallway. The sound of their feet on the stone floor made a young girl look up from behind a trestle table she was using as a desk. She rose, and came over.

"Hello." Her hair was long and straight and chestnut, almost down to her waist. She had dark eyes, a snub nose, and was still in her teens. She was wearing a grey wool shirt and Gordon tartan trews. "Can I help you?"

"I hope so." Thane matched her smile. "I'm looking for the manager, Peter Crossley."

"He's in a meeting." She hesitated. "He said he couldn't see any-one—"

"Ask him." Thane showed his warrant card.

The girl took it, read it slowly, and still hesitated.

She sighed. "He said no-one. But I'll try."

She left them, the Gordon trews moving in an easy, teenage swagger, and disappeared down a corridor. There was a noticeboard along most of one side of the hallway, beside a large-scale map. Sandra drifted over to the noticeboard, then moved on to the map. After a moment, she stared closer then glanced round.

"Sir—"

Thane joined her. The map took in the north end of Loch Lomond. It was large scale and took in every detail of the network of tracks that led to Fean Cove.

They heard footsteps approaching and turned as the girl came back followed by a tall, thick-set man with sandy hair. The sandy hair was thin on top, and the man's broad, slightly fleshy face didn't offer any wel-come.

"We only had a sergeant last time." He kept his hands in the pockets of the blue tweed jacket he wore over an open-necked shirt and grey trousers. "What's happened now, Superintendent? I'm Peter Crossley."

"The death of Mary Dutton—we're making some new enquiries," said Thane with deliberate formality. "This is Detective Constable Craig. We need a few minutes with you."

"That's what we—what I thought." Crossley glanced at the girl, who was still beside him. "Get lost, Mandy. Nothing to do with you." He waited until she was back at the trestle table, out of earshot. "I told the little I know. Anyway, I thought your people had finished."

"We've started again," said Thane.

"I see." For a moment, a flicker of what could have been apprehension showed in the man's blue eyes. Then he sighed. "My boss is here—she'd better hear this. You picked a bad day for me, Superintendent."

"Because of your boss?"

The Peace Camp manager nodded. "Mrs. Thornton. Her father started this place, she owns it now, and she arrived a couple of hours ago. Out of the blue—she does things that way." He looked across at the girl and raised his voice. "Hold the fort again, Mandy. But nobody else, no matter what—understand?"

Then he beckoned and they followed him down the corridor to a door partly hidden by a decorative archway. Knocking, opening the door, Crossley ushered them into a large, shabby room which had a log fire burning in its stone hearth. A man and woman seated at a large, old-fashioned table looked up at them. The table was covered in files and papers.

"This is Superintendent Thane," said Crossley gloomily, closing the door behind him. "It's about the accident at Fean Cove."

The woman rose and came over. She was small and neat, in her mid-forties, her short dark hair lightly flecked with grey. The man had followed her. She gave him a glance then her deep-set brown eyes, sharp and appraising, switched back to Thane.

"I'm Barbara Thornton, this is my husband." Her voice was crisp. "I don't know what you want, Mr. Thane. But we'll help if we can."

Hastily, Crossley completed the introductions. Magnus Thornton was a tall, mousey-haired man with a thin build and an irritated expression.

"Don't worry about my husband, Superintendent," said Barbara Thornton dryly. "He's an accountant, he often looks miserable."

"There's a reason." Thornton grimaced back at the papers on the table. "It's called total chaos."

"But nobody's fault," soothed his wife.

"That doesn't help," said Thornton.

Two more chairs had been brought to the table by Crossley. While the Peace Camp manager quickly cleared most of the files and papers, Barbara Thornton returned to her seat and waited for the others to join her.

She had a heart-shaped face with high cheekbones and a small mouth. Her dark green velvet jacket and matching skirt went with a grey silk blouse and a single string pearl necklace. There was a large solitaire diamond ring beside the gold band on her wedding finger. Sitting next to her, Magnus Thornton wore a grey business suit with a white shirt and plain maroon tie. He was about the same age as his wife. Irritation faded a little, he relaxed back and rubbed his long, narrow hands together.

"So what's this about?" he asked with an air of resignation. "Peter told me about the accident, about the local police coming here—what now?"

"A few things have changed," said Thane. He looked past them. The room had bare floorboards and a minimum of furnishings. At the far end an uncurtained window gave a view of the paddock and the donkey. "We've re-opened the case."

"I see." Barbara Thornton glanced at her husband, then at Crossley. "Superintendent, as far as the Peace Camp was concerned, she was just another guest. She came and she left—nobody knew she was a police-woman until the local sergeant told Peter."

Crossley nodded. "We never ask people what they do for a living."

"That's deliberate. One of the reasons they come here." Barbara Thornton frowned. "Superintendent, people your rank don't have time to waste. You said things have changed. What does that mean? It wasn't an accident?"

Thane nodded.

"Murder?" asked Magnus Thornton bluntly.

"We're treating it that way."

Thornton stopped rubbing his hands, his eyes narrowing. Barbara Thornton stared across at Sandra, as if seeking confirmation, while Peter Crossley took a deep breath and let it out as a sigh.

"Now we know." Magnus Thornton was the first to speak. "But I wasn't here, my wife wasn't here." He twisted a humourless grin at Crossley. "That leaves the question to you, Peter."

"I told Sergeant MacLean all I knew," said the Peace Camp manager. "Mary Dutton booked in to stay a week, then after two days she said she was going to move on." He shrugged. "That happens. She left the next morning."

"Did you see her go?" asked Sandra Craig.

"No." The man's beefy face flushed. "She paid her bill the night before, when she told me. After that—well, this isn't an hotel."

"If it was, my wife wouldn't have so many problems," said Magnus Thornton.

"Magnus." Barbara Thornton made a quick, irritated gesture. "Don't —not now." She fingered the pearls at her throat. "Superintendent, you haven't told us how she died. Was she—well, was she raped?"

Thane shook his head.

"Then—" she looked puzzled.

"I can't tell you more, Mrs. Thornton." Thane rubbed a thumb along his chin. "Why did you think sex was involved?"

"Because I'm a woman." Barbara Thornton pursed her lips. "It—I suppose it was the first thing that came into my mind."

Magnus Thornton gave a grunt which could have meant anything. But she wasn't finished.

"Peter said this isn't an hotel, Superintendent. Can I explain? It might help. We've no real rules, because that's the way my father founded this place. People arrive, they're welcomed, we leave them to come to us."

"What about meals?"

"They can prepare their own food in the cabins, or there's a cafeteria in this house—they decide."

"Who cleans, who makes the beds?" asked Sandra.

"We offer maid service." It was Crossley who answered, leaning forward, anxious to contribute. "Not many want it. Usually, we just clean up after they've gone."

"Clean up? It can be more like a rebuild," said Magnus Thornton. He gave Sandra a cynical grin. "Some of these people behave like a wrecking crew."

Outside the window, the donkey gave a sudden bray, made a mad gallop across the paddock, then stopped and shook its head. In the background distance, the handbell was clanging again.

"Crossley." Thane spoke quietly. "How well did you know Mary Dutton?"

Crossley stiffened. "What do you mean?"

"This wasn't her first visit."

"That's right." Crossley nodded carefully. "She stayed a few days last year. But—"

"You saw a lot of her, didn't you?"

"I took her into Arrochar village for a drink a couple of times, that's all." Crossley flushed a deeper red and ran a hand over his thin, sandy hair. "Nothing else happened, if that's what you're hinting." He moistened his lips. "In fact, I don't think I like this."

"It's easier here than in a police station." Thane let the warning sink home, ignoring Barbara Thornton's muttered protest. "You knew her. She suddenly said she was moving on. Didn't she give a reason, didn't she say where she was going?"

"I asked." Crossley shrugged. "She wouldn't tell me."

"You're sure?" asked Thane grimly.

"Yes."

"Do you have to bully him?" asked Barbara Thornton. "He gave you an answer."

"It's all right, Mrs. Thornton." Crossley drew a deep breath. "Go on." He scowled at Sandra Craig. "Shouldn't she be writing this down?"

"Not yet." Thane tapped his fingers lightly on the table for a moment. "Mary Dutton was here two days. Did she meet anyone, talk with anyone?"

"I don't think so." Crossley shook his head. "I didn't see much of her."

"Do you keep a guest register?"

The man shrugged. "Yes and no."

"Meaning?"

"We handle a lot of group bookings. Suppose—well, suppose a party of ten want one of the large cabins. We deal with the party leader, the booking is in his or her name. That's all we need."

"Sergeant Dutton didn't have a car," said Sandra Craig quietly. "How did she get here?"

"We sent the camp mini-bus to pick her up at Arrochar." Crossley's heavy face cleared a little. He was on surer ground. "People phone and we do that."

"How did she leave?"

"On her own, as far as I know."

"Tell me something, Superintendent." Magnus Thornton broke in, with thinly veiled sarcasm. "Are you planning to harass all the staff like this—or is Peter special?"

"Nobody is special yet, Mr. Thornton." Thane kept a stonily polite front and turned to the Peace Camp manager again. "This 'yes and no' register you keep—do you take any note of guests' car registrations?"

Crossley shook his head.

"Are we breaking any laws?" asked Barbara Thornton, a dangerous glint in her dark brown eyes. "Or have you some real kind of reason for all this?"

"Just one," said Thane unemotionally. "A dead policewoman, Mrs. Thornton." It silenced her. He turned back to Crossley. "Do you remember a metallic blue Toyota being here about the same time as Mary Dutton?"

"I can't remember." Crossley floundered for a moment. "I—I'm not very interested in cars."

"Try," invited Sandra Craig.

"Toyota—it's a Japanese make, I know that much." Crossley bit his lip.

"Toyota, metallic blue—maybe two men aboard," prompted Thane.

Magnus Thornton gave a murmur of interest and glanced at his wife. She was frowning.

"You've a line on someone?" asked Thornton.

Thane shrugged. "Crossley?"

"I'm not certain. There may have been." Crossley nursed his head in his hands for a moment, elbows on the table, then looked up. "It could have been people passing through, stopping for a meal or a look around the place—that happens. But I can't help you. Maybe someone else will remember."

"We'll ask," said Thane.

They did.

The interview session over, the atmosphere in the Peace Camp office suddenly became less frigid with Crossley almost friendly again in his relief and both Thorntons making noises about being willing to help.

There was a staff of seven, which was fewer than Thane had expected. They ranged from a cook and a gardener to cleaning staff, a general handyman, and Mandy, the young receptionist. Thane gave the job of talking to them to Sandra Craig and Magnus Thornton surprised him by immediately volunteering to act as her guide.

They went off, Thornton smiling, Barbara Thornton watching them go with a total lack of expression on her face. Then she went back to the files and papers while Crossley took Thane out into the lobby area, where the Peace Camp register was kept.

It didn't take long to check; it was just as sketchy as Crossley had indicated. A typical entry was a pencilled tick opposite a cabin, a scribbled name, the number in a party, and arrival and departure dates. Sometimes there was even less.

"But we'll have letters on file, telephone numbers, things like that," said Crossley apologetically. "If you want any of them—"

Thane nodded. "I'll need a copy of the entries covering when Mary Dutton was here. Can I see the cabin she used?"

"Yes." Crossley checked the register. "It's empty. I'll get the key."

He left Thane, went back to the office, and returned with the key in a few moments.

"Anything else?" he asked.

"No." Thane looked at him. "Unless you've remembered something."

Peter Crossley stiffened. "If you mean the way things were between me and Mary, I told you."

"Suppose she said differently?"

"No." Crossley shook his head vehemently. "No chance—and if she did, she was wrong."

Thane took the key, left him, and went out into the grounds. The team of joggers led by the woman with the handbell had vanished; the saffron-robed footballers were in a silent circle under a tree. He passed other people, some alone, some in twos and threes. An elderly man strolled past, in shorts and a sweater, spindle-like legs in open-toe sandals, and gave him a slight nod of recognition.

Thane stared after him. He was a senior High Court judge and his name certainly wasn't on the Peace Camp register.

Mary Dutton had occupied a single-room cabin, one of four in a block. Unlocking the door, he went in. Basic in style, it amounted to one room with a tiny kitchen area and a separate shower, washbasin and toilet. The main furnishings were a bed, a large locker and two upright chairs.

He tried the bed. It sagged comfortably and he let himself sink back on it, hands clasped behind his head, staring at the pinewood ceiling. As usual when he was trying to think, he would have given a lot for a cigarette.

From all the talk there had been in Crossley's office, one aspect still nagged at his mind.

Detective Sergeant Mary Dutton had been no schoolgirl in her outlook or emotions. She wouldn't have come back from her first Peace Camp visit talking so much to Sheila Swann about Crossley on the strength of a few kind words and a couple of drinks. She wouldn't have tried so hard to get her friend to come with her on a return visit.

Crossley had to be lying. Maybe, in part, he wanted to protect his job. But if he could lie determinedly about one thing, did it stop there? Thane scowled at a crack in the wood overhead. Against that, the Peace Camp manager didn't tie in with that all-important postcard or the flecks of paint.

He sighed and elbowed himself up from the bed. Maybe something else would surface through Francey Dunbar at Arrochar or Joe Felix back in Glasgow. There was even Jock Dawson, probably still padding around with his dogs at that lonely corner of Loch Lomond.

Something had to surface. Something usually did.

Because it was on his list, he spent a few minutes checking through the cabin. It had been thoroughly cleaned since its last occupancy; every surface had been polished. He'd still have to ask for a Scenes of Crime team to run a routine check, but Thane knew it could almost be guaranteed to be a waste of time.

Eventually, he went out again, locked the cabin door behind him, and walked for a spell around the rest of the Peace Camp area. Eventually, he was back near the house and beside the paddock area.

The donkey ambled across to meet him. Thane pulled some grass from his own side of the fence and offered it. The donkey looked over, nuzzled his hand, then drew back with a snort.

"The same to you," said Thane sourly and leaned on the fence.

"I know the feeling," said a voice.

Barbara Thornton was standing behind him. She came over to the fence, produced a sugar lump from one pocket of her dark green jacket, and the donkey took it from her hand.

"We call him Lester." She leaned her elbows on the fence. "Well, now you've seen the place, what do you think of it?"

"It's different," said Thane carefully.

"At least you're diplomatic now and again." In profile, her face with those high cheekbones was hard to read. "I wouldn't take another one in a gift."

"Problems?" asked Thane.

"More than a few. If Magnus and I had our way, things would change." She shrugged. "It began as my father's idea. Did you know?" He nodded.

"He had his reasons, I suppose." Her voice softened a little. "He was a bomber pilot in World War Two, he came back with plenty of medals and a badly damaged conscience. For a few years he made a lot of money in business, then one day he suddenly bought Glen Torbat house and set up this place." The donkey had returned, but she ignored it. "The Peace Camp—the name was his choice, but it wasn't any kind of political label."

"That damaged conscience?" Thane nodded. "What went wrong?"

"Nothing, till after he died. Then inflation, rising costs, and a trust deed I can't break." The donkey tried to nuzzle her across the fence. Barbara Thornton gently pushed its face away. "Financially, it barely breaks even. But I'm stuck with the place."

"If you could, what would you do?"

"Sell, or build an hotel." She gave a dry laugh. "Either way, sleep easier."

"How does your husband feel about it?"

"Magnus?" For a moment, the same strange expression he'd seen back in Crossley's office crossed her face then had gone. "He's an accountant, Superintendent." She paused, and her mood changed again. "I'm sorry about the way I snapped at you—you know, when you were questioning Peter Crossley. When you told us about the car—"

"I had to do it that way."

She nodded. "Do you really think something happened here?"

He shook his head. "I don't know."

"Which could be police-speak for mind your own damned business." She smiled wryly. "But I know Peter, he's been manager here for years.

He's not brilliant but he's harmless." She paused again and looked thoughtful. "You know, I've an idea where your policewoman could have headed when she left here—if she was the type."

"Tell me," invited Thane, puzzled.

"Maybe she wanted something more committed than this place, one of the real peace camps—the kind where they squat outside defence bases and shout a lot. She wouldn't have to travel very far." Barbara Thornton saw his expression. "You don't think so?"

"I doubt it." He shook his head. "But I'll keep it in mind."

"It's just a notion." She stepped back from the fence. "If you're finished, come back to the house. I told Peter to organise something to eat."

They went back together. Peter Crossley had soup and sandwiches waiting in his office and also had the details from the Camp register ready. Sandra Craig had returned before them and was eating at the table, but there was no sign of Magnus Thornton.

"It's my fault, Mrs. Thornton." Sandra gave an apologetic grimace and reached for another sandwich. "We were in the cafeteria kitchen, looking for the cook. I'm afraid I knocked over a bowl of salad dressing—just being plain clumsy. He got most of it, and he's cleaning up some-where."

Barbara Thornton looked at her through narrowed eyes for a moment, then shrugged.

"At least your own clothes weren't damaged, Constable Craig," she said softly. "I'm glad you escaped."

Magnus Thornton still hadn't reappeared by the time they left. Thane let Sandra take the wheel and waited until the Ford had driven out of the Peace Camp's gates.

"So what did happen?" he demanded.

"Wandering hands." Sandra Craig changed gear and swung the car on the hill road back towards Arrochar. "Nothing subtle about it, just plain grab and grope. I warned him off first, twice," she grinned. "I thought of breaking his arm."

"Common assault, police brutality. He could sue us for the cleaning bill." Thane sighed and settled back. "Apart from that, what did you get?"

"Not a lot." She shook her head. "It's the way we heard, sir. People come, people go, nobody pays much attention. Mandy on reception and one of the cabin maids both remember Mary, but nothing more. The gardener thinks he may have seen a blue Toyota because his brother-in-law has one. The only real thing I did get was something interesting about the mail arrangements."

She stopped it there for a moment, sawing at the wheel to avoid a suicide dash by a rabbit. It left Thane clutching the dashboard.

"Rabbits rule—don't do that." He released his grip. "What about the mail?"

"They've their own private collection box in the Camp. Someone empties it each morning and drives all the mail to Arrochar post office." She gave him a sideways glance. "Mary's postcard was date-stamped Arrochar, wasn't it?"

Thane swore. It knocked part of their basic reckoning sideways. Mary Dutton might never have reached Arrochar, despite the postcard. She could have been killed any time from the night before—anywhere.

But the postcard had been sent. If there was any real link with the Peace Camp, if it had been posted in the private mail box, someone had slipped up.

Sandra Craig seemed to read his mind. "What do you make of Crossley, sir?"

"I don't buy his story when he talks about Mary."

"I feel that way." She steered the car round a bend. "But I talked to people who say he didn't leave the camp that night."

"Would they remember?" asked Thane cynically.

She shrugged. "What about the Thorntons?"

He grinned. "You're the expert on Magnus."

Sandra grimaced. "I think his wife has an idea what happens. But he's still nobody's fool."

"True." Thane opened the glove-box, took his pack of cigarettes out from hiding, and saw her frown. Sighing, he put them back again. "All right, let's hear the rest of it."

It was background, and it didn't take long to tell.

The Thorntons had been married about ten years, lived in a luxury farm cottage conversion on the southern edge of Glasgow, and had no family. No-one at the Peace Camp knew much about their private lives. Magnus Thornton was a former banker who ran Gordon Hope Management, a one-man companies servicing firm in the city. Barbara Thornton controlled Thornton Travel, a small string of travel agencies she had inherited from her father.

It was seven years since Barbara Thornton's father had died and she'd taken over the Peace Camp, three years since she had appointed Peter Crossley as manager there—and Crossley had told the truth about one thing. No-one ever knew when either Barbara Thornton or her husband were going to make a surprise visit. When it happened, particularly when they appeared together, it was totally business and no time was wasted.

"What do they drive?" asked Thane.

"Two Jaguars, both white." A note of envy entered his voice. "Did you see that diamond solitaire?"

He grinned. "Maybe you could have earned one."

Her reply was even ruder than he'd expected.

They passed the same tramp at the roadside another two miles on. This time he was ready for them. As the Ford swept towards him, he turned his back and dropped his trousers to his ankles.

Sandra Craig gave a horn-blast and waved as they passed.

Thane looked back. The tramp, trousers still around his ankles, stood open-mouthed in disappointment.

CHAPTER FOUR

They reached Arrochar village at 3 P.M. to meet a rising, gusting wind. Loch Long's shingle beach was being washed by a low, grey swell from the Atlantic, the scatter of dinghies off-shore tugged at their moorings, and dark rain clouds were heading in from the west. The radio aerial on the roof of the village police station had begun quivering its own comment.

A storm was on the way. The first rain drops began pattering down as the Crime Squad car parked in the station yard and the real downpour started as Thane and Sandra Craig hurried into the shelter of the building.

The public office had a customer. A young constable behind the counter faced an angry, shabbily dressed man who had a small child clutching at his trouser leg and an even smaller one perched beside him on the countertop. The man's tirade ended in mid-sentence and he gave a suspicious glare. His left eye was blackened, swollen, and completely closed.

"Wait, Davie." The constable came over, straightened as Thane showed his warrant card, and nodded. "Your sergeant is using Sergeant MacLean's office—through at the back, sir." He winced as the child on the counter gave an impatient yell. "Sergeant MacLean was called out, but he should be back soon."

The child on the counter howled again, the man with the black eye scowled.

"Trouble?" asked Thane.

"Yes." The constable's schoolboy face shaped a grimace. "We locked up his wife after she hit him with a bottle—they're regulars. Now he wants her out."

"Doesn't he know when he's lucky?"

"He says he'll risk it—he can't cope with the kids." There was another yell from the counter. The constable gave a groan. A patch of wet was spreading out from under the child. "Hell, now what do I do? I'm on my own till MacLean gets back."

"Think positive," suggested Sandra Craig. "Get a cloth."

The other child began howling. Easing away, they found Sergeant MacLean's office. The door lay open, and they saw Francey Dunbar slouching in a chair with his feet up on the Strathclyde sergeant's desk. Behind him, a collection of posters on the wall ranged from Wanted notices to details of a charity dance in the village hall.

"Busy, Francey?" asked Thane dryly.

"Thinking, sir," said Dunbar cheerfully. He swung his feet down, rose, and considered the rain beating against the office window. "Looks like you just made it in time."

"Any word from Jock Dawson?"

"Not yet." Dunbar grinned. "Any chance he could drown in this lot?"

"His dogs have life-saving medals." Thane dropped into the vacant chair. "Where's MacLean gone?"

"A break-in at a farmhouse." Dunbar saw Sandra eyeing the empty coffee mug on the desk. "There's a kettle next door. He keeps the coffee in the first-aid cabinet."

"Sir?" She raised an eyebrow at Thane.

He nodded and she went out. They heard the kettle being filled.

"What about here, Francey?" asked Thane.

"Fairly good." Dunbar propped himself on the edge of the desk, dug a notebook from his pocket, and flipped it open. "Two good descriptions plus one witness definite about the Toyota and another saying maybe."

"You've passed them on?"

"To our people and Phil Moss." Dunbar sucked an edge of his thin moustache. "Two men, early thirties, well dressed—they used the credit card names Harold Evans and John Wilton. Evans about five foot ten, thin, dark hair, sallow, spoke with an accent—some say English, some say foreign. Wrote with his left hand." He glanced at the notebook. "Wilton five foot seven, medium build, spectacles, small scar on his chin, light brown hair, probably a Scot. Said they were salesmen passing through."

"Not bad." The descriptions were good, if the witnesses' memories could be relied on. Any cop knew the gamble, the frustration involved, the way memory and reality could be totally different. "Anything else I should know about?"

Dunbar shook his head. "That's it—except Linda Belmont is still waiting for that call from Katie's pal. Uh—any luck at the Peace Camp, sir?"

"Ask Sandra."

"He means I got my bottom felt." She could hear them from the next room.

"A brave man," said Dunbar quietly. "Crossley, the manager?"

"No, an accountant named Thornton. He was there with his wife— she owns the place." Briefly, Thane sketched their visit. His account left Dunbar frowning.

"I don't buy some of it." His sergeant scratched absently under the neck of his sweater. "Why would Crossley be twitchy about Mary Dutton?"

"Either he's hiding something or he's scared of Mrs. Thornton." Sandra Craig returned, a mug of coffee in each hand. She set one down in front of Thane and nursed the other. "She's the type who'd scare a few men."

"Like you," suggested Dunbar.

Thane stopped them. "I want a Scenes of Crime team at Glen Torbat tomorrow, Francey. Tell them to go through the motions at the cabin Mary Dutton used, then make a show of trying the camp register for fingerprints. After that, they'll need to fingerprint the staff for elimination."

"Including Crossley?" Dunbar understood. "Want me with them?"

"No." Thane eyed him over the coffee mug. "Go in separately— helmet, leathers and the B.M.W. Book a cabin for a couple of nights, nose around, but keep out of trouble."

"Expecting something?" Dunbar raised an eyebrow.

Thane shrugged. All he knew was they weren't finished with the Peace Camp connection. He needed someone inside able to ask around and Francey Dunbar was tailor-made for the role.

The rain stopped as suddenly as it had begun. They heard the police station door bang as the constable finally got rid of his complaining visitor and family, then a few minutes later Sergeant MacLean's car drove into the puddled police yard. As MacLean climbed out, Jock Dawson's grey Land-Rover rolled in.

Thane went through to the front office to meet them. Dawson walked in first and shook his head.

"Nothing, boss," he reported laconically. "Me and the dogs worked that whole Fean Cove strip—topsides, then along the beach."

Thane remembered the special constable. "What about Harrison?"

"Dropped him at his house." Dawson had more important things on his mind. "Rajah and Goldie should have been fed an hour ago. I won't be long."

Turning on his heel, he ambled out leaving Thane with MacLean.

"How was your break-in?" asked Thane.

"A kitchen window left open, so someone climbed in and stole a few bits and pieces—mostly tins of food." MacLean loosened his tie and unbuttoned his tunic, then sighed. "They saw Big Angus earlier on. I'll have to find him, I suppose. He's what social workers call a 'travelling person,' sir. Meaning, in Big Angus's case, a damn thieving tramp. He could be anywhere by now."

"Try the road between here and Glen Torbat," said Thane. "I think we passed him—a heavy beard and his own line in greetings."

MacLean winced. "Those damned trousers again? I warned him, next time I'd have him for indecent exposure. But as soon as he gets some money for booze—"

"Big Angus celebrates?" Thane tried not to grin. "Pick him up later. Think back to when you told Crossley that Mary Dutton had been a policewoman. Did he seem surprised?"

"That's hard to say." MacLean was cautious. "He was more interested in telling me the Peace Camp couldn't be involved."

"Ever met his boss, Barbara Thornton?"

"Aye, once sir." The local sergeant sucked his lips at the memory. "Pleasant enough, but I wouldn't want to cross her."

"What about her husband?"

"No. Though I've heard he's a match for her." A telephone began ringing somewhere, they heard the constable answer, and MacLean strained to hear what was happening. "Eh—anything else right now, sir?"

"Mrs. Thornton suggested Mary Dutton might have headed off to some anti-nuclear camp outside a defence base. Where's the nearest?"

"A long way from here, sir." MacLean was still trying to listen to his constable's telephone conversation. "The Polaris base at Gareloch is the closest I know." He grinned a little. "That's right outside of my patch, thank the Good Lord."

"Nothing nearer, any size?"

"Nothing."

"Right." Thane hadn't expected a different answer. "Thanks for your help, sergeant."

"You're—uh—finished here? asked MacLean cautiously.

"For now." Thane saw the relief in the local sergeant's eyes. "I'll stay in touch." He could have mentioned Francey Dunbar but didn't. The fewer people who knew Dunbar was going into the Peace Camp at Glen Torbat, the less risk there was of its leaking out. "Good luck with your tramp."

"The damn car that brings him in will have to be fumigated," grimaced MacLean. "Best o' luck with—well, your business too, sir."

He headed off purposefully towards the back office and the telephone. Thane heard him taking over the call from the constable, chuckled, then went outside into the puddled yard. He was spotted. A low, warning growl came from the Labrador bitch. She was standing guard at the open rear of the Land-Rover.

"Goldie, shut up," ordered Jock Dawson, sticking his head out into view. "That's the boss."

The Labrador subsided and Thane went over. Dawson was sitting on the Land-Rover's flat floor with the black bulk of Rajah lying across his lap. Looking up, the German Shepherd gave a soft whine.

"Easy," soothed Dawson. He gave an apologetic grin in Thane's direction. "We've a wee difficulty. Don't move for a moment."

Thane froze. Dawson had one of the dog's massive front paws between his hands. Suddenly he bent, his head close against the animal's strong, white teeth. His fingers shifted, gripped, then the dog-handler bit at something in one of the dog's pads. Rajah jerked, then Dawson brought his head up again. Letting go the animal's paw, he spat a long, sharp thorn into the palm of his hand.

"Got the devil." He grinned at Thane, slapped the German Shepherd on the rump, and the dog rose. It licked the paw briefly then sprang down to the ground to join Goldie.

"Back in business?" Thane sat on the edge of the tailboard.

Dawson nodded. "He must have picked it up at Fean Cove. Want us for something, boss?"

"No. But let's talk for a minute."

"Right." Dawson made himself more comfortable, his back against the Land-Rover's sidepanels. Producing a small metal tin, he took out tobacco and papers and hand-rolled a cigarette. He struck a match, the cigarette flared, and he took a long, satisfied draw. "Look, boss, will I make it easier? This morning was fine, but you don't really know what the hell to do with me?"

"That's not exactly how I'd put it," said Thane.

"Ach, I was warned." Unperturbed, Dawson let the crumpled cigarette dangle from his lips. "Don't worry about it, boss. You know the saying—never look a gift dog in the mouth."

Thane winced. "How long have you worked with dogs?"

"I grew up wi' them." Dawson grinned. Goldie had come over and was rubbing herself against Thane's leg. "I was told you've a dog at home."

Thane nodded.

"They know it." Dawson drew on his cigarette again. "They know a hell of a lot. Rajah, now—he knows Sergeant Dunbar isn't too happy about him. So he'll make Sergeant Dunbar's life a misery for a spell, for devilment. But they'll know you all well enough soon. No problems."

He was serious and it mattered to him, despite the grin. Thane guessed that, as far as the lanky dog-handler was concerned, it amounted to a speech.

"I'll use you when I can—any way I can, Jock," he promised. "First thing, when we get back, draw a Squad radio for this vehicle. How about food for the dogs?"

Dawson shook his head. "No worries, that's fixed. Rajah doesn't officially retire for a spell yet, they both draw rations."

"Good." Police dogs drew standard rations, scaled by a veterinary professor. It worked out at one and a half pounds of meat and one pound of meal per dog per day. Thane had heard some grudging cops complain they didn't eat as well. "How about you? How do you feel about things?"

"Me?" Dawson looked surprised. "If the dogs are happy, I'm happy."

They left Arrochar as another rainstorm swept in, met better weather as they headed south, and reached Glasgow in bright sunlight. The city was beginning to empty for the evening as the two vehicles crossed the Kingston Bridge and reached Crime Squad headquarters.

Parting from the rest of his team in the parking lot, Colin Thane went into the building and straight to his office. A small pile of message slips had accumulated on his desk. Beside them, someone had placed half a dozen copies of a new head and shoulders photograph of Mary Dutton. The prints had been weighed down with a metal box he used for paper-clips, the sun had got at them, and they had warped at the edges.

He looked at them for a moment, the snub-nosed face and dark, thoughtful eyes seeming to make their own silent protest, then tucked two into an inside pocket and put the rest in a drawer, out of sight.

The message slips were a mixed batch. Some concerned other cases and would have to be passed on. One that mattered to him, timed 3 P.M., was from Linda Belmont. Katie's friend had called, they had a meeting arranged for early evening, and the blond detective sergeant would let him know later. Thane felt a mild sense of relief, then smiled at the message that followed. Millside C.I.D. wanted him to know that Tank Mallard and his sister had appeared in court and had been re-manded.

The next slip, a telephone message, was different and formal. The Strathclyde laboratory had finished their analysis of the samples of grit found on Mary Dutton's clothing. They were a mixture of rock dust and road asphalt, and the sources could be anywhere.

Joe Felix knocked on his door and came in while he was sorting through the remainder. The stocky, balding detective constable had his tie loosened and was in his shirt-sleeves.

"Francy told me you were back, sir." Felix had the tired-eyed look of a man who had had his own kind of full day. "I've had Commander Hart on the prowl, wanting an up-date."

"I'll go along." Thane discarded the last of the message slips. "What about here?"

Felix shook his head. "Not a lot. I went through Mary's apartment like you asked—nothing. I can't make any kind of match with the two descriptions Francey phoned down from Arrochar, and she wasn't in-volved in any credit card case in her time with us." He shrugged. "I checked with Inspector Moss. He says he'll keep trying with his lists."

"The Toyota?"

"Several outstanding as stolen, but the computer says none with that respray." Joe Felix was disappointed and showed it. "Uh—Francey says you're putting him in undercover tomorrow."

"That's right." Thane sensed something coming. "What else did he tell you?"

"He thinks Dawson's Land-Rover smells like an old boot." Felix grinned. "I thought maybe you could use me as back-up to Francey, with a radio link. There's that miniaturised unit I borrowed—"

"Stole," corrected Thane. Somehow, Joe Felix had acquired the tiny unit from a military research and development establishment. They were screaming for its return. "No, he'll be all right."

"Someone said that about the *Titanic*," said Felix doubtfully. "I think it sank."

"Out." Thane noticed him on his way, checked the message slips again, then went through to the Commander's office.

Jack Hart was at his desk, scowling over the budget requisition file. He looked up, closed the budget file with a grunt of relief, and waved Thane into a chair.

"Have a nice day?" he asked sarcastically.

"Some have been better," admitted Thane.

Hart nodded, sat back, and clasped his hands behind his head. He sighed. "Tell me."

Sketching what had happened didn't take long, and Hart already knew about the two descriptions from Arrochar. Lined face impassive, he listened through the rest in silence then swore under his breath.

"I'd give a lot to be an optimist—say that we're after two small-timers who were kiting stolen credit cards. That they panicked and killed her." He shaped a scowl. "But does it smell right to you?"

"No," admitted Thane. "Not unless we rake up a pair of psychopaths." He eyed Hart across the desk. "There's Crossley."

"The shrinking boy-friend?" Hart grunted. "He's a lot better, if it wasn't for that damned postcard." He got up, went over to the window, and glared out at the bright, warm sunlight. "Perfect evening. Every punter will be out playing golf, every ned will be out screwing houses. So what are you going to do about it?"

"Stay with what we've got." Thane was used to the Squad commander's mental somersaults. "Including Crossley."

"Crossley." Jack Hart nodded. "But tell Francey Dunbar we don't pay detective sergeants to contemplate their navels. He'd better come up with something." Returning, he picked up the budget requisition file and weighed it in his hand. "Anything urgent your people should be told?"

Thane shook his head.

"Right." Hart tossed the file into his Pending tray. "You can buy me a beer—I deserve it."

They were on their way out of the building when Maggie Fyffe beckoned urgently from the reception desk. But the Commander's secretary wanted Thane.

"A call for you." She pointed at the telephone on the reception counter. "Mrs. Thornton, from the Peace Camp."

Jack Hart raised an eyebrow. Crossing over, Thane lifted the receiver and took the call.

"I've been thinking since we talked, Mr. Thane." Barbara Thornton's voice came briskly over the line. "This isn't urgent, but could we meet tomorrow? It would help me—it might help you."

"You want to leave it till then?" He was puzzled.

"Yes, it's nothing dramatic," she said dryly. "Do detectives eat lunch?"

"It's not unknown." He frowned at the receiver. "Where?"

"I'll call back and let you know." The line went dead as she hung up.

"Well?" asked Hart.

"She wants to talk again."

"Good," said Hart with minimum interest. "How about that drink?"

Thane followed him out.

Commander Jack Hart felt he was suffering, Commander Jack Hart wanted a sounding board, and he had Thane.

They went to a small south side bar called the Grey Pigeon, where the manager was an ex-cop and knew most of the Crime Squad by their first names. The Grey Pigeon was quiet, they settled at a corner table once Thane had paid for the beers, and for the next fifty minutes Hart launched quietly spoken thunderbolts at "bloody bureaucrats" and the world at large. It took two more beers before he ran out of steam, and they decided against another round. The ex-cop behind the bar counter had been Traffic. He was still a walking reminder about things like blood alcohol levels.

"And it's time I got back," said Hart. "That damned requisition has to be finished tonight."

They left, parted, and Thane drove home. Mary met him at the door. She had been washing her hair; her head was still wrapped in a towel.

"Are we eating curry?" asked Thane.

"Rat." She sniffed suspiciously as he kissed her. "Also a lucky rat. You've been drinking."

"With Jack Hart." Thane followed her in as Clyde padded through from the kitchen, stumpy Boxer tail wagging a greeting. "Jack has problems."

"And we haven't?" She rested her hands on one of his shoulders for a moment. "Kate has gone out."

"Has she said anything more?"

"A little. She waited till we were on our own."

Thane nodded. It was Tommy's weekly swimming club evening, meaning he ate and ran.

"Katie is going along as moral support when her friend meets Linda Belmont tonight. She wanted me to know, I was to tell you." Mary shook her head, the worry back in her eyes. "That's all I got from her, but I've a feeling it's nasty, Colin. At their age—"

Early teenage. Colin Thane wished he wasn't a cop, wished he didn't know from hard experience the kind of possibilities that could exist.

"I'll hear soon enough," he said quietly.

"Kate knows that. But she wants someone else to tell it." Suddenly, unexpectedly, Mary kissed him again. "Leave it till then." Her mood changed, deliberately. "You'd better eat. Phil is coming over—he phoned about ten minutes ago and said he had to see you."

That sounded hopeful, but he was still thinking about Katie as they went through. It wasn't long since they'd had to ease Tommy out of potential trouble, but that had been different, straightforward. But Katie—

"Aren't you going to wash first?" asked Mary. "It's a rule we have around here."

Meekly, he obeyed.

The meal was one of his favourites, a mixed grill and fry-up which would have reduced any dietician to despair. Then came a thick slice of a home-made cheesecake. Mary disappeared briefly then returned with her hair hot-brush styled. She had changed from shirt and jeans into a cool blue linen dress.

The doorbell rang as Thane poured them coffee. Mary went through; he heard Clyde barking enthusiastically, then Phil Moss's voice. They came into the kitchen. One sight of the grin on Moss's thin face told him he'd been right.

"Have you eaten, Phil?" asked Mary.

"Well—" Moss's grin wavered then widened. His bachelor eating habits varied, even though he had a landlady who had spent years trying to fatten him up. "Not a lot. Then I got a chance of a ride out here."

She produced another plate. By a probably pre-planned miracle, she had food left to fill it.

"Maybe I've earned this." Moss produced an envelope from an inside pocket and handed it to Thane. "We've an ID on your two travelling credit card aces, otherwise James Friend and Herbert John Balfour. Everything matches, Colin."

He pulled up a chair. While Moss began eating, Thane opened the envelope and took out a slim batch of photocopy record sheets.

The stark, typewritten lines spelled it out. James Friend, age thirty-four, height five foot ten, thin, with dark hair and sallow complexion, matched the "Harold Evans" description from Arrochar. He wrote with his left hand, and he was Australian by birth. That tied with the "spoke with an accent—some say English, some say foreign" puzzle they'd been handed. He had fifteen previous convictions, a mixed bag beginning in Australia, picking up again in London, and the last few in Scotland. The smudged copy photograph above his fingerprints showed a lean, smugly handsome face smiling at the police camera.

Then came Herbert John Balfour, known to his nearest, if not necessarily dearest, as "Inky." Again everything matched with the "John Wilton" they'd been seeking—age thirty-two, height five foot seven, medium build, small scar on his chin, light brown hair. Born in Edinburgh, twelve previous convictions scattered up and down Britain; the helpful note added, "Sometimes wears spectacles when working." His copy photograph showed a plump, round face with a faintly puzzled expression as if he was determined to tell the world it was all a mistake.

"I'll help you through it." Moss glanced up from his plate for a moment. "Friend and Inky Balfour have worked together for the last five years. They met up in prison. Balfour has the brains, Friend is the nasty —he likes using a knife. We've two instances where the charge should have been attempted murder, but it couldn't stick."

Thane walked round the table, lifted his coffee cup with his hand round the rim, and took a gulp.

"Can we tie them in with Mary Dutton?"

"We can." Moss forked another mouthful, chewed, and swallowed. "No problem."

Thane drained the rest of his coffee, set the cup down on the table, and read on through the rest of the Records data.

"I'm glad, Phil," said Mary quietly.

"That makes two of us. I haven't exactly covered myself in glory on this." Moss finished the food on his plate, and made polite, reluctant noises before starting on a wedge of cheesecake.

Thane finished the last of the sheets. Mouth tightening a little, he turned back to the one before it and a paragraph that mattered. It was a note from Criminal Intelligence. They had information that James Friend had acquired a heroin habit, still comparatively low-grade, but his danger rating, in terms of possible physical assault, had definitely grown.

"How did we miss them earlier?" he asked bluntly.

"Because they weren't on your list, they weren't on mine." Moss wiped a hand across his mouth and sat back. "Mary Dutton was temporarily attached to Fraud Squad before she transferred to your mob."

"I'm getting lost," said Thane slowly.

"I don't blame you, but that's how she knew them." Moss's thin face showed an acid satisfaction for a moment. "She was there, back-up, when some of the Fraud Squad mob picked up Friend and Balfour on a stack of charges. In fact, she brought down Inky Balfour when he tried to run—damned nearly killed him." He paused. "But it wasn't her case, before or after."

"Except Balfour would remember her." Thane understood. It often happened—the nearest handful of cops act as reserve troops, have a few minutes' involvement, then forget it.

Usually forget it. Both Inky Balfour and Detective Sergeant Mary Dutton would have had reason to remember their meeting.

"Phil." Mary had been listening; she was puzzled enough to chip in. "How did you put it together?"

"Credit cards and Arrochar." Moss gestured good-humouredly in Thane's direction. "He nudged me, I shuffled some print-outs, and we'd a small string of frauds just like it, all between Glasgow and Arrochar."

"Recent?" asked Thane.

"Over the last three or four months, nothing big, usually a couple of weeks or so apart, always the same descriptions. Three linked a metallic blue car." He gave a soft, satisfied sound of mock modesty. "Mary Dutton's service record mentioned the Fraud Squad, so I pestered a few of them."

"Nice work," said Thane softly. Phil Moss's kind—dig and keep digging, don't stop till you get there.

"Thanks." Moss's eyes became hard and bleak. "But I owed her—and we've still got to find this pair. They're not exactly on the Voters Roll."

"No leads?"

Moss shook his head.

Mary still smoked, about ten a day. Thane took one from her pack, lit it while she poured more coffee, and felt his head swim a little at the first assault of nicotine.

"You'd stopped," said Moss.

"He's a liar," said Mary. "That's another he owes me."

She chased them through to the living room, knowing they wanted to talk. Then she looked at the waiting dishes, swore under her breath, and began gathering them up. When she heard the telephone ringing, she thought of Katie, abandoned everything, hurried out to the hall, and answered the call.

Thane emerged from the living room, the same thought in his mind. But she shook her head and handed him the receiver.

"Duty officer, for you." She didn't hide her disappointment.

The Crime Squad duty officer, a detective inspector from Aberdeen, was apologetic. He'd never known a senior officer who enjoyed being phoned at home.

"I've got a call from a woman, sir—she's holding on another line. She says you know her and that it's urgent."

Thane sighed. "Does she have a name?"

"All she'll say is you asked a question and that she's old enough to be my grannie." The duty officer made a sad noise. "That's leaving out a few words I never heard my grannie use."

"I know her." Thane saw Moss had joined Mary in the background. "Can you patch her through?"

He heard a couple of clicks that weren't British Telecom approved then a familiar voice complained in his ear.

"Shut down, Brenda." He waited until the elderly woman quietened. The best part of a lifetime fencing stolen jewellery had left Brenda with a hair-trigger temper. "What have you got?"

"You asked about your policewoman. I've a name for you. Do you know Billy Greenan? He's in the car trade."

"Yes." Billy Greenan was a car thief, occasionally hiring out as an armed robbery wheelman—but non-violent, almost a pacifist. Thane was puzzled. Greenan didn't fit into anything they knew. "What about him?"

"He told someone he did a favour for someone else, that it involved a car and a policewoman."

Thane stiffened.

"I'm interested." He kept his voice as casual as he could. "Does he have a watering hole?"

She cackled. "No. But if you want him, he spends seven nights a week at a place called Jacko's Amusements in Firland Street—that's unless he's working. Billy Greenan is the original Space Invader, crazy about computer games." Her voice switched to a wheedle. "You'll remember I told you?"

"Next time you'll have pink ribbons on the handcuffs," promised Thane.

He hung up on another cackle.

"Worth while?" asked Moss.

He nodded. "It might be."

"Going out?"

Thane hesitated and exchanged a glance with Mary. Her eyes told him she already knew the answer, and she gave a slight nod.

"Yes," he told Moss. "It's Billy Greenan. Something about a police-woman and a car—he's worth turning over."

"I'm ready," said Moss. "You'll need someone, and it's a joint opera-tion."

Thane knew better than to argue. Anyway, there was nothing wrong with the idea. But when Katie got back, or if Linda Belmont called—

"I'll be here," said Mary, reading his mind.

He'd left his jacket in the living room. He went back for it, checked his car keys were in their usual pocket, and Moss followed him out.

It was close on nine-thirty, the evening just beginning to shade into dusk in that slow way it does in Scotland in May, when Colin Thane drove the Crime Squad car into Firland Street.

They were not in the pleasantest part of town. A long time before, when Glasgow had been second city of an unshakeable empire, when it made steel and built ships, when its engineers and craftsmen never thought that could end, Firland Street's tenements blocks had been built of solid red sandstone and its shops had been as neat and clean and as debt-free respectable as the customers who used them. There were factories within walking distance; the shipyards were a brief tram-ride away.

Now it was grimy, neglected and crumbling. The factory sites had become waste ground; most of the people had gone, and the ones who had remained or who had moved in didn't hope for anything better because they knew it wouldn't happen. Some were thieves; one family were small-time drug pushers; others were stranded on social security. The few shops that remained kept steel shutters over their windows by night. The shutters had been made in Japan.

"I never did get the up-market jobs," said Phil Moss acidly. But he was pleased, like a schoolboy playing truant, back in a world he knew. Straightening, he peered ahead. "Jacko's Amusements—hell, I remember when I had a beat near here and that was a baker's shop."

They stopped near the dingy little amusement gallery, got out, and walked the rest of the way along the empty street. Jacko's Amusements still had the old bakery shop front window, but the glass had been painted over in a rainbow mix of colours. They could hear a subdued electronic piping and chatter from inside, then as they pushed open the door and went in, it met them full volume.

The gallery was dimly lit, but random patterns of colour flashing from the machines ranged round the shabby walls and scattered around the floor space. It seemed almost deserted; only a handful of customers in sight, an elderly attendant on duty in a booth near the door.

"Billy Greenan here tonight?" asked Thane.

The attendant stared at him, swallowed, and gestured toward the back of the gallery. They headed there, past unused machines which pulsed invitations to defend Mars against purple invaders or attack a variety of electronically generated monsters with your own personal ray-gun.

There was something wrong. The handful of customers farther down the gallery had stopped playing and were waiting, grinning. Thane glanced back, saw stark fear on the old attendant's face, understood, then heard Moss swear as the gallery door swung open and two more figures walked in.

The door slammed shut again. The new arrivals both wore leather jackets and denims; one held a sawed-off billiard cue at his side, and the other had a leather cosh and was slapping it lightly against the palm of his hand. From the rear of the gallery, the players were gradually closing in.

It was an ambush. They'd walked into it, and there was no way out. Instinctively, Thane and Moss backed towards a patch of wall, counting heads.

There were six of them, all in their late teens or early twenties, all armed with some kind of club. They were easy to label, hired trouble, ready to cripple or kill—for money, if it was on offer, for kicks alone if they felt that way.

"Here we go," said Moss softly. A small black detective-issue baton had appeared in his grip. It was scarred, and it had a lead insert which no Chief Constable would ever have approved. "When?"

"Wait." Thane kept his hands at his sides. They had done it before, though this time the odds were bad, almost hopeless. "Now—"

The grinning half-circle hadn't spoken, were still closing, and were caught off guard. Intended prey weren't supposed to attack, weren't supposed to get in the first blows.

Thane heard a howl of pain and caught a glimpse of one thug staggering back as Moss's baton slammed like a blunt rapier-tip into his stomach. He took another, tall, unshaven, with yellowed teeth, who was starting to swing a baseball bat. Thane kicked him hard in the crotch, hammered a fist into those yellowed teeth, and the tall figure overbalanced. He crashed into the nearest games machine, and it fell in a smash of glass and a violent sparking of broken circuits.

Then the rest were on them, swearing, clubs swinging.

Something hard and unseen grazed Thane's head. He fended off a swinging billiard cue, taking the blow on his arm, gasping at the pain it caused, then was caught up in a punching, kicking struggle. He had to stay close in, must—two more of the amusement machines tumbled and smashed. Phil Moss was down, was being kicked, was trying to get up, had been clubbed again.

Suddenly, the chirping machines went dead and the gallery's main overhead lights blazed on. For a moment, startled, their attackers hesitated in confusion.

A deep, low, chilling growl came from near the door.

"Go, Rajah," said Jock Dawson, his voice no longer lazy. "Stay, Goldie."

A heavy black thunderbolt sprang through the air, crashed into the nearest thug, and slammed him to the floor. The giant German Shepherd landed neatly, white fangs bared, and seemed to catapult on. The next man screamed in terror as those massive jaws clamped down on his upper arm. Rajah gave a quick, worrying twist of his head and a leather jacket sleeve ripped like paper. Flesh torn, blood spurting from the wound, the man screamed again.

"Rajah, stay."

The German Shepherd froze, tail thrashing. At the attendant's cubicle, Jock Dawson stood totally assured and relaxed with Goldie poised eagerly at his side.

First one, then all of the men retreated. The retreat became a scrambling run towards the rear of the gallery. Only one figure made a desperate, foolhardy charge at Dawson. He had an iron bar.

"Go, Goldie," said Dawson crisply.

Rajah had been a black thunderbolt; Goldie was yellow lightning. She sprang, took the man high in the chest, and he went down. She was on top of him with her teeth inches from his throat.

"Hold, Goldie," ordered Dawson.

There was a back door; it had been thrown open; the rest of the gang were struggling to escape—while Rajah watched them balefully. Dawson puckered his lips and gave a soft whistle.

The black thunderbolt erupted across the floor, the German Shepherd's full weight took the last man between the shoulders, and he went down as if pole-axed.

"You." Dawson swung to the thug pinned down by Goldie. The Labrador's teeth were still bared, a soft noise coming from deep in her chest. "Listen, bampot. This is a young dog, she gets excited. She'd like to have your throat—understand?"

The man gave the faintest of terrified nods.

"Then don't move." Dawson loped down the length of the gallery, kicked the rear door shut, and bolted it. Grinning, he scratched Rajah lightly between the ears then stooped and handcuffed the German Shepherd's dazed captive. He looked round at Thane. "You two all right, boss?"

Leaning on one of the overturned amusement machine cases, several parts of him aching, Thane pursed his lips. Phil Moss was still sitting on the floor, his thin face grey with pain, his left shoulder hanging oddly, his right hand supporting his left elbow.

"Phil?" he asked.

"They broke something," said Moss bitterly. "Damn my luck, I don't like hospitals. They're all the same—patients they can do without."

As long as Moss complained, he couldn't be too badly damaged. Wincing, Thane straightened, brought out his handcuffs, and tossed them to Dawson. Dawson caught the handcuffs, went back to Goldie and her prisoner, and gently toed the Labrador out of the way. Less gently, he handcuffed the frightened thug and made him stay face down.

"Dear God," said a quavering voice. The old gallery attendant had made a cautious appearance from his booth. Shaking, he stared open-mouthed at the damage. "Look at the mess—who'll pay for it?"

"That's the least of your worries, sunshine," said Dawson. "And stay clear of that dog. Maybe she doesn't like you."

The attendant skirted carefully round Goldie, making a pleading gesture to Thane.

"These neds just marched in and took over, mister," he said hoarsely. "They—they said they'd kick my head in. I know their kind, they'd have done it."

"I believe you." Thane stopped him. "Have you a phone?"

"They cut the wires, mister."

"I'll radio," volunteered Dawson. "Garbage collection, boss?"

"And an ambulance," said Thane.

"Right." Dawson turned to his dogs, crouching menacingly beside their catches. "Rajah, Goldie—guard. I won't be long."

He was back in a couple of minutes with the inevitable news that Firland Street was still empty. The local population had no intention of showing interest in what was going on. By then, Thane had helped Moss into a battered chair brought from the attendant's booth. The two hand-cuffed captives had hardly moved. Any time either had as much as quivered, there had been a low, warning growl.

"Let's have that one." Thane pointed at the nearest.

Dawson obliged, hauling the chosen prisoner into a sitting position by the hair. Then, with some disgust, the dog-handler carefully wiped his hand clean on the young thug's jacket.

"Right," said Thane softly. The ned could be no more than twenty;

he had pimples; his face was a mixture of hate and fear. "Going to tell me about it?"

There was a moment's hesitation then a reluctant, sullen nod.

"Who set this up?"

"I don't know—who cares?" Their prisoner shrugged and the hand-cuff links jingled. "One o' my mates got the offer—a hundred notes in his hand, another hundred later."

"To do what?"

"Fix any cop that walked in here." The young face twisted in a scowl. "Nothin' was said about damned dogs, or—"

"What about Billy Greenan?"

"He'd be out chasin' his tail, thinking he'd a job lined up."

The other man, slightly older, still dazed, equally unhappy, told the same story. Neither would name any of their companions. That was the way Thane had expected it would be. Keeping their mouths shut meant they'd serve a modest, untroubled year or so in prison with no hardships involved. Go the other way and, even if they lasted that year or so, retribution would be waiting on the outside.

He left them and crunched over the broken glass to Phil Moss. He was still pale, but he was sipping whisky from a flask the attendant had produced.

"How do you feel?" asked Thane.

"Like I'm probably dying," snarled Moss. He scowled. "What do you think? Did Brenda sell you out?"

"This way?" He'd thought of it, rejected it. "Too crude, Phil. More likely she was used."

"Then somebody knew how to do it." Moss chewed his lip. "The car —you still want Billy Greenan?"

He did, more than ever. But there was one mystery he could deal with straight away. Jock Dawson had taken his dogs into a corner. Thane went over, stopped, and stared. Rajah's great black paws were playing with a yellow rubber duck. Goldie was gnawing happily at a bright red rubber mouse which squeaked a little at each chew.

"Just relaxing them," said Dawson. "They can get a bit uptight, like people."

"Your idea?" asked Thane.

Dawson shook his head. "It's standard just about anywhere, boss. Every police dog has a personal toy—it saves them chewing the handler."

"Right." Thane drew a deep breath. "But you popped up with them like the original Demon King. How?"

"Bein' nosey I suppose, boss." Dawson looked embarrassed. "Remember you told me to get a radio fitted in the Land-Rover? I stayed on to get it done, then I was talking with the Duty Officer when that woman called in—"

"So you both listened?" asked Thane. "Heard what she told me?"

Dawson nodded sheepishly. "I just thought I'd come along an' see what happened. You know, what exactly you'd do—I'm trying to learn this plain-clothes business." He shrugged. "Your car was outside, empty, I saw some o' the opposition going in and—"

"You stuck your nose in." Thane gave a sigh, though it made him wince, and gave up. "All right, buy those two terrors an extra bone each. I'll pay. Better still, make it three—I don't want you quarrelling."

Dawson looked at his dogs and winked.

CHAPTER FIVE

Two car-loads of Central Division C.I.D. arrived first, then the ambulance. The detective sergeant in charge of the C.I.D. contingent quickly made it plain he wasn't going to ask awkward questions about how an inspector from Headquarters staff and a Crime Squad superintendent had become involved in a small war in Central Division territory. He even made a determined effort to ignore Jock Dawson and his dogs.

They tidied up. The two prisoners vanished first. Phil Moss stubbornly got out to the ambulance on his own feet, then was gone. A cursory check around the nearby streets and lanes yielded nothing, and the lights in Jacko's Amusements went out as the attendant willingly closed up for the night.

"That looks like everything, sir." The detective sergeant eyed Thane warily as they stood together in the street. "Need any more help here?"

Thane shook his head. The Central men had filled a plastic sack with discarded weapons and had a chance of fingerprints. He'd told them enough to keep them reasonably happy, and the police-speak phrase "in the course of enquiries" covered in a way any cop was prepared to accept. Jacko's Amusements would be just one more incident report to be filed.

"If anything needs squaring at Division, I'll take care of it in the morning," he promised. "Call it a close-down."

Jock Dawson had already taken his dogs and gone home. As the last of the C.I.D. men departed, Colin Thane walked back through the grey dusk to where his Ford still lay untouched. He knew he was being watched from some of the tenement windows, that Firland Street had decided it was safe to breathe again, and as he got behind the wheel, one or two braver souls began appearing in doorways.

He started the car then let the engine idle for a moment while he used the radio to check in. The Crime Squad duty officer came on the air and sounded relieved to hear him, but apart from ordering a general lookout for Billy Greenan, there was nothing more Thane wanted done that night. Signing off, tossing the radio microphone back on its shelf, Thane slipped the car into gear and set it moving. There was one last thing he had to be sure about before he took his aching body home.

Phil Moss had been taken to the nearest hospital, the Royal Infirmary. It was big, it was old, and its Casualty Emergency department prided itself in being one of the busiest in Europe.

They were still dealing with Moss when Thane walked in. They were also stitching up and patching up a variety of other patients, from a drunk who had had most of one ear bitten off in a fight to a teenage girl brought in from a road accident.

The girl died while he waited. The drunk shouted, swore, fainted at the first stitch, then came round and was hustled out by two uniformed cops. Two workmen came in on stretchers from a night-shift factory accident, a small boy was carried in after being rescued from a house fire. But no-one had been brought in with a dog bite.

Thane had seen it all often enough, tried as usual to shut himself off from it, and as usual knew he'd failed. Some of the staff knew him by sight. One of the nurses brought him a mug of tea; another loaned him an early edition of the next day's newspaper. Almost an hour passed before one of the duty casualty surgeons came in, looked round for him, and beckoned.

"Maybe we should check you over too," said the casualty surgeon dryly, watching the way Thane limped over. "If your lot won, what are the enemy like?"

"Not too happy." Thane followed him down a corridor. "How is he?"

"Complaining." The casualty surgeon chuckled. "I know his type— scrawny yes, but made out of steel wire and old boots, you have to hit them with a telegraph pole to do any real damage." He stuffed his hands into the pockets of his white coat and became professional. "His shoulder is broken, but the X-rays show a fairly clean fracture. We've had him through theatre and we'll keep him in for a spell—if the nurses can stand it."

"No other injuries?"

"Someone used his ribs as a football but didn't win any prizes." The casualty surgeon frowned again. "Really, I'd be happy to give you a quick going over. You look fairly rough, Superintendent."

Thane shook his head. Sighing, the casualty surgeon stopped at a door, opened it, looked in, then smiled and stepped back.

"Sleeping like a babe. We had to give him a general anaesthetic before we set the shoulder—with any luck, I'll be off duty before he comes round."

Thane took a couple of steps into the room. Absurdly thin between the bed sheets, eyes closed, snoring gently, Phil Moss had one arm encased in plaster from neck to elbow. His thin face seemed grey against the white of the pillows, but his breathing was steady.

"How will he mend?" Thane asked soberly.

"If he behaves, like new. But it'll be a couple of months before he can even sneeze at a parking ticket." The casualty surgeon led Thane out and walked with him to the main desk. He stopped. "Do me a favour. Wait."

He vanished briefly, returned and handed Thane a small bottle of pills.

"Yours," he explained. "Old-fashioned painkillers, take as required. The way you look, you'll feel worse by morning."

Thane thanked him and left.

Sheer relief made him feel better on the drive home through the night. It was close on midnight when he arrived there and his house was the only one in the street still showing lights. Leaving the car, locking it, he used his key to open the front door and went in. Mary appeared from the living room, stared at him, then moistened her lips.

"What happened?"

"The natives got restless." He forced a grimace. "I got some lumps. Phil's in hospital, but he'll mend."

"Are you sure?" She didn't hide her doubt and concern.

He nodded. "I was at the hospital. He's in the Royal—they say a broken shoulder is the worst of it."

Mary gave a long sigh, a blend of relief and resignation. Ready for bed, she was wearing a dressing gown and her dark hair was tied back with a thin strand of red ribbon. Thane caught the scent of her favourite perfume but felt too tired, too sore to care.

"We'll get you fixed up." She took his arm, her eyes narrowing at the way he winced. Once she'd settled him on the couch in the living room, she looked at him again. "For a start, you could use a drink."

Thane caught her hand as she turned away.

"What happened with Katie?"

"She's fine. She got back looking a lot happier." A faint smile lightened her face. "She thinks your Linda Belmont is wonderful."

"Did Linda call?"

"About an hour ago. She said not to worry about Katie, that she isn't involved. But the rest is nasty, if it's true."

"What kind of nasty?" asked Thane grimly.

"Drugs and a teacher. Maybe more. She said she'd talk to you in the morning."

He nodded. Without realising, he had tightened the grip on her hand. There had been other options, but drugs had been near the top of his list.

Mary sensed his mood.

"Katie isn't in it," she said quietly.

But she so easily might have been, and they both knew it.

Colin Thane woke to Thursday morning stiff and aching. When he showered, his body seemed patterned in technicolour bruising and he gave in, taking two of the painkiller tablets he'd been given by the casualty medic. By the time he'd shaved and dressed, they had worked and he went down to breakfast feeling reasonably able to face the day.

Mary was busy. It was one of her duty days at the clinic, and she always made a determined effort to get as much done around the house as possible before she left. Tommy and Kate were having a minor squabble at the breakfast table, but let it cool when he joined them. He looked at Kate.

"Good meeting?" he asked obliquely.

"Yes." She gave him a smile which was a blend of child and woman, which reminded him once more how closely she resembled Mary. "Thanks, Dad."

"What meeting?" demanded Tommy.

"Mind your own business." The squabble began again.

Later, Thane gave Mary a hand to clear up. Then it was time to go.

"You'll find out how Phil is?" She knew he would, but it was more than a reminder.

Thane nodded. "And don't worry about today. The most dangerous thing I know about is a woman who wants to buy me lunch."

"Enjoy it," she said dryly, then grinned. "If it's your body she wants, she's in for a disappointment." She changed the subject. "I've got Monday off."

"Monday?" He was puzzled.

"It's a public holiday, the clinic will be shut." Mary eyed him thoughtfully. "You're due some time off. You also need a break. We could drive to a beach or somewhere."

He'd forgotten about the May holiday. "I don't know—we can see how things are."

She nodded. They both knew the odds were against it.

Radio Clyde predicted a warm day. When Thane drove into the Crime Squad parking lot, a section from the Strathclyde mounted branch were cantering past. The men and women were in shirt-sleeves order; their horses' coats gleamed in the sunlight.

Things began reasonably. He made a phone call to the Royal Infirmary, where a ward sister with a pleasant Irish accent told him Phil Moss had come round, had eaten breakfast, and was comfortable.

"But he's a dreadful man," she said resignedly. "I'm not going to repeat what he called me when I said he wasn't to get out of bed."

"Tie him down," suggested Thane. "Tell him I'll look in as soon as I can."

It was still early; most of the Crime Squad teams were just arriving. He heard the rasp of Francey Dunbar's motor cycle and a little later his sergeant came into the room. Dunbar seemed ready to blend into the Peace Camp scene. In place of his usual plain riding leathers he was sporting patched denim trousers, ornamented knee-length boots and a camouflage jacket which looked as if it could have started off life in the Falklands campaign.

"You should do." Thane considered Dunbar's outfit with a slight grin. "But remember what I told you. Sniff around, yes. Any kind of hassle, no. If anyone even looks twice in your direction, get out."

"Fast," agreed Dunbar. He hooked his thumbs into the pockets of his camouflage jacket and frowned. "I heard about last night. You should have hauled me in."

"I didn't go looking for trouble," said Thane.

"Jock Dawson and those damn dogs." Dunbar shook his head. "I'd have liked to have seen it." He indicated the overnight print-out sheets on Thane's desk. "Anything yet on—well, anything?"

"No." It had needed only a fast skim through the print-outs. So far, the search for James Friend and Inky Balfour had drawn a blank. The two credit card hustlers could be anywhere, and Billy Greenan, the new possibility, still hadn't surfaced.

"Then I'll get on my way." Dunbar glanced at his wristwatch. "I want to arrive just ahead of the Scenes of Crime mob—it'll look better." He started to leave then stopped at the door. "Uh—say hello for me to Inspector Moss."

"I will."

Thane watched him go, waited until he heard the motor cycle start up again, then opened a desk drawer and took out the small black notebook he kept at the back. Checking the number he wanted, he lifted the telephone and dialled. The number barely rang out before it was answered, as if the receiver had been snatched up.

"Good morning, Brenda," he said grimly. "Give me one good reason why I shouldn't wring your neck for last night."

"I've heard, Mr. Thane—everybody's heard." The grey-haired woman sounded nervous. "But I thought the Billy Greenan story was straight, believe me." A wheedling note entered her voice. "You don't really think I'd set someone like you up that way, do you?"

"Only if you thought you'd get away with it," Thane told her bluntly. "So what happened, Brenda?"

A sound like an angry hiss came over the line. "I think I know, Mr. Thane. The bit about Billy Greenan was real, the rest—well, it was deliberate, meant to bounce back on me."

"One of your friends?" asked Thane sarcastically.

"Someone who knows you and I sometimes talk to about things." The anger spilled over. "Someone else you talk with, Mr. Thane—a jealous someone who'd like to squeeze me out, for maybe more than one reason."

He frowned at the telephone mouthpiece, trying to follow her. Part of it made sense, the rest was just possible.

"Can you give me a name?" he asked.

There was a long, empty pause on the line before she answered.

"Not this time. I'll make sure first, then if I'm right I'll ask some people I know to make what you could say was a social call."

"Brenda." He made it a warning. "You'd better go easy on that line. I'm warning you."

"Sorry, Mr. Thane." She spoke firmly. "But I've a reputation to protect. All I'll promise is there won't be reason for you to worry."

She hung up on him, something he hadn't expected. Thane put his own receiver down slowly, lips pursed. Someone, somewhere had a bad time ahead, a very bad time. But Brenda wasn't fool enough to let it go too far—and beyond that, did he really care?

He put the black notebook back in its drawer and rose from his chair, intending to go through to the duty room. But as he stepped out into the corridor, he almost collided with Tom Maxwell. For a moment the Squad's two deputy commanders eyed each other warily, then Maxwell gave a cautious nod.

"You've been busy." He gave an approving grunt. "That other day, when we were talking about who should handle things—"

"I'd have felt the same way," said Thane.

"That's it, then." Maxwell gave him a lopsided hint of a smile then his expression hardened again. "I've read the reports, lumps and all. How close do you think you'll be to a wrap-up when you get those two card-kiters?"

"Friend and Balfour?" Thane eyed him frankly. "I've got enough to hold them, but I don't know about a murder charge—not yet. It'll be like picking at a scab, wondering what's underneath."

"I had that feeling." Maxwell took out a handkerchief and blew his nose, noisily. "I'm due in court this morning, I'll be stuck there. But if it does happen, call Mary Dutton's mother, will you? She wants to know—from us, not from some damned newspaper."

Thane promised, and Maxwell limped off.

The main duty room was in a noisy, good-humoured mood. Someone safely in the background gave a dog-bark as Thane walked in; someone else gave a mock cheer; others grinned. He returned their interest with a gesture that wasn't in the Training Manual, saw Linda Belmont at her desk, and went over.

"Good morning, sir." The blonde detective sergeant greeted him with the heart-melting smile that was one of her main assets. But it had sympathy at the edges. She gestured at the report sheet still in her typewriter. "I was going to bring this through."

"Tell me." Thane propped himself against the edge of her desk, easing the load on some of his aching muscles. "What have we got?"

"Something that could have crawled out from under a stone." She gave a grimace of disgust. "The girl is a Jean Fraser—age fourteen, in the same school year as your daughter but in a different section. She says you've met her."

Thane nodded, with a vague memory of a plump, attractive girl with plaited, straw-coloured hair. Kate had brought her home a couple of times.

"Jean Fraser's class teacher is a John Quanton—early thirties, joined the school staff a few months ago." Linda Belmont shaped a shrug. "Quanton gives private little parties for some of his girls—giggles and a glass of cheap wine. Then there's a second time. One girl on her own, more giggles and wine, 'Try a little sniff of this funny powder—it's called cocaine.' "

Thane swore under his breath.

"Have we names?"

"So far, two others she knows about and some possibles. Until now, they've all been too scared to talk about it—and he moves on after that one session." Linda Belmont's voice stayed empty of emotion. "He's a genuine weirdo. The way she tells it, Quanton doesn't try to get them into bed. He produces a camera and takes photographs."

"Do we know anything about him?"

She shook her head. "He's on file, but only for a possession of drugs charge, years ago. The Fraser girl says his last teaching job was in London—I've telexed down."

Thane nodded. There was another question, one that mattered.

"What chance have we more of the girls will talk?"

"That depends." Linda Belmont scratched a fingernail across her desk in pensive style. "None of the parents know, the kids are terrified of that aspect on its own. I'll have to work on them." She looked up. "Presuming it's true, his kind worry me. Sick, yes—but suppose the next girl starts screaming?"

"Yes." Thane knew what she meant. The girl concerned could end up dead. Yet even now they knew, it wasn't going to be easy. "You'll have to talk to more of the girls, be sure of them."

"Then we can go for a Moorov?" She understood. "How many girls?"

"Three at a minimum, I'd feel safer with four."

Scottish law demanded a minimum of two witnesses' evidence before anything could be treated as established fact. Sometimes circumstantial evidence, including medical or scientific, could bridge the gap—but not always and what had begun as a safeguard for the innocent could become a disaster for truth. A victim's story, no matter how harrowing, wasn't enough. No court would or could convict on that alone.

Or it had been that way, until the Moorov Doctrine had been fought through by two policewomen. A factory operator had been charged with molesting several girls he employed, always when the girl concerned was alone. There was no other evidence—but the judge had agreed that several similar incidents put together amounted to proof of a pattern of actions.

If Jean Fraser's classmates would talk, they had their case.

"Four of them." Detective Sergeant Belmont gave a resigned nod. "I'll leave that till this afternoon, after school—less chance of trouble that way. How about the parents, sir?"

"They'll need to know—eventually." Thane paused. "I asked a favour, this doesn't have to be your headache. We could turn it over to the local cops, or the Drug Squad."

"No way." She flared at the idea. "Look, sir, I remember when I was their age. Things happened to me. He's a reptile, I want to nail him."

Thane thought of Kate and didn't argue.

Sandra Craig and Joe Felix were waiting patiently on the other side of the duty room. He went over to them, looking around for Jock Dawson, seeing no sign of the dog-handler.

"Where's Jock?" he asked.

"Up to his eyeballs in report forms," said Joe Felix. "The dog-bite kind—in triplicate. He says any time a police dog takes a lump out of anyone there's more red tape than blood." He grinned. "But I think he enjoyed last night."

"I'm glad someone did," said Thane. "Have either of you spoken to Central Division?"

Sandra had. The two prisoners would be in court that morning on assault charges, but there was still no hospital report of a patient being brought in with an interesting dog-bite—and the Central men were still waiting for the results of the fingerprint checks being made on the weapons they'd recovered.

"Then there's Billy Greenan—" She left it there, half statement, half question, and took a bite at the chocolate bar she was nursing.

"He'll surface soon enough." Joe Felix was confident. "I know our Billy—he hasn't the brains to do anything else."

Thane nodded. The timid-mannered car thief's name was on the current wanted list circulated to every Scottish force. The same applied to the two men who really mattered, James Friend and Inky Balfour. But they were different, considerably trickier, operators used to living by their wits and moving one jump ahead of the next situation. By now they could be anywhere—except that he had a stubborn, increasing hunch that they might still be in the city, or somewhere close to it.

"Keep stirring, keep prodding," he told Sandra and Felix. "Greenan, yes—but the main effort stays Friend and Balfour. I want anything we can get on them, from what they like for breakfast onward."

Sandra nodded, her mouth full of chocolate. Joe Felix hesitated, frowning a little.

"Joe?" Thane looked at him.

"The Peace Camp connection, sir. You've got this Aussie and his pal Balfour working regularly between the city and Arrochar, Glen Torbat is within spitting distance." Felix stuffed his hands in his pockets and looked worried. "If Francey trips over them out there, how do we hear?"

"He climbs on that damned great B.M.W., finds an outside phone, and calls in," said Thane patiently. "I didn't send him out there to be a hero, and he knows it."

Felix nodded, obviously with another question on his mind. Before he could ask it, a detective looked up from answering one of the duty room phones.

"For you, Superintendent," he called. "Line three, a Mrs. Thornton."

"Well now," murmured Sandra Craig, sucking a smear of chocolate from her lips. "Your dragon lady. Nice timing, but don't let her talk you into anything, sir."

'She's buying me lunch." Thane ignored the redhead's grin, and took the call on a phone beside them.

"Superintendent, I still haven't changed my mind," said Barbara Thornton as she heard his voice. "But I should have told you there's a condition—that my husband doesn't get to know that we've talked."

"How much would that matter?" asked Thane.

"It wouldn't be the end of the earth, but I'd rather avoid it," she said. "I think I can save you from arresting someone and then regretting it."

"All right." He looked round at Sandra and Joe Felix and shrugged. "When and where, Mrs. Thornton?"

"That's another problem. I suppose you know I run a travel agency?"

"It came up," agreed Thane.

"You checked us out." She gave an amused chuckle. "Something turned up. I've got to have lunch with some advertising people—I'm sorry. But before that I'll be at the Thornton Travel main branch in Wellington Street. Could you make it there, about noon?"

"Yes, as things stand."

"And if you're in touch with Magnus—"

"I won't mention it."

"Thank you." She made it a purr, said goodbye, and hung up.

Thane replaced his own receiver and saw the quizzical expression on Sandra Craig's face.

"Don't start," he warned. "God knows what she wants, but I'm ready to listen." He turned to Felix. "Still doubtful, Joe?"

"You mean about Francey, sir?" Felix's face went slightly pink. "No, but—"

"Well?" Thane waited while the noise of the duty room flowed around them. Felix was earnest, Felix was willing, a genius in his own electronics world, but a pessimist at other times.

"You're going to see this Thornton woman." Felix's pinkness spread up to the roots of what was left of his thinning hair. He glanced at Sandra for support. "On your own—we don't know much about her or her husband yet."

"That's one of the reasons I'm going," said Thane patiently. "But what we've got up front is still the credit card scene—Friend and Inky Balfour, whatever hole they've crawled into. Maybe Peter Crossley at the Peace Camp ties in with them, maybe he doesn't—I'm ready to bet he's lying about how things were between him and Mary Dutton, but that could be plain panic. So let's stay with Friend and Balfour till we've something better."

Felix nodded. He still didn't look totally convinced.

Thane left them and went back to his room, closed the door. On his own again, he thought for a moment, then phoned Mary at her reception desk at the medical clinic. She had just arrived, the clinic was always busy in the morning, and he could hear plenty of background bustle at her end of the line. But she was glad he had called, coldly angry by the time he'd told her what Linda Belmont had put together so far.

"How soon will you know?" she asked.

"Whether the other girls will talk?" There was no way of telling. The one thing Linda Belmont daren't do was try to force the pace with her young witnesses. "As long as it takes."

"Ask a damn fool question and you'll get a damn fool answer," she said with wry resignation. "Just don't let me get anywhere near him meantime—or you could have another murder on your plate."

A few minutes later he made another call. It took longer, it was to Strathclyde Headquarters, and it took a little time to track down the man he wanted, the detective who had linked Mary Dutton to that past case involving James Friend and Inky Balfour. His name was Alex Riney, he was a detective inspector, and he already knew that Phil Moss was in hospital.

"How can I help?" he asked Thane.

"Some background."

"Friend and Balfour?" Riney made an apologetic grunt. "I can't help you find them, Superintendent. They faded off the scene months ago—we thought they'd gone south till this happened."

"We could still talk."

"No problem. When? I'm tied up this morning, but after that—"

Thane thought. "Early afternoon. I wanted to look in on Phil, but that could wait."

"No need," suggested Riney. "He's a troublesome devil, but I was going to visit and annoy him. How about at the hospital, around two o'clock?"

Thane agreed and hung up. Soon after that, Maggie Fyffe appeared and summoned him through to Jack Hart's office. The Squad commander's mood hadn't improved overnight and he listened dourly to Thane's update on the situation. When it came to what had happened at Jacko's Amusements, he was caustic in his comments on senior officers who wandered in where no self-respecting angel would have gone without a back-up team.

But he had something else on his mind.

"The media are picking up some whispers about what's going on," he said grimly. "I've called in some past favours and they're sitting on the story for now. But that won't last for ever. How much will it matter to you if we go public?"

Thane grimaced. It was a regular problem. Sometimes it helped to have press, radio and television sniffing at their heels. Unexpected witnesses could be turned up that way, often were, if the timing was right.

Hart's telephone rang, saving him from having to answer. Hart lifted the receiver, grunted, listened, then sucked his teeth with a sudden interest.

"I'll tell him," he said, and hung up. He gave Thane a slight grin. "Maybe you're going to have a better day. Billy Greenan has been picked up over in Govan. Somebody called Sergeant Mackenson would like the pleasure of your company and says you know him."

"I do." Thane drew a deep, thankful breath.

"Then get on with it," suggested Hart. "Move."

Thane moved. Govan was an independent-minded area of Glasgow, most of it along the south bank of the Clyde. It had a history that went back to stones carved by the early Druids; it had been a thriving village of weavers where the parish minister had prospered on having the right to catch salmon from the one-time clean and sparkling river.

Govan had grown up to be tenements, shipyards and engineering works before it was finally swallowed by its giant neighbour. Like most of the city, it had been hit hard by the depression of the 1980's; it had its derelict factories and its unemployed. But Govan was the kind of place that battled through—and the parish minister might have to think of fishing again. Salmon had been sighted in the cleaned-up Clyde, the first time in many generations.

The police station for Govan Division was a new building, out of the school of shoe-box architecture. It was at its busiest when Glasgow Rangers football club played a weekend home game, when rowdies, hooligans and pick-pockets were brought in by the van-load.

Through the week it was quieter, with the usual trade of thieves and hard men, well-heeled drug pushers and the occasional high-class embezzler from its suburban fringe. When Thane arrived, parking his car in the station yard, a patrol van was unloading a collection of school-age shoplifters.

He went in, jumped the queue at the inquiry desk, and a few moments later a booming voice announced Sergeant Mackenson's arrival.

"Good to see you, sir." Charlie Mackenson was big and ugly, bulging out of his uniform, and grinning from ear to ear. "It's been a few years."

"A few, Charlie," agreed Thane. Mackenson had once almost killed him in the third round of an amateur boxing final. Since then he'd heard of Mackenson now and again—a legendary brute as a cop, but the kind of brute who off duty ran a wheelchair basketball team for handicapped kids. "You haven't changed."

"Like hell I haven't." Mackenson chuckled at the notion. "I'm fat, over the hill, and burned out. But I've got your Billy Greenan for you, gift-wrapped."

"How?" asked Thane, following Mackenson along one of the police station corridors.

"We were told you wanted him at this morning's muster, then I'm just strolling around, minding my own business, and damned nearly trip over him." Mackenson shrugged. "This isn't his usual patch, maybe I should have waited. There's a supermarket near where I got him, with a parking lot full o' shoppers' cars—he was probably going to work. But I didn't want to risk losing him."

They reached a door marked Interview Room with a constable standing outside. Mackenson nodded, the constable faded away, and they went in.

The interview room had a table, a few chairs, a plain linoleum floor, and little more. Billy Greenan was standing beside the table, a small, frightened rabbit of a man in his late twenties. He had a thin face, short brown hair, a choirboy expression, and big ears.

"Hello, Billy," said Thane gravely. "Sit down."

Greenan hesitated.

"Sit," snarled Mackenson.

The car thief scrambled to obey, and sat quaking on the edge of his chair. Smartly dressed in a blue suit, white shirt, dark red tie and matching handkerchief, he could have been a bank clerk hoping for early promotion. It was part of what Greenan liked to call his "style"—that he blended in with the respectable section of the population. One lapel of the suit was torn; there was a red patch that would be a bruise on one side of his face. Thane decided not to ask why.

"Cautioned him, Charlie?" he asked.

"Chapter and verse," said Mackenson, leaning against the wall. "Like it was set to music."

"But I hadn't done anything, Mr. Thane—" began Greenan.

"Shut!" Mackenson's bellow made even Thane wince and left Greenan staring in near terror. "Son, this is Govan Division. We eat little neds like you between meals. You speak when the Detective Superintendent says so, not before."

Greenan swallowed and gave a quick nod.

"Sir." Mackenson gave Thane a fractional wink, his voice still like thunder. "I think he maybe understands."

"We've been looking for you, Billy." Thane brought another chair over, swung it round, then sat on it saddle-style, the chair back facing Greenan. "You're what's called 'helping with enquiries.' You want to do that, don't you?"

A low menacing rumble escaped from Mackenson's lips.

"Yes." Greenan managed a whisper.

"Right." Thane rested his hands on the chair back, his voice almost gentle. "First time you've been involved in a murder, isn't it, Billy?"

"Me?" Greenan's eyes widened; he swallowed; his voice was a forced squeak. "Come on, Mr. Thane. You—you know me. You're joking, eh?"

"No."

"But—" The thin-faced car thief gave a terrified glance towards Sergeant Mackenson. Mackenson showed his teeth in a sardonic grin.

"Two fraudsters—an Australian named Friend, the other Inky Balfour," said Thane. He stabbed a forefinger in a way that made Greenan jerk. "You did a job for them, Billy. Will I tell you what it was? I think they wanted a blue Toyota to disappear. You obliged."

"They only told me—" Greenan stopped and licked his lips. "I mean—"

"Didn't they tell you they'd killed a policewoman?"

"No. No, they didn't, Mr. Thane." Greenan made a noise like a moan. "Look, they only said they had a problem. Then that maniac Jimmy Friend made some kind of a—a joke about a woman cop."

"She was Crime Squad, a detective sergeant." Thane rose from the chair and stood over Greenan. He gauged he needed only one thing more to crush the little thief completely. "You helped them dump her body, didn't you?"

"Me? No, Mr. Thane, no way." Greenan almost blubbered in horror at the thought. "I wouldn't have touched that car if it hadn't been Jimmy Friend. He scares hell out of me—I had to do it."

"That's not the story I heard," said Thane softly.

"Things get twisted," said Greenan earnestly. "Look, a few of us were drinking two, maybe three nights after that. You know how it is—maybe I shot my mouth off too much." He shook his head at the memory. "Then I woke up in a sweat the next morning in case Jimmy Friend got to hear."

Thane believed him. Still leaning against the wall, Mackenson gave no impression of even listening. Outside, in the corridor, someone went past whistling.

"Where do I find them, Billy?" demanded Thane.

"I don't know, Mr. Thane. They found me. We—we've done a thing or two together now and then." Greenan moistened his lips. "I could use a cigarette."

"Hard luck," said Mackenson unfeelingly. "Anyway, they're bad for your health."

"You're going to tell it from the beginning, Billy," said Thane. "You understand?"

Greenan nodded.

Mackenson reached into a pocket and started to produce a notebook. Thane shook his head. Formal statements could wait.

"They—they knew where I was living. They hauled me out of bed, an' it was about four in the morning. They had this car, a blue Toyota, and they wanted it to vanish, permanent." A faint spark of pride entered Greenan's voice. "That isn't easy, Mr. Thane. You've got to know what you're doing, believe me. You don't just dump the thing in the river—"

Thane cut him short. "You took the job?"

Greenan nodded. "An' I haven't seen them since, didn't want to—that's the truth."

"So what happened to the car?"

Greenan hesitated, fear struggling with the way he earned a living. "No names, Mr. Thane?"

"I'll listen. But don't push your luck."

"I didn't like doin' it—that Toyota was in good nick, I could have unloaded it no problem." The little man sighed. "Still, when someone like Jimmy Friend—"

"Tell," snapped Mackenson from the background.

"I've a wee arrangement, there's a trawler that operates out of one o' the fishing villages down the coast." Greenan eyed him warily. "Sorry,

Mr. Thane, that Toyota is under sixty fathoms of wet in the middle o'
the Irish Sea. Even the people who dumped it couldn't find it again."

"All right." Thane cloaked a bitter sense of disappointment, accepting
Greenan was still telling the truth. "When you first saw the car, was it
damaged?"

Greenan shrugged. "It was dented at the front end, nothing desperate. I wasn't too interested in anything but gettin' shot of it."

"And what exactly did Friend say about the 'woman cop'?"

"I'm not sure." Greenan looked down at his hands, rubbing them
nervously.

"Try," said Thane grimly.

"I—" Greenan swallowed. "You won't like it." He waited for some
kind of response, got none, and licked his lips. "Friend said he'd have got
more of a kick out o' things if she'd been in uniform—then Inky Balfour
shut him up."

"You stinking little maggot." Mackenson took two lumbering,
theatening steps towards the car thief then stopped reluctantly, rumbling angrily, as Thane gestured him back.

"I'm finished with him for now." Thane drew a deep breath. "Can
you hold him here for me, Charlie? I don't want him out and about for a
day or two."

Mackenson grunted. "No problem. Any particular charge?"

"Not yet."

"We'll think of something." The Govan sergeant's face brightened at
the thought. He beckoned Greenan. "On your feet, sunshine. Let's start
on it."

Colin Thane checked with the Crime Squad duty room by phone
before he left Govan. Very little was fresh, beyond the news that Central
Division had looked up another of the neds from the Jacko's Amusements ambush. They'd identified him through fingerprints and more
conclusive evidence was the massive dog-bite on one arm. He'd been
seen by a police surgeon, whose treatment had included a painful and
allegedly precautionary injection of penicillin into the young thug's
rump.

But their prisoner was from the same mould as the two before him.
He wasn't talking.

Thane established there was nothing else that mattered, then hung up.

It was a fifteen-minute drive back into the city. Wellington Street, where Barbara Thornton's travel agency office was located, was long and straight and climbed through the heart of Glasgow's business area. It was also a no man's land when it came to parking, patrolled by traffic wardens with hearts of stone and faces to match.

Thane squeezed his car into the nearest sidestreet space he could find and walked the short distance from there to the travel agency. It had a modest window area offering bargain flights to Majorca and the Costa del Sol. When he went in, an assistant was preaching the delights of the Greek Islands to an elderly customer who looked as though he'd rather stay at home.

A second counter assistant, a woman, stopped painting her fingernails and came over. Thane gave his name, asked for Barbara Thornton, and she used an internal phone, then wafted her nails in the direction of a stairway at the rear.

He went up and Barbara Thornton met him when he reached the top. She was wearing a tailored navy-blue skirt, plain white blouse, and navy-blue pumps, efficiently executive but softened by a large Wedgewood blue cameo brooch.

"You're punctual, Superintendent." She greeted him with a satisfied smile. "But then, I expected you would be."

Thane followed her through what seemed to be an accounts office, where two middle-aged women were working, and into a separate room. It was comfortably furnished, more like a corner of a hotel lounge than an office, despite the scatter of letters and invoices on a low, glass-topped coffee table.

"For important clients—not that we have many. I use it most of the time." Barbara Thornton settled him into one of the black imitation leather chairs. "I backed out of lunch. Can I give you a drink?"

"Well—"

"I've a decent malt whisky, a present from one of the airlines." She settled it for him, went over to a small drinks cabinet, and came back with two cut-glass tumblers. There was a stiff measure of whisky in each, and she splashed in some water from a jug before taking the chair opposite. "Thanks for coming."

"You made it sound interesting." Thane sipped his drink. It was a very good malt. He looked around and saw a stylised brown statuette of a horse on a shelf above a bookcase. It had to be Chinese in origin; he'd seen one like it somewhere before and it had been valuable.

"No, that's a copy." She had been watching him, seemed to read his mind. "The original is Tang dynasty and if I owned it I wouldn't be working for a living."

"Another present?" asked Thane.

"From my husband," she said it dryly. "For our wedding anniversary —he's a romantic at heart. Maybe you noticed. I think that red-haired policewoman of yours did."

Thane smiled and let it pass. "You said there was something I should know."

"Yes." Barbara Thornton tasted her own drink, the solitaire diamond ring on her wedding finger sparkling in the light. "Can I ask you a question first?"

He nodded.

"You know how I feel about the Peace Camp, Superintendent. I'd get rid of it tomorrow if I could, despite what my father thought of it. But maybe I still respect some of the things he respected—and I care about the people out there." She eyed him carefully. "Do you really think there's any connection between your sergeant's death and Glen Torbat?"

Thane shrugged. "I can't rule it out, Mrs. Thornton."

"And the police are back this morning. I had a phone call about them, and that they're taking fingerprints."

"Routine."

"If you'd said anything else I'd have been surprised." She sighed. "And don't call me Mrs. Thornton—even the clients call me Barbara. Not that we've too many of them."

"Barbara. You mean trade isn't too good?"

"It breaks about even. Thornton Travel goes for the economy end of the market and that's where money is really tight now—if you're unemployed, you don't splash out on holidays abroad. You're too damned busy trying to feed the family. Then on top of that, I've got the Peace Camp hanging round my neck." She pursed her lips. "That's not why you're here. I've still your word—?"

"The way I said, Where is your husband?"

"Magnus? He took a flight to Aberdeen this morning. Chasing some client—at least, that's what I was told." Two small patches of colour showed on her high cheekbones, but her voice stayed almost empty of emotion. "We've run our own lives for some time now, Superintendent. We manage a fairly civilised arrangement."

"I didn't know." It was easier to lie. Thane could picture that style of "civilised arrangement" only as a refined kind of hell. He searched for something to say. "With his line in work, I suppose he's away a lot."

"It's been that way lately." She used her free hand to brush away a stray strand of her short, grey-flecked hair. "I'll tell him you came here and asked more questions about the Peace Camp set-up."

"All right." It was the kind of half-truth which could be easier to maintain. Thane had a feeling Barbara Thornton had been down that way before. "So—why am I here?"

"Stay with your drink." She rose and smiled at him. "I'll only be a moment."

She went out, closing the door behind her.

Thane sat back, puzzled and wary. Barbara Thornton was certainly demonstrating the way she was used to managing situations—or maybe the word was nearer to manipulation. She'd surprised him with her open attitude to her marriage situation; it made her insistence on secrecy about whatever was next even harder to grasp.

He shrugged and looked again at the Tang horse. It nudged at his memory, then suddenly he remembered. It had been a few months back; he and Mary had spent a day on a long overdue visit to Glasgow's new Burrell Museum, the city's latest pride, home for a magpie collection of art treasures gathered by an eccentric Scottish shipping magnate. When he died, he'd gifted the multi-million-pound collection outright to a startled Glasgow.

The Burrell ranged from Rembrandts to Rodins, from chunks of Spanish castle to medieval English silver and Babylonian pottery. One of the richest, most colourful areas was its Chinese section—and the Tang horse had been there, proud on a pedestal.

Barbara Thornton was right. Owning one like it, she could have seen off any cash problems. Except if you did own something so perfect, could you allow yourself to be parted from it?

Thane was still musing over that unlikely prospect when the door opened again. He looked up, blinked, and tried to mask his surprise as Peter Crossley came awkwardly into the room with Barbara Thornton close behind. The thick-set, sandy-haired Peace Camp manager, tense and unhappy, looked uncomfortable in ill-fitting suit and tie. Crossley glanced round quickly as Barbara Thornton closed the door, as if she was cutting off his last chance of escape.

"You remember Peter," said Barbara Thornton.

Thane nodded, set down his glass, and got to his feet.

"He's what this is about." She gave Crossley a slight encouraging touch on the arm. "I had him come here because—well, I'll let him tell you."

"Tell me what?"

"Barbara reckons it's better I don't wait till you find out," said Crossley reluctantly. He took a deep breath. "I've got a record, Superintendent. I—I was in my twenties, I got drunk one night and I killed someone."

"Someone?" Thane stared at him.

"A woman—a girl." Crossley moistened his lips. "My wife—we'd been married a year, I caught her with someone else." He gave a wan attempt at a smile. "I was lucky, I suppose. The jury called it culpable homicide, I got twelve years, came out after eight."

Barbara Thornton nodded calmly. "One of my father's old friends sent him to me, Superintendent. We needed a manager at the Peace Camp, I gave him the job. He hasn't let me down. Of course, I suggested he changed his name. That wasn't too difficult."

Thane looked down at the whisky left in his glass and wished he hadn't abandoned it.

"What was your name when you were convicted?"

"Peter Brylie—Barbara said it would be easier if I kept the same first name."

Thane turned to the small, watchful woman beside him. "You've never told your husband?"

"I don't think he'd feel very happy about it—particularly now," she said in a matter-of-fact voice. "Do you?"

"That's not my problem." Thane pursed his lips. "I suppose there's more?"

Crossley glanced again at Barbara Thornton. She gave a slight nod.

"I'm a convicted killer," said Crossley wearily. "You've a murder on your plate—I nearly panicked yesterday, when you started questioning."

"So you lied?"

"Just a little," said Barbara Thornton.

"How little?" asked Thane.

"Mary and I—" Crossley shrugged miserably. "It wasn't serious as far as I was concerned. I couldn't get serious that way again—no matter how she might feel. But—"

"She was more than just one of the camp guests?"

Crossley looked down at his feet then nodded.

"So what about the rest of it?"

"The rest was true," said Crossley earnestly. "She just suddenly told me she was leaving, wouldn't say why."

"And you still can't remember the two men or the blue Toyota?"

Crossley shook his head.

"Now maybe you understand, Superintendent," said Barbara Thornton quietly. "I told you, you might have plunged in, jumped to the wrong conclusions."

"He didn't make it easier for us." Thane considered the sandy-haired camp manager unemotionally. "That's all?"

"Yes," said Crossley.

But Thane was sure he was lying.

CHAPTER SIX

Colin Thane spent another ten minutes with them then left. There was a parking ticket on his car—there was a parking ticket on every car in the sidestreet. He started to shove the parking ticket in his pocket, one more for Maggie Fyffe to sort out, then paused, grinned, and replaced it. Once you had a parking ticket, you might as well use the thing. He felt hungry, and there was a small Italian restaurant round the corner where the food was good.

Getting into the Ford, he used the radio on the Squad's low-band secure frequency. The call was patched through to Joe Felix.

"Still nothing at this end, sir," reported Felix gloomily. "Unless you want a minus. Scenes of Crime have finished at Glen Torbat but say Crossley wasn't there."

Thane gestured toward the hand-set's "send" button. "I've talked with him. He's with Barbara Thornton in Glasgow. See what Records have on a Peter Brylie. He got twelve years for killing his wife."

He released the "send" button, heard nothing but a purr of static for a moment, then Joe Felix replied with a sad curse.

"Brylie is our Crossley?"

"Yes. But he's clinging to the rest of his story." Thane glanced at his wrist-watch as he spoke. "I'm going to eat, then I'll be at the Royal Infirmary. Out."

He tossed the hand-set on its shelf and left the car.

The restaurant had an empty table and he ordered the chef's special, a Cotoleta Milanese. When it came, Thane ate slowly, mentally isolating himself from the buzz of conversation at the other tables, thinking over what had shaped into a very odd morning.

Billy Greenan was a straightforward situation, or as straightforward as anything involving the little car thief could be. He'd done a job, he'd dumped the Toyota, and it was gone for good unless someone was prepared to drain the Irish Sea. His story pointed totally at the two credit card fraudsters, Friend and Balfour, and Greenan's fear of Jimmy Friend had seemed very genuine.

Then there was Peter Crossley—it came easier to think of him that way. Crossley, the self-confessed killer who had served his sentence and now hid behind another name, was very different.

It was one thing for him to admit how things had really been in his relationship with Mary Dutton, and that she had known nothing about his past.

For the rest, Crossley still stuck fast to his original story. But even with Barbara Thornton there to give silent support, the Peace Camp manager hadn't been totally convincing. There had been a hard-to-define uneasiness, almost a scent of fear, the impression that Crossley somehow knew more than he admitted.

Thane stopped it there, finished his meal, paid, and left the busy restaurant. He paused at a news kiosk and bought a couple of health fad magazines that might interest Phil Moss, then walked back to his car.

It was 2 P.M. by the time he drove to the Royal Infirmary and found a parking place in the hospital yard. Going in, he discovered that Moss had been transferred to a side-room in another ward. The irate nurse who directed him pointed frostily at the door then departed in a swish of starched apron.

Phil Moss was sitting up in bed, shoulder still in plaster, but grinning and his face back to its normal wrinkled grey pallor. He already had his other visitor. Detective Inspector Alex Riney was a fat, soft-bodied man with a cheerful face, and not long to go before he reached pension age. Thane shook hands with him then tossed the magazines on the bed.

"Thanks." Moss glanced at the titles and grunted. "I've seen one of them. But I'll give it to a nurse—if I can find one that reads."

"Feeling better?" asked Thane mildly.

"Fit enough to be out of here if anyone would listen." Moss was on the mend. Alex Riney had brought grapes and Thane helped himself to a couple then settled into the chair waiting on the other side of the bed.

"Do we talk about this in front of him?" asked Riney good-naturedly.

"It'll keep his little mind occupied," said Thane.

Riney chuckled; Moss muttered an obscenity and shifted into a more comfortable position against the pillows.

"Right." Riney stroked a hand comfortably across his plump waistline.

"Credentials first, I suppose, Superintendent. I'm with the Credit Card and Cheque Squad—there's so damned much of it now the bosses set us up separate from the Fraud Squad, where I was before. You're interested in Friend and Balfour, I know them. But like I told you on the phone, I can't help you find them. They're floaters, always have been."

"It didn't connect when they started kiting between here and Arrochar?"

"To be honest, no." Riney looked slightly embarrassed. "Look, it was small-time, not their usual style, pretty irregular. The descriptions we got weren't wonderful, we'd plenty of bigger things on our plate. So"—he gave an apologetic shrug—"no, we didn't connect."

"That happens." Thane gave a nod which held a degree of sympathy. It was the same picture in too many police areas, forced economies that left unfilled gaps in manpower, which meant battles over overtime claims, which even brought complaints if cars clocked up too high an operational mileage. "But we want to hear about them."

"Aye." Riney grimaced. "If you've read the files I don't need to tell you Friend is the one to watch—I'd call him Australia's revenge for the old convict ships. Friend met up with Inky Balfour in prison, they held hands from then on, and I'd just hoped they'd finally moved to someone else's patch."

"What's their usual scene?" asked Phil Moss. He scowled as Thane helped himself to more grapes. "There's thieving—and thieving."

"Not with them. They stick to kiting, even if Friend is violent at the edges." Riney was positive. "You want the standard lecture?"

Thane rescued a grape seed from his mouth and nodded. Riney was their expert; it always paid to listen.

"Well, forget the counterfeited cards, the forged cheque books—who needs them? The real things get stolen all the time, maybe in handbag snatches or a mugging, burglary or whatever. The neds know the market, they'll get twenty pounds for a credit card, up to fifty for a full cheque book with its guarantee card. Specialists like Friend and Balfour maybe pay double that when they buy from a middleman, and they buy in quantity."

"Then off to work?"

Riney grinned. "First they've got to change the signature on the plastic—use the same name that's on it, but substitute their own handwriting. That's not too much of a problem."

"Why not?" Moss frowned at him. "I thought the banks and the credit card outfits had some new ideas?"

"They keep trying. It used to be your villain just bleached out the original signature—all he needed was a tin of brake fluid and something out of the kitchen cupboard." Riney grinned. "Try that now with some cards and a rude message comes through from underneath. So the latest trick is to remove the signature strip and paste on a new one. If you've the know-how and a tame printer, then you're in business—just stay under the authorisation limits."

Thane had heard some of it before, had seen some of the statistics. Cheque and credit card frauds had mushroomed in every civilised country; losses were rated in millions every year.

There was no limit to the number of times a credit card could be used in a day; the con artist could keep going until his luck ran out—or, more likely, he wanted a rest.

But signing a stolen cheque then getting money for it across a bank counter had to be more difficult. He grimaced. It was sometimes difficult enough when everything was genuine.

"Suppose you're cheque kiting, Alex. The banks don't make it easy—any time I've had to cash a personal cheque out of town, at a strange bank, they want the cheque book too. Then they either mark a page at the back or slap on a date-stamp."

"That way, you can only draw out one lot of cash a day—and there's a tight limit. I know." Riney gave him a slightly pitying smile. "But your problem is you're honest. When your real pros hit a town they move in for the day, there are maybe half a dozen in the team. They've cars, a van as an office and travelling wardrobe, they work to a schedule, they'll maybe use thirty or forty cheque books between them, and they'll use every last cheque they've got."

"But how?" demanded Moss. "What about the date-stamps?"

Riney shrugged. "That's where the office in the van comes in. They've got the gear along to bleach out the stamp. Or if they're organised, they've a bundle of substitute date-stamp pages someone ran off. They just take out the old one, staple in another."

"I'll be damned," said Moss with grudging respect. "Uh—how much could they take?"

"In a day?" Riney took a dig at the grapes, gathering a handful. He popped one into his mouth and sucked pensively. "The last time we had a real team operating, they cleared twenty thousand pounds in credit card purchases on day one, stayed overnight in a five-star hotel, then took the local banks on day two for fifty thousand in cash. We never got as much as a smell of them."

"Were Friend and Balfour in on it?" asked Thane. Riney knew his subject, but they were drifting.

"Maybe." Riney shrugged. "All we knew was the team was made up of four men and a woman. They switched clothes, switched wigs, about the only thing the woman didn't try was a moustache." He paused and frowned. "You know, talking like this—yes, I'm getting a nasty feeling."

"You've lost me." Thane was puzzled. "Why?"

"Well, you want to know about Friend and Balfour. They're regular operators, yet we haven't really heard of them in months." Alex Riney's big, amiable face showed a dawning alarm. "Come to think of it, they're not the only ones. There are a few more who've sort of slipped out of the frame, like they'd emigrated."

"All about the same time?"

Riney nodded.

"How many?"

Riney hesitated. "I know Glasgow, I'm not sure of the Edinburgh scene, or the rest—but I can make a few calls." He heaved himself out of his chair, suddenly business-like. "I'll get back to you."

He left, letting the side-room door bang shut behind him. For a moment, Thane and Moss looked at each other in silence.

"Fifty thousand—and the rest." Moss scratched at the edge of the plaster cast on his shoulder in a restless indignation. "Well, he called it a blitz. Maybe—"

Thane nodded. Maybe Mary Dutton had walked into something much bigger than she realised. Maybe, for the first time, they might have a positive motive for her death within their grasp.

"And I'm stuck in a damned bed. It's getting to be a habit." Moss scowled as a trolley squeaked past outside in the corridor. "Look, Colin, about last night—"

"We've got three of them so far."

"Those dogs were damned good." Moss sucked his lips in wry admiration. "That handler who was with them—"

"Jock Dawson."

"He seems all right."

Thane chuckled. "He'd probably agree." He got up to go. "Anything you want sent in?"

"An escape kit." Moss stopped him. "How are things at home, with Katie?"

"Sorting out. Her school has a problem teacher."

"They should ship the basket here," grumbled Moss. "Give them a chance, and some of them would put barbed wire in the bedpans."

It was mid-afternoon by the time Colin Thane returned to the Crime Squad Headquarters building. By then, the effect of the painkiller tablets had begun to ease and some of the aching and stiffness was returning to his body. Once in the building, he went to the men's room, took two more of the hospital tablets, and washed them down with water. Then he went along to Jack Hart's office.

Hart was out, Maggie Fyffe was fending off any calls, and the Squad Commander's secretary's temper showed signs of fraying at the edges.

"Someone been rattling your cage?" asked Thane.

"Don't you start." She glared at him.

"Forget I asked," said Thane mildly.

"Sorry." She sighed and shook her head. "It's not your fault."

"But?"

"He disappears, Tom Maxwell disappears, you disappear, everyone disappears. Then the phones start ringing." Maggie Fyffe drew a deep breath. "What am I supposed to do when some moron of a civil servant starts bawling me out?"

"Tell him to go to hell," suggested Thane.

"I did—and the same to another couple of idiots." She sat back, anger evaporating. "I've a message from the boss for you. This Peace Camp place you're interested in—you saw a High Court judge among the guests?"

Thane nodded.

"No, you didn't—and he went home this morning. He spotted Francey arriving and decided it was time to leave. But he'll keep his mouth shut."

"Sensible judge," said Thane. The legal profession knew how to steer clear of trouble. "As for you, Maggie, I think you're wonderful."

"That's a hell of a help," said Maggie Fyffe, and the phone beside her began ringing again.

Thane left her and went through to the duty room. It was quiet, almost deserted, but Sandra Craig was pecking out a report on a typewriter, with Jock Dawson peering over her shoulder. A length of yellow tail protruding from under her desk showed that at least one of Dawson's dogs had moved in. The tail twitched as Thane went over, Goldie's head peered out, then the Labrador retired again.

"Where's the big fellow?" asked Thane.

"Rajah?" Dawson gave him an easy grin. "Out in the van, sir. Want me to bring him in?"

"No. We've enough troubles." Thane sat on the edge of the desk. "Where's Joe Felix?"

Sandra stopped typing. "Chasing the Scenes of Crime report from Glen Torbat, sir." She gave an appreciative grimace. "But it looks like you got the part that matters. He left the Peter Brylie print-out on your desk."

"Does it match with Crossley?"

She nodded. "Yes, and Francey knows—he phoned half an hour ago from some place in the wilds, and I told him. He says Crossley is back at Glen Torbat." She anticipated Thane's question. "Crossley arrived on his own."

"Anything else?"

"Not yet. Francey says the weather is lousy up there. He'll try and call again tonight."

Translated, it meant Detective Sergeant Francey Dunbar felt fed up, forgotten, and far from home. But that might change. Thane thumbed at the report sheet in the typewriter.

"What have you got?"

"I ran that check on the Thorntons." Sandra Craig's voice was enough to indicate the result wasn't a happy scene. "It looks like their kind of marriage wouldn't win any prizes. They may live together, but they've both had a few outside interests."

"Both?" Thane raised an eyebrow.

"Mrs. Thornton likes to maintain a front, but it ends there." Sandra shrugged. "I'd say she's still an attractive woman, sir—at least, to older men. You know, not exactly geriatrics, but—"

"Older," suggested Thane. "Anyone current?"

She shook her head. "No-one seems to know and I didn't push it too far."

He didn't ask who Sandra Craig had asked, how she'd put it together. The red-haired girl sitting in front of him always knew something, someone, somewhere, always seemed able to separate gossip from fact. Once, only once, after he'd joined the Squad, Thane had doubted what she had put together. He'd run his own checks, had discovered it was accurate to the last detail. Next day, without a word, she'd handed him a list of the people he'd contacted and what they'd said.

"So they don't win a prize for wedded bliss." He shrugged. "What's the rest of it?"

"So far, sir?" Sandra removed the report sheet from her typewriter. "Barbara Thornton seems to have a reputation for helping waifs and strays—I'd say Crossley is probably just the latest on the list, no sexual involvement."

"But?"

"Well, she doesn't flaunt it. But the travel trade get glenty of 'research trip' invites for weekends abroad and she never arrives alone."

Jock Dawson chuckled to himself. "Waste not, want not, eh?"

"Down, Jock," said Thane wearily. "What else? She told me Thornton Travel wasn't doing too well."

Sandra nodded. "It seems that way. There's a rumour one of the major travel operators has made noises about buying her out and that she hasn't much choice. But she'll still have some private money of her own."

Thane whistled thinly, thoughtfully, through his teeth. The Labrador at his feet stirred at the sound, looked up, then subsided again with a grunt. He ignored the movement, still thinking. Maybe he'd hoped for more; he wasn't sure.

"What's the story with her husband?"

"He gets around," said Sandra Craig. "But nobody long-term—that's not his style."

"Money?"

"I think Barbara pays the bills. His own operation, this Gordon Hope Management, doesn't amount to much. He acts as registered office for some small companies with fairly vague backgrounds." She shrugged. "Some probably only exist on paper, keeping someone's tax bill down. But he travels a lot—or he has lately. He's up in Aberdeen today."

Thane stared at her. "How the hell did you find that out?"

Sandra Craig blinked. "His secretary says he flew up this morning."

"You spoke to her?"

She glanced at Dawson, and the dog-handler gave an embarrassed grin.

"I did," he admitted. "But no problem, sir. I told her I was in the dog business and that I had some tax problems. Then once she told me the boss was out of town—"

"He turned on the four-footed-friend charm," said Sandra dryly. "Francey couldn't have done better."

"Well"—Dawson cleared his throat hastily—"she sounds all right. She's having a problem with her dog, probably feeding it wrong, and—"

"Why Aberdeen? Did his secretary say?"

"Some client up there has a problem. But Thornton is due back on the evening flight to Glasgow." Dawson hesitated. "Uh—I never met Detective Sergeant Dutton. But didn't she come from that area?"

"Farther out," said Thane. "So do a lot of other people—forget that one. But I still have a feeling I want to know if Magnus Thornton made the trip."

"We can check." Sandra Craig was puzzled.

"Do it, but quietly," said Thane. "And you and Jock can take a trip out to the airport. I want to be sure Thornton gets back this evening."

Magnus and Barbara Thornton were beginning to worry him though he wasn't totally certain why.

He left the duty room and went back to his own office. There were a few message slips waiting on his desk, but none required any urgent attention and he turned to the print-out sheet from Criminal Records.

Peter Crossley who had been Brylie seemed to have told him the truth. He had been twenty-five years old, married just over a year, when he had killed his wife. Most of his twelve-year sentence, reduced to eight with normal remission, had been served in an Open Prison. To get there, even as a first offender, meant he had to have been regarded as low-risk.

Moodily, Thane discarded the print-out and sat back. There was blue sky outside his window again; a small fly was moving lazily along the inside of the glass.

What was he really trying to prove anyway? Everything he had pointed directly to Friend and Balfour; the two-man fraud team had gone to earth; the real effort remained trying to find them.

He knew from experience what that meant, a monotonous round of knocking on unfriendly doors, asking questions, getting little in the way of answers. Unglamorous, except that when a cop knocked on a door, he never knew what might happen when it opened.

And that made it worse.

Giving up, Thane went along the corridor to Maggie Fyffe's domain. She was in a slightly better temper and he managed to cadge a mug of coffee from the pot she kept simmering for Jack Hart's benefit, coffee that was like nectar compared with the Crime Squad's regular instant variety. Nursing the mug, he returned to his room and found Joe Felix waiting.

"Maggie's brew, sir?" Felix treated his achievement with open respect. "With her, that's like pulling teeth. How do you manage it?"

"Natural charm. You can quote me." Thane set the mug on his desk. "Did you get the Scenes of Crime report?"

"On Glen Torbat?" Felix nodded. "But I thought you'd want to hear about something else first. One of Tom Maxwell's men has called in. We've got a sighting on Friend and Balfour. Two days old, but here, in Glasgow."

Thane tensed. "Where?"

"City centre, near St. Vincent Street, mid-morning." Felix shrugged. "His contact knows them, says they got into a taxi—he got a clear view and he's positive."

Two days old it might be, but it placed both men in the city. It was the first recent sighting, and it fuelled Thane's stubborn hunch that they hadn't fled. He nodded with a degree of relief.

"What about Scenes of Crime?"

"They're not too happy," admitted Felix. "First they miss Crossley when they know he was the real reason they went, then they drew a total blank in the cabin Mary used. Not as much as a smudge that mattered."

"They fingerprinted the rest of the staff?"

"The way you wanted, but on a first run there's no match with any." Felix paused. "That's the way you expected?"

"Yes." But it tidied some of the edges. "Did they notice Francey?"

"In the background. Some female with a handbell had him jogging in the rain." Joe Felix enjoyed the thought, then moved on. "Sandra confirmed Magnus Thornton was on the morning flight to Aberdeen. He is booked back this evening."

"I still want her out there."

"What about tonight?" Felix shifted his weight from one foot to the other. "We've been talking. We think we should stay on for a spell."

"You mean nursemaid duty, in case I stray?" asked Thane. But it saved him asking. "We'll see how things shape."

The afternoon dragged on, the kind of waiting with little happening which was always frustrating. He had Joe Felix run a check on the vague chance that either Jimmy Friend or Inky Balfour might have known Crossley in prison. The result was a negative—their paths couldn't have crossed.

Tom Maxwell drifted in. His witness-box stint in court had finished for the day and the defence case had sprung a decided leak. Maxwell lingered until Thane, knowing what he really wanted, gave him an update on what was happening.

As Maxwell left, the telephone rang. Alex Riney was at the other end of the line and the Strathclyde detective inspector could have sounded happier.

"Don't ask me to explain why, Superintendent," he began gloomily. "But I can give you a list of at least nine high-class cheque-kiting operators who have melted off the scene—that doesn't include your two. I can only trace one of the nine for sure, a woman, and that's because she's in gaol down in London."

Thane frowned at the receiver. "When did they start fading?"

"All round about the same time, a few months ago. Every one of them in Glasgow or Edinburgh based, none of them seems to be active." Riney paused hopefully. "Do you believe in miracles?"

"Not that kind."

"That makes two of us," said Riney bitterly. "Maybe I should have worried about it earlier, but we've been too busy chasing working villains."

"We let sleeping dogs lie," agreed Thane.

Riney grunted. "What about when they wake up?"

"You tell me—any ideas?"

"I sent in my crystal ball for repair," said Riney. "Their kind seldom get careless. We've had no whispers."

Neither of them said anything for a moment, then Thane broke the silence.

"Glasgow and Edinburgh—how about Aberdeen?"

"Up north among the oil wells?" Riney used sarcasm to hide his gloom. "No, we don't know of any resident kiters up there—none that matter, anyway. When Aberdeen has real trouble, it usually arrives on a day trip from Glasgow." He brightened a little, glad to move on to something positive. "I've made a list and put together photographs. I'll send them over."

Thane thanked him, promised to keep in touch, and hung up. Then he glanced at his wrist-watch, the digital with the chrome steel casing and matching bracelet which had been Millside C.I.D.'s parting gift. It was almost 5 P.M.—seventeen hundred hours on the digital—and Mary should be home from the clinic. Lifting the receiver again, he dialled the number and she answered.

"How was Phil?" she asked.

"Planning a mutiny."

She chuckled. "And how about you?"

"Stiff but surviving." He knew the other thing she wanted to know. "There's nothing fresh on the schoolteacher front. But—"

"You're going to have to stay on?" Mary Thane had heard him shape towards the same thing often enough. "Mary Dutton?"

"Yes. It's just grumbling on, but something could break."

"Last time, it was Phil's shoulder," she said pointedly.

"This time, I've got nursemaids. How was the clinic?"

"Like a production line," she said wryly. "That woman was in again, the one who had her cheque book stolen." There was a strange noise in the background. "That's Clyde. I think he's going to be sick—on the carpet. Take care."

Her phone slammed down.

Minutes later, he had another visitor. Jack Hart came barging in, grinning from ear to ear.

"Had a good day?" asked Thane.

"Very good." The Crime Squad commander stuffed his hands in his pockets and looked out of Thane's window for a moment, humming under his breath. "I think we're winning."

"Another budget meeting?" Thane tried to appear interested.

"Except this time I played them at their own game, cost-effectiveness. They didn't like it. So maybe I can soon get back to being some kind of a cop again." Hart came over. "Tom Maxwell says you've been busy. What's the real strength of it?"

Thane told him. It was the same story he'd told Maxwell, with a few additions.

"A hell of a lot of loose ends, but you need Friend and Balfour to pull them together." Hart delivered his verdict with a sharp-eyed understanding. "Need any more help?"

"Not till something happens."

"If Friend and Balfour are just the tip of your iceberg then we've got real trouble." Hart's lined face hardened. "I want to know as it develops. Your other problem will be tomorrow's newspapers. They're going to run some kind of a story about Mary Dutton and there will be an official statement from Strathclyde. I've a guarantee it will be as dull as their Force Information Office can make it."

Hart left; Linda Belmont came in. She looked more like a college student than a detective sergeant, in a casual outfit of white shirt and tailored sky blue trousers topped by a white nylon jacket.

"This is from Maggie, sir. She says it just arrived." She laid a large brown envelope on his desk. "I'm on my way to see those schoolgirls."

"How many?"

"Five, if they turn up. The Fraser girl helped me organise it and they'll be at a local tennis club."

Thane pursed his lips. "Do they know the reason?"

"No." She shook her head. "But there's nothing to stop them guessing."

"Are you taking the Animal?" He couldn't see her hairy, muscle-bound detective partner blending into a tennis background.

"No, sir." Linda Belmont almost giggled at the thought. "I spoke to one of the girls on the Drug Squad. She'll be there."

"Remember they're juveniles and we're on thin ice. If you get enough from them for a case, talk it over with Commander Hart before you bring in Teacher."

It would be safer to have Hart as senior officer from that stage, with no fringe interest.

He waited until Linda Belmont had gone then he opened the envelope. A collection of playing-card-sized record shot photographs tumbled out, each with a name inked on the back, then a typewritten master list. Alex Riney had kept his promise.

Ten photographs, eight men and two women. Thane spread them on his desk, putting Friend and Balfour in centre position. Their photographs were the only ones he knew, Jimmy Friend's lean features in that mocking smile, Inky Balfour showing that injured innocence.

All the others had faced the police camera with varying degrees of resignation or defiance. They looked the kind of people who might be in business or who could turn up supporting some charity fund-raising. People who wouldn't stand out in a crowd, people it would be easy to trust.

That was their stock in trade. He glanced at Alex Riney's master list, winced at the total of fraud convictions the ten had accumulated, and wondered how many more cases weren't known about or couldn't be proved.

Thane gathered up the photographs then dealt them out again, slapping each one down on the desk.

Specialists. Yet all had faded from the scene.

What the hell was going on?

He was still frowning at the photographs when his telephone rang and the duty officer patched through Sandra Craig on a low-band call from her car.

"We're leaving the airport," she reported. "Thornton came off the Aberdeen flight and collected his car. Jock and I are tailing him, and he's heading south—probably heading for home. Do we stay with him?"

He thought quickly.

"Yes, but don't crowd him. Let me know when he gets there."

"When he gets there." Sandra Craig was disappointed, but went off the air.

Another half-hour slipped by, then she radioed again. Magnus Thornton had arrived home; both white Jaguar cars were parked in the driveway of their cottage conversion.

"Keep an eye on the place," Thane told her. "I'm going to pay them a visit."

"On your own, sir?" She disapproved. "Jock thinks—"

"Tell him I'm housetrained," said Thane sarcastically. "Where did he leave Rajah and Goldie?"

"At the Dog Branch kennels—he says they need a rest."

"Don't we all?" said Thane, and hung up.

What he was going to do might be a mistake, but he had to take that chance. If either of the Thorntons was involved, then something had to be made to happen. He gathered up Alex Riney's collection of photographs, put them in an inside pocket of his jacket, and went out to his car.

It was a pleasant, sunlit evening and he almost enjoyed the drive once he was out of town.

The Thorntons' cottage was in a strip of dairy farming country about two miles south of the last of the suburbs. It was a narrow strip, the Glasgow skyline on the horizon on one side, the low, bleak hills and bogland of the Fenwick Moor on the other.

Thane caught himself wondering how much longer the farmers would survive so close to the spreading city. They were fighting. The traditional small farms had mostly given way to larger units running larger herds.

But a lot of the grazing land had long since become golf courses with clubhouse bars. Developers kept on nibbling out another few acres for house building, someone found a prime site and built an hotel, someone else sneaked in a small workshop. . . .

And so it went on.

Any old, abandoned farm cottage was now being snapped up for conversion, the kind of conversion which only retained the original stone walls, the scarred timber beams, and the dark grey country roof tiles. No farm labourer had ever enjoyed the double-glazed picture windows, the patios with fish ponds, or the built-in bars which became standard fitments.

A cottage conversion home had become a status symbol for people who had made it in the city, wanted out, but couldn't stray too far from the business world.

Thane was glad the dairy cattle were still around. They ate their grass and didn't give a damn about the new neighbours; they still wandered down the same country roads at milking time.

He met one herd at about the same time as he decided he was near the Thorntons' home. Forced to stop, he watched the fat, amiable, brown-and-white Ayrshires amble by on both sides amid a buzz of flies. One of them stopped, gazed in at him through the driver's window, then gave an indignant bellow as her rump was thwacked by a herdsman's stick.

The cow shifted and Thane wound down his window.

"How do I get to the Thornton cottage?" he asked the herdsman.

"Straight on, then first right. You're not far from it." The herdsman considered him carefully. "Know them?"

Thane nodded.

"Aye, well tell them to keep their eyes open." The herdsman's frown became a scowl. "There's a couple o' folk parked in a car in the next road, doin' damned all but waiting. They look the thieving kind."

The herdsman walked on after his charges. Grinning, Thane switched channels on his radio and used it.

"Hearing me, Sandra?" he asked.

Jock Dawson's voice answered him. The dog-handler sounded bored. "She's out of the car, boss. Stretching her legs or whatever she wants to call it."

"Find a better spot," said Thane. "The locals think you're big-time criminals."

Dawson swore and acknowledged.

Thane set the Ford moving and the herdsman's directions brought him to the Thorntons' cottage in a couple of minutes. It had grey stone walls and ivy, garden furniture on a patch of lawn, and the two white Jaguars were parked on the gravel driveway.

He left the car, walked through the evening sunlight to the cottage door, and used the heavy brass knocker. After a moment, Magnus Thornton opened the door and gave a surprised grunt when he saw his visitor.

"I didn't expect you out here, Thane. I suppose there's some kind of a reason?"

"I need some help," said Thane simply.

"Do you?" The tall, mousey-haired accountant leaned against the doorpost for a moment. He was wearing a plaid sports shirt and casual trousers; his feet were in sandals. He shrugged, his thin face unimpressed. "Come in. But I've had a damned hard day—don't make it worse."

Thane followed him through to a large, comfortably furnished living room. Barbara Thornton stared up at him in surprise from one of the armchairs ranged around a natural stone fireplace which had a copper canopy.

"Sorry to break in on your evening, Mrs. Thornton," he told her.

"That's all right." She recovered quickly, glancing at her husband. "I —I was just telling Magnus how you'd been at my office—"

"With those questions about the Peace Camp?" Thane saw the flicker of relief that crossed her face. "This is something new that turned up."

"Sit down and let's hear about it then, get it done with." Thornton flopped into the nearest chair. "I said I'd had a rough day—I meant it. I'm not long back from Aberdeen and the damned plane shook all the way."

Thane chose a chair between them. Thornton's briefcase lay at the man's feet beside a half-filled glass and an opened copy of an Aberdeen evening paper.

"I'll keep it short. You know we've been trying to trace two men with a blue Toyota." He reached into his inside pocket and brought out Alex Riney's photographs. Fanning them, keeping the faces hidden, he selected Friend and Balfour and handed the two prints to Thornton. "Ever seen these two before?"

"Where?"

"Anywhere."

"All right." Thornton glanced at them. "No, never."

"Mrs. Thornton?"

She took the photographs, studied them for slightly longer, then shook her head.

"Have you caught them?" asked Thornton.

"Not yet."

"Then who are they?"

"Two cheque-book artists who were seen at Arrochar."

Barbara Thornton studied the faces again. "And they killed your policewoman?"

"Good thinking, Barbara," said Thornton sarcastically. He indicated the other photographs. "More faces?"

"None that matter." Thane took the two prints from Barbara Thornton and returned them all to his pocket. "Thanks for trying. Maybe someone on the Peace Camp staff will remember them."

"You can try." Thornton shrugged. "I'm just glad we were at home that night. Remember we opened that bottle of wine, Barbara?"

She nodded.

"That reminds me." Thornton lifted his glass and got to his feet. "Like a drink, Thane? I'm topping this up." He refilled his glass to the brim.

"No—but thank you. I'll get on my way." Thane rose. A display case filled with a collection of small pieces of antique glass and silver caught his eye and he went over to look at them. "Are you a collector, Mr. Thornton?"

"Not guilty—at least, not as far as that lot is concerned." Thornton gave a sardonic grin. "That's mostly junk."

"They belonged to my father," said Barbara Thornton quietly.

"Who didn't know any better," said Thornton. "I'd have done better." He turned away, ignoring her. "Before you go, Thane, any ideas yet about why that girl was killed?"

"That's something we're still putting together, Mr. Thornton," said Thane. "But we're getting the pieces—it won't be too long."

Thornton's thin face didn't alter. He waited while Thane said good-bye to Barbara Thornton, then went with him to the door.

It was early dusk outside, the sun beginning to glint red on the cottage windows. Starting the Ford, setting it moving, Thane heard Sandra Craig's voice murmur from the radio.

"Everything okay, sir?"

Reaching for the handset, he waited until the first curve of road masked him from the cottage.

"Just fine," he said sarcastically. "Where are you?"

"Behind the trees to your left. It's an old track, mud and damn great biting midges."

He saw the trees, silhouetted against the skyline on a slight rise of ground.

"Got you." From up there, they had a clear view of the cottage.

"You've to call the duty officer." Her voice was blurred by static as the Ford passed the remains of an old barn. "He's been trying to raise you."

"What's worrying him?"

"Francey is on his way in. He says he wants you to be there." She paused. "What about us, sir?"

"Stay where you are, keep watching the cottage." Thane winced as the Ford juddered through a deep rut. "Radio me if there's any movement—in or out."

There was a moment's silence, as if Sandra was sharing her dismay with Jock Dawson.

"Till when?" she asked.

"Till you hear differently," said Thane.

He changed the radio's frequency, and called the duty officer.

It was almost 10 P.M. when Colin Thane stopped the Ford in the Crime Squad parking lot. Darkness had arrived; the Glasgow skyline was a blaze of lights. The night man on the main door greeted him with a grin as he went into the building.

"Has Sergeant Dunbar arrived?" asked Thane.

"Yes, sir." The man's grin widened a little. "He's in the duty room."

"Something amusing you?" asked Thane.

"No, sir." The man retreated, still grinning.

Thane went through, reached the duty room, then stopped short as he saw the bulky figure of MacLean, the Arrochar sergeant. Ill at ease, in unfamiliar surroundings, MacLean looked anything but happy.

"What the hell brought you here?" demanded Thane.

"Him, sir." MacLean gestured. "Big Angus."

Thane stared past him, to the far side of the busy, smoky room. Francey Dunbar was there, standing guard over the shaggy, bearded figure of the wanted tramp. Big Angus sat handcuffed, the ancient coat he was wearing was tied at his waist with string, but at least, for the moment he was wearing his trousers.

Thane went over. Dunbar greeted him cheerfully; Big Angus scowled.

"Are you going to tell me he's why you pulled out?" asked Thane, bewildered.

"Yes, sir." Dunbar reached down under the desk, straightened, and dumped a blue back-pack in front of him. One of the shoulder straps was broken. "He had this—it was Mary Dutton's." He gestured toward the tramp. "I thought you'd want to hear how he got it."

Big Angus glared and muttered under his breath. The tramp had piercing green eyes. At that range, he also had a foul, stale liquor breath.

Thane ignored him. The back-pack was still almost new and the initials "M.D." had been inked on the front flap. It had been opened and emptied, the contents dumped on the floor beside the desk. They seemed to amount to Big Angus's spare rags of clothing, a few tins of food, some rabbit snares, and a battered cooking pot.

"All right, Francey," he said resignedly. "What happened?"

"My part?" Dunbar shoved his hands into the pockets of his ornate leather jacket and chuckled. "I got lucky, nothing much more. I left the

Peace Camp to phone in—told them I was going to bike into Arrochar for a beer." He motioned toward Big Angus. "I met him on the road, saw the back-pack, and got curious."

Thane nodded at the handcuffs. "But he wasn't friendly?"

The tramp protested. He had a deep, gravelly voice and a strong West Highland accent.

"Man, I was attacked! Och, how was I expected to know what he was?"

They ignored him. Still grumbling, Big Angus subsided.

"Did he give you trouble?" asked Thane.

"A bite on the leg—MacLean reckons I'll need rabies shots." Francey Dunbar shook his head. "But I dragged him into Arrochar, got MacLean, and he drove us here." He turned to the tramp. "Let's hear the story again, Angus. None of the trimmings this time. You're talking to my boss, understand me?"

"Aye." Big Angus's handcuffs jingled as he scratched awkwardly somewhere deep under the old coat. He eyed Thane cautiously. "Man, I just found the damnation thing—"

"The night Mary Dutton was killed," said Dunbar softly. "He saw it happen."

"It was dark," protested the bearded tramp. "I didn't see anything for sure, mister."

"Francey?" It would save time.

"He says it was late and he'd camped for the night about a mile from the Arrochar end of the Glen Torbat road. He saw a car's lights, then something seemed to happen and it stopped."

"That's right." Big Angus licked his lips. "But—"

"By then he was interested," said Dunbar. "He says two men got out and loaded something or someone into the rear seat."

"I thought it was maybe someone hurt, mister." The tramp bared his yellowed teeth in what was meant to be an apology. "You know, that they were helping—then they drove away."

"Heading where?"

"The same way they'd been going—Arrochar." The unkempt figure was eager to get things finished. "That's when I walked down to the road, to take a wee look around." His eyes strayed to the back-pack. "I found that thing in the heather beside the road, like it had been thrown there when—well, when whatever it was happened."

"Found it, kept it, sold Mary's things a couple of days later to a travelling dealer for five pounds," added Francey Dunbar with a grim disgust. He saw Big Angus tried to rise and shoved him down in the seat again. "Stay there. Tell the rest of it."

"You mean when they came back?" The tramp gave a sullen shrug. "That was later, a lot later—I think it was the same car and another one. They stopped at the same place and they searched around with torches. I was well clear o' the road, so that didn't worry me."

"When they gave up, both cars headed back towards Arrochar again," said Dunbar. He touched the blue back-pack, his eyes ablaze. "I've taken him through the story half-a-dozen times, that's always how he tells it."

Thane said nothing for a moment. Big Angus's story gave them some kind of an eye-witness, then more—someone else had come to the aid of the men who had killed Mary Dutton, could even have been the one who realised her back-pack had been forgotten and who insisted they tried to find it. Maybe there had been other attempts, later. Maybe they had just given up.

"What about the cars, Angus?" he asked quietly. "Would you know them again?"

"No chance of that." The tramp shook his head. "I told you, mister— it was dark. Anyway, most cars look the same to me." He raised his handcuffed wrists indignantly. "How about takin' these things off?"

"Later." Thane signalled another man over to watch their prisoner then took Dunbar out of earshot. "Take him through it again, just in case. Then we need a full, signed statement."

"What about after that?" Dunbar indicated Sergeant MacLean, still hovering in the background like a lost soul. "MacLean wants him back in Arrochar on that housebreaking charge."

"He can have him as long as he keeps him locked up."

As he said it, Thane was thinking again. The tramp's story placed Jimmy Friend and Inky Balfour as coming from the direction of the Peace Camp. But they hadn't gone back that way; their help had come from the other direction. Allow the length of time Big Angus claimed had passed, and that help could have come from Glasgow.

Stay with that possibility—

"There's something else, sir." Dunbar paused, making sure he had Thane's attention. "Do you remember Mandy, a girl at the Peace Camp?"

"The reception desk." Thane nodded. "Young, grey wool shirt, Gordon tartan trews—"

"We got talking. She's into Animal Rights. She told me a long story about how Peter Crossley is a reasonable enough boss but is scared stiff of Magnus Thornton."

"So?" Thane tried not to sound impatient.

"So Thornton has the only key to one of the cabins and nobody else gets to use it—a private arrangement with Crossley. When Mandy found out, Crossley told her to keep her mouth shut. Particularly when Barbara Thornton was around." Dunbar's tanned face shaped a grimace. "Maybe it's just where Thornton takes the occasional woman, but—"

"But we don't know," murmured Thane. "Has Mandy ever seen who uses it?"

"No. She only works part-time, mostly mornings." Dunbar shook his head. "But why don't we bounce Crossley off a few walls?"

"We will, tomorrow," promised Thane. "Thanks, Francey."

He left Dunbar to organise Big Angus's statement, took time to talk to Sergeant MacLean in a way that left the Arrochar man happier, then was heading back towards his own office when Linda Belmont appeared in the duty room. She looked tired but she was smiling and she came straight towards him.

"We've got our Moorov, sir." She was totally confident.

"Good." Thane drew a deep, relieved breath. "How many girls talked?"

"You wanted four, I've got six." She grinned. "Two extras turned up at the tennis club, only one of the bunch backed down. We've got your kinky schoolteacher by his proverbials—and I'm not letting go."

It was the one really good piece of news he'd heard the entire evening. Thane could have hugged her.

"What about their parents?" He had to be sure.

"I've talked with them. They want his head on a plate—well, not exactly his head." She chuckled. "Can I go ahead and pick him up?"

"Now?"

"No, sir." She eyed him deliberately. "In the morning, at the school gates."

He winced then heard his name called. One of the night shift duty men gestured urgently, pointing to a telephone.

"Wait." Thane left her and took the call.

"Is that you for sure, Mr. Thane?" asked a gruff voice over the line.

"Yes."

"Good." He heard a grunt of relief. "It's me, Tank Mallard." The Millside ned paused awkwardly. "Spare me a moment?"

"Stretching it, yes," said Thane flatly. "I thought you were out of circulation."

"Me and my sister got bail." Mallard chuckled. "Look, I reckon I owe you, Mr. Thane. You didn't put the boot in, and me in more trouble, over that bit of a misunderstanding we had."

"I get weak moments then regret them," said Thane dryly.

"Well, I'm doin' a lady named Brenda a wee obligement and she says you're trying to find that Aussie madman Jimmy Friend an' his fancy pal Inky Balfour."

Thane froze where he stood. "That's right."

"An' they killed a woman cop, or it looks that way?"

"Yes."

"I never grassed on anyone before, Mr. Thane." Tank Mallard's voice became an even deeper growl. "But like I said, I owe you—an' I don't hold with killin' women, even women cops. You follow?"

"I follow." Thane tightened his grip on the phone. "Tank, if you know anything—"

"You can have them gift-wrapped, Mr. Thane, a wee token of thanks from Sadie an' me." Mallard spoke tersely. "Top floor, 42 Graduate Street—the name on the door is Bridges, they've rented it for the last couple o' months. He paused then added anxiously. "You'll forget who told you, and—well, about me doing this wee favour for Brenda?"

"I've a bad memory—if you're sure."

"I'm sure," said Mallard with conviction. "An' I've a favourite cousin who'll get his head kicked in if I'm wrong."

He hung up. For a moment, Thane didn't move then he slammed down the receiver and drew a deep breath.

"Sir—" Linda Belmont was at his side.

"Talk to Commander Hart about it, Linda." He brushed her aside, looking for Dunbar. "Francey—"

"Here." Dunbar materialised at his elbow.

"Get Joe Felix, grab any spare bodies you can. I need two cars, a full team."

"Friend and Balfour?"

Thane nodded.

"Two minutes," promised Dunbar, spinning on his heel.

They made it in less.

CHAPTER SEVEN

As a city, Glasgow is a place where a considerable part of the population still goes along with the Victorian edict of "early to bed, early to rise."

Not many of her citizens are outstandingly healthy, wealthy and wise, as the rest of the verse promises. But it is a practice which provides a useful, frequently blessed watershed for the police. Give or take a few exceptions, it means that after 11 P.M. anyone still out and about can be slotted into a few specific categories.

There are night-shift workers, fellow-sufferers with whom any cop can relate. There are party people, usually homeward bound. If they are in a car, with a woman driving, they are married and the woman won't fail a breathalyser test. There are men who have been sent out to walk the dog.

Anyone else could be a potential criminal.

All of which is sound, practical policing in the eyes of any citizen who has ever been vandalised or mugged, robbed, raped or knifed, or been forced to identify his or her religion by a mindless gang of young drunks.

It meant, specifically, that most of the city's traffic lights were controlling almost empty junctions by the time the two Crime Squad cars reached Graduate Street. They drifted to a halt some distance from number forty-two, joining the many other cars already parked at the kerb for the night.

Graduate Street was on the fringe of Northern Division territory, on one side of the University hill. Francey Dunbar knew it, had even lived in it for a spell. Most of Graduate Street was made up of large old houses long since converted into modest hotels or student hostels. The hotels catered to elderly permanent residents; the hostels were places where students ate, slept, swopped tips on how to fiddle pre-payment electricity meters or learned the art of persuading a telephone dial to give you a ten-minute call to Australia for free.

But number forty-two was a modern maisonette block, meaning five storeys of brickwork with garage parking, an elevator, garbage chutes, a fringe of grass the letting agents called "secluded gardens," and high rents to match.

Colin Thane was in the lead car. Only a few lights still showed at the windows of the maisonette block, which made the task ahead fractionally easier.

"We're going in quietly," he warned the men with him. "If Friend and Balfour are here, we take them with as little fuss as possible—and we make sure they're here before we start."

"No misfires," murmured Francey Dunbar.

It could happen. The wrong house raided, an innocent couple startled in bed, howls of protest that were a gift to any local politician and meant a carpeting for the officers concerned.

There was another, purely practical problem.

"Joe." Thane glanced round at Joe Felix, the middle man of three in the rear seat. "Francey thinks the main door could have an electronic lock."

"I've got my kit," said Felix confidently. "But how about the apartment, sir? Jimmy Friend on drugs means it could be a steel plate job."

They all knew what he meant. Drug addicts and pushers often sheltered behind reinforced doors, the kind that would delay a raid long enough for any drugs they possessed to be safely flushed down a lavatory.

"I brought the Big Key," said Dunbar. The Big Key was one of the Squad's standard issue ten-pound sledgehammers.

"Then let's do it." Thane opened his car door.

Both cars emptied; no-one had to be told anything more about what to do. Two men departed for the rear of the building; two more would take position in the entrance hall as soon as they were inside; the rest would go up.

A mail truck drove past, the only vehicle moving in the street. At the entrance to No. 42 a lurking tabby cat arched its back then made a dignified retreat.

"Joe." Thane beckoned Felix forward.

The heavy glass door was closed, a steel panel beside it housed call buttons and a two-way speaker grille, and the lock was an electronic security type.

Humming under his breath, Felix considered the door for a moment then opened the small canvas bag he was carrying. He took out a metal box which had a meter and two switches, positioned it carefully, then flicked a switch. The box gave a soft hum, the meter needle bounced as power flowed to a transistorised electro-magnet, and there was a loud click as the door's security lock sprang open. Felix grinned, switched off, and put the box back in his bag.

Thane first, the others following, they went into the brightly lit lobby. The elevator was in front of them, doors open.

"Nice place, sir," muttered the hulking figure at Thane's side. The Animal, temporarily divorced from Linda Belmont, had been at a loose end. He looked around with a degree of admiration. "We're getting a better class of criminal these days."

Someone chuckled, then they waited. Francey Dunbar had used the stairway, going to the floor above. They heard a doorbell, a soft, brief murmur of voices, then he hurried down again.

"The way you were told it, sir. Newish tenants, top floor left, Bridges on the door—two men and descriptions match."

Six detectives were enough to cram the little elevator. The nearest pressed the top button, the doors closed, and they went up. When the doors opened, they spilled out on a carpeted corridor. Moving silently, Thane checked the apartment doors. Top floor left had "Bridges" on a small white-on-black plastic nameplate.

He stood for a moment. There was no sound of any kind coming from inside; the next step was his responsibility if anything went wrong.

"Key it," he ordered curtly.

The Animal had the sledgehammer. Positioning himself, he gave the long wooden shaft a practice twitch then swung. The ten-pound metal head slammed the keyhole with a noise like an amplified drumbeat and the door burst open, flying back on its frame. There was no steel lining, the lock had vanished, and the hammer's head was trapped in splintered wood.

Francey Dunbar was first through, into total darkness. Nothing moved, the others crowded in, someone tripped and cursed, and someone else found a switch. An overhead bulb lit the tiny lobby.

The man who had tripped took a quick step backward. There was a dead man at his feet, shirt-sleeved, sprawled on his back in a pool of congealed blood. Most of his nose had been destroyed by a bullet as it drove a path into his brain. Staying clear of the blood, Dunbar knelt beside the body then looked up at Thane.

"Jimmy Friend?"

Thane nodded. The dead man matched in height and build and hair, and in what was left of that face.

They found Inky Balfour in the living room. He had fallen across a couch, shot through the back of the head. He was dressed in a bright blue rollneck sweater and grey trousers. Death and the way he had fallen had twisted his face into a near comical expression of surprise. Like Friend, he had been dead some time.

"Well, at least we can stop looking for them," said Dunbar bitterly. "That's always something."

There were voices outside in the corridor, some alarmed, others querulous. The dead men's neighbours had begun to emerge.

Thane ignored them, even shutting Friend and Balfour from his mind for a moment as he looked around. The living room had been ransacked, left in a chaos of cleared shelves and emptied drawers. The back of the TV set had been removed, the carpet had been turned over, and pictures had been torn from the walls. Nothing had been overlooked.

They checked the other rooms. It was the same situation in every one —whatever he was trying to find, the killer had searched everywhere with an obvious cold determination which had taken a lot of time.

But had he found what he wanted?

"Call it in, Francey," said Thane wearily. "Our people and Northern Division." He heard the voices in the corridor growing louder and pursed his lips. "Soothe these people and get them back where they came from." He glanced at the rest of his men. "Let's get started."

They left the Animal guarding the broken door. Nothing short of a tidal wave would get past him. Then they got down to work.

The first arrivals were from Northern Division, beginning with a patrol car crew then two C.I.D. men, rising steadily in rank after that and culminating in the tall, ginger-haired shape of Detective Superintendent Havergall, the divisional C.I.D. chief.

Johnny Havergall took a jaundiced view of what he found. He'd been happily at home, watching a pirate video tape seized in a raid. He wasn't wearing a tie; he didn't like smashed doors, dead bodies or a team of Crime Squad heavies turning up unexpectedly on his patch.

"It's damned uncivilised," he complained.

"Next time I'll send invitations," snapped Thane.

They glared at each other for a moment then Havergall was the first to give a wry, resigned grin.

"All right, mark my card on it," he said. "Who are they, what have we got?"

Thane told him and Havergall sucked hard on his lips. He looked around again at the ransacked chaos.

"Stupid question. Can we rule out robbery?"

"Yes." Thane took him into one of the bedrooms. A money clip filled with banknotes was lying on top of the dressing table and a gold bark-finish ID bracelet had fallen on the floor. The mattress had been dragged off the bed. Stepping round, Havergall grunted as he saw an emptied wallet and a scatter of credit cards lying behind it.

"Goodbye, robbery," he agreed. "Any luck with the neighbours?"

"No."

Joe Felix had taken on that job. But almost all of the tenants of the Graduate Street block were business or professional couples, out during the day, their homes left empty. They knew nothing; they'd seen nothing. The one exception was an elderly woman on the second floor, disabled and housebound. But she lived with her television set at permanent full volume.

Havergall sighed. "Well, I'll start stirring the rest of the pot. Anyone done the garbage chutes?" He grimaced as Thane shook his head. They both knew it had to be done. "All right, I'll put a couple of my lads on it. Divisional C.I.D. always get the dirty jobs."

The specialists and the other inevitables started to arrive. The Scenes of Crime team took photographs, prowled with tweezers and plastic evidence bags, began puffing fingerprint powder in all directions. A mortuary wagon joined the growing clutter of vehicles outside, the crew content to wait and share a flask of coffee until they were summoned. The duty police surgeon appeared. He was young, new to the job, and flustered at being late.

"Calm down," soothed Havergall sympathetically. "We're not complaining, they're not complaining—there's no problem."

Everyone cleared a path for the next two arrivals. Jack Hart had turned out, and the big, heavy-faced man with the Crime Squad commander was Buddha Ilford, the Strathclyde A.C.C. Crime. Jimmy Friend and Inky Balfour were being given full honours.

Havergall was nearest the door and was Ilford's immediate target.

Seeing them talking, Thane made to come over but Jack Hart warned him off with a slight headshake. It was a moment for diplomatic protocol; Ilford wanted to hear the story from his own man.

At last, Ilford came over with Hart and Havergall close behind. He considered Thane with a stony lack of approval.

"So—you've had your tail caught in a mangle on this one. Any chance you know who turned the handle?"

"Not yet." Thane made himself remember that Ilford had been his boss before he was posted to the Crime Squad, would be his boss again when the posting expired.

"Give him a chance," murmured Hart with some sympathy. "I told you how things stand."

"They don't stand this way too often, thank God." Ilford mellowed a little and looked around. "How do you read it, Thane? That they were killed because someone wanted them out of the way?"

Thane nodded. "Then he made sure he wasn't leaving anything behind that mattered."

Ilford grunted. "Any luck with papers, documents?"

"Not yet."

A Scenes of Crime man went past nursing a plastic evidence bag.

"Anything from them?" asked Hart.

"Nothing that matters." Havergall took the question. "It looks like we can forget fingerprints. They say the door handles were wiped, that most of the obvious touch surfaces seem the same."

Ilford uttered a low-grade obscenity then he and Hart went off on a brief inspection tour. They returned together.

"No apparent sign of a break-in—at least, not before Thane and his wrecking crew arrived." Ilford pursed his lips. "That has to mean someone they knew." He glanced hopefully at Hart. "Any suggestions, Jack?"

Hart shook his head. "It's still the way I told you. We're certain these two killed Mary Dutton, but any further and we're floundering."

Ilford grunted. "You go along with that, Thane?"

Reluctantly, Thane nodded.

"Then we'll talk politics." Ilford looked at Thane and Havergall. "Commander Hart and I have sorted this out, accepted priorities. Strathclyde will front things here—present it as a straight double murder being handled by Northern Division. That means no mention of Crime Squad involvement, no mention of the Mary Dutton link. That means

Northern Division handle the local legwork, Crime Squad stay with the wider picture." He shrugged. "It may make no difference or it may protect the little we've got, leave whoever did this feeling happier. Understood?"

"What about the media, sir?" asked Havergall gloomily. "Who'll handle them?"

"I will." Ilford bared his teeth in a humourless grin. "We know Friend used drugs. What's wrong with an off-the-record hint to a couple of reporters that there could be a drugs-related angle in their story—a dealer-pusher style fall-out? They'll grab that."

"Anything that keeps them off our backs." Jack Hart frowned as the police surgeon made a diffident approach. "Finished, Doc?"

"Yes." The young medical man looked slightly pale. "Move them when you want."

"And?" asked Hart.

The police surgeon hesitated.

"He means can we presume they're dead?" asked Ilford sarcastically.

There was still a hesitation. "One of the sergeants says this is linked to the Mary Dutton case."

"Which sergeant?" Thane sighed as a glance went across the room towards Francey Dunbar. "What difference does that make?"

"Anything linked with Mary Dutton has to be referred directly to Professor MacMaster—"

"God has spoken," said Havergall. "You sound like you're scared of him."

"Not scared, terrified." The police surgeon gave them a weak smile. "So—anything I tell you—"

"Won't be used in evidence against you," said Ilford. "MacMaster isn't here, I am. Get on with it."

Even junior police surgeons knew the A.C.C. Crime by reputation.

"I'll tell you what I can. Cause—apparent cause of death, gunshot wounds in each case. Apparent time of death approximately noon today in each case—that's based on body temperature and general stiffness." His medical bag was still open and the police surgeon closed it with a decisive snap. "I'll contact Professor MacMaster. I think he'll want to take personal charge of the post mortems."

"You said noon." Thane held him by the arm. "You're sure of that?"

"Yes." The police surgeon managed to free his arm and made a quick escape.

"Noon," said Hart in a flat voice.

At noon they placed Magnus Thornton in Aberdeen. At noon, Thane had been talking with Barbara Thornton and Peter Crossley. Estimated time of death was anything but an exact science; there were any number of factors including body weight, clothing, temperatures and air currents that could cause minor variations. But if it had been noon, or any time around noon—

"There's more than your tail in that mangle, Thane," said Ilford cruelly. He glanced at his wrist-watch. "Coming, Jack? It's time I fed the media their poisoned corn."

Hart nodded, gave Thane a shrug, then A.C.C. Crime and Squad commander left together. Havergall relaxed with a sigh and turned to Thane.

"Not your night?"

"It's been that way." Thane needed time to think.

"Praise be it's your end of the deal." Havergall turned away as one of his men came over. He listened to the man and brightened a little. "I've hauled in the landlord. Let's see what pearls of truth he can produce."

The plump, well-dressed, middle-aged man waiting in the apartment lobby was anxious to explain he wasn't the landlord. His name was Planter; he was the property management agent and the owners lived abroad.

"But you arranged the let of this apartment?" asked Havergall.

"Yes." Planter moistened his lips, pretending not to watch as the mortuary attendants arrived and started to ease Jimmy Friend's body into a black zip-fronted plastic body-bag. He had a precise, almost prissy voice. "Not to—ah—that gentleman, though we met. I dealt with his friend, Mr. Bridges."

"Come through," invited Havergall.

Planter went with them, saw Inky Balfour's body still sprawled over the couch, and shuddered.

"Yes—that one."

They took him back into the hallway.

"Did you ask them for references?" asked Thane.

"No." Planter winced as the body-bag's zip rasped shut, enclosing

Jimmy Friend. "But they seemed to meet our requirements. I—they took an initial three-month lease. It was due to expire."

"When?"

"Next week." Nervously, Planter went on the defensive. "Naturally, I reminded them, but they said it didn't matter, that they weren't interested in an extension because they were leaving."

Havergall frowned. "Going where?"

"I didn't ask." Planter had a more important worry on his mind. "This will bring a lot of bad publicity for the block. I suppose there's no way of avoiding it?"

Thane shook his head.

Planter sighed. "That won't help me find new tenants, will it?"

"Who knows? If you're lucky, you might pull in some weirdo—black drapes and bongo drums," suggested Havergall unfeelingly. "How did this pair pay?"

"The three months in advance, cash."

"Did you ever hear anything about them from the other tenants—complaints, trouble of any kind?" asked Thane.

"None." Planter was positive. "Everyone seemed to find them acceptable. Perhaps a little—ah—withdrawn, reserved. But—"

"Acceptable," said Thane dryly.

It matched anything else they'd heard from Joe Felix's tour of the neighbours. Jimmy Friend and Inky Balfour had been hardly known, hadn't encouraged any kind of approach, and there was only a vague impression from some people that they might have had occasional visitors.

"Thanks, Mr. Planter," said Havergall briskly. "One of my people will see you out to your car."

Planter frowned. "What about the damage to the door, the mess in here? Who'll pay for that?"

The two detectives looked at him, saying nothing, Havergall smiling a little. Swallowing, Planter turned and went away.

"Sod him," sighed Havergall. "Well, what's left for tonight?" He gave a slightly puzzled frown at the closed black body-bag near their feet. "This one was supposed to be into drugs, right?"

Thane nodded.

"Yet the best we've found is some aspirin in the medicine cabinet." Havergall shrugged. "Anyway, I'll extend the door-to-door routine in the morning—the rest of the street and anywhere else that might be useful. If you need more, let me know."

The mortuary wagon attendants had moved into the living room. Thane could hear them working straightening Inky Balfour's body enough to get it into a second body-bag. The Scenes of Crime men were still moving around but they'd be gone soon, heading back to base to collate what they'd gathered, type initial reports, fill in their overtime sheets. Then, if MacMaster was conducting the autopsies . . .

He saw Havergall was waiting patiently.

"Tomorrow," he agreed.

"Good." Havergall was glad. "I'll hang on for a spell, then leave a couple of the troops behind as night watchmen."

Thane left him and went into the living room. Francey Dunbar was watching the mortuary wagon men finish their task.

"We're pulling out," Thane told him. "Home—pass the word."

"To everyone?" Dunbar gave him an odd look.

"Yes. I'll bed down in my office—" Thane stopped. It was 2 A.M. Sandra Craig and Jock Dawson would still be sitting in their car in that patch of trees. "Everyone, Francey. Including Sandra and Jock—you tell them."

"Sandra will be in one hell of a mood," said Dunbar ruefully. He yawned. "What about tomorrow?"

"We'll start early." There was one thing he wasn't giving up on. "I'll arrange another car to be in position at the Thorntons' cottage from first light."

From habit more than anything else Thane took a last walk around the apartment then left it and went out into the corridor. The mortuary wagon crew were there, waiting on the elevator, the two closed body-bags on folding trolleys beside them. They greeted him affably, their night's work almost done.

"But I'll tell you this, Superintendent," said the nearest, taking another stab at the call button. "There's no way you'd get me dying in a place like this." He sniffed. "Architects! You'd never get a decent coffin into this size of elevator—not even on its end."

The elevator arrived.

Thane changed his mind and took the stairs.

The duty officer at Headquarters had to be briefed, but after that Thane had a few hours' sleep in the folding camp bed which normally stayed stowed in a cupboard in his room. When he wakened, it was a grey, drizzling dawn of a Friday, which reasonably matched his mood.

He kept a spare razor, a clean shirt and a new pair of socks in the bottom drawer of his desk. As far back as when he had walked his first Glasgow beat, he'd learned that fresh socks mattered in a cop's life. Going along to the washroom he showered, shaved, and dressed. By then it was 7 A.M. when the Squad canteen began serving breakfast.

At that hour it was still deserted. He saw Joe Felix at a table, exchanged a nod, then Thane went to the counter and ordered orange juice, a bacon sandwich and mug of tea. The counter waitress had a transistor radio tuned to Radio Clyde and the duty disc jockey was trying to make the local weather forecast sound happy.

It wasn't. As the music took over again, Thane carried his breakfast across to join Felix. The plump detective constable was eating his way through a mountain of scrambled eggs and had Friday's morning papers scattered beside him.

" 'Morning, sir." Felix grinned at him. Felix could be insufferably cheerful. He also usually ate breakfast in the canteen because his wife was a night-shift hospital technician. They were a contented couple who claimed that being apart so much kept them together.

"Anyone else in yet?" asked Thane.

"Jock Dawson." Felix chewed another mouthful of scrambled egg for a moment. "He took his dogs for a walk."

"Anything happening?"

Felix shook his head. "All quiet. The car at the Thornton cottage is in position—no sign of movement there yet." He used the handle of his fork to stir his mug of coffee. "What about Crossley, sir?"

"He's on today's list, once I know the rest of it."

Thane lapsed into silence, sampling his way through the newspapers while he ate. The double shooting at Graduate Street had broken late for the news desks; only two papers had managed to give it any kind of real space on their front page, and both carried an "exclusive" tag on the suggestion of a drugs connection. He smiled a little. Buddha Ilford had pulled his strings.

It was harder to find any mention of Mary Dutton, but it was a morning when there were other attractions. There was a new international crisis, a new economic crisis, and a real-life scandal, with pictures, of what a TV actress of dubious age had said to a bishop of dubious political outlook. Detective Sergeant Mary Dutton rated an inside single-column report of "enquiries re-opening" in one paper, only a brief mention in the rest.

Things could have been worse. He turned to the comic strips in search of some sanity.

Joe Felix finished his food, lit a cigarette, and went over to the counter for another mug of coffee. As he got there, the canteen phone began ringing and the counter waitress answered it. She handed the receiver to Felix, who listened, spoke for a moment, then hung up. Collecting his coffee, Felix ambled back.

"You've an invitation." He lowered himself into his seat and took a gulp of coffee. "That was someone at the City Mortuary. I'm to tell you MacMaster has practically finished both autopsies. He'd like you to look in."

"Now?" Thane regretted the bacon sandwich.

"That's the message, sir." Felix gave him a sympathetic shrug. "As long as you keep moving they let you out again, don't they?"

The City Mortuary was an anonymous brick building located like a halfway house next to Glasgow High Court and close to the River Clyde. A steady part of its throughput came from the river, and a considerable proportion of the High Court's trade had its roots in what happened inside.

Colin Thane got there shortly before 8 A.M. The same grey drizzle of rain was still falling, the morning traffic hadn't reached its peak, and Glasgow wore a drab face. He left his car close to the mortuary. MacMaster's old black Daimler limousine, like a hearse with passenger seats, was parked outside. Despite the drizzle, the patch of road under the Daimler's body was dry. It had been there a long time.

The main door squeaked as he went into the building. A cleaner using a mop and bucket looked up, recognised him, and muttered a greeting. Thane went past the man and down the tiled corridor, his nostrils under attack from the strong smell of disinfectant in the air.

"There you are, Mr. Thane!" An attendant, a small, plump gnome of a man, bustled out of a sideroom. "Nice timing—the Professor is cleaning up. I'll tell him you're here." He paused and winked. "Here, I've got a new one for you. What do you call a kid who eats his mother and father?"

"Tell me, Frank," said Thane resignedly. It was part of the ritual.

"You call him an orphan. An orphan—not bad, eh?" Chuckling to himself, the attendant crossed to a washroom door, tapped on it, and looked in. "He's here, Professor—"

MacMaster emerged. Clean-shaven as ever, still adjusting his tie a fraction against his collar, the thin, elderly professor wore a green linen hospital coat over his regular clothing. He looked fresh enough to be starting his day.

"Still raining outside, Thane?" MacMaster gave a twitch of a smile which made his dentures clack. "Never mind, I've something interesting for you—quite fascinating."

"Now?" asked Thane.

"Why not?" In a surprisingly good mood, MacMaster took him by the arm. "It'll only take a moment." He glanced at the attendant. "Frank, can you find us some of your excellent coffee?"

"No problem." The attendant grinned and left them.

"Not my ideal companion for a journey across the Styx," murmured MacMaster. "But his coffee is reasonable—provided he washes his hands."

Humming under his breath, something even more unusual, MacMaster led Thane along to one of the autopsy rooms. Pushing open the door, ushering his visitor in first, the professor went over to the steel-topped table in the middle and switched on the big overhead lights.

A sheet covered the body on the table but hugged the physical contours close enough to show MacMaster's subject lay face down.

"The man Balfour—cause of death, a gun-shot wound in the head." MacMaster spoke with a concise, clinical clarity but gave Thane a sideways glance. "You haven't found the weapon?"

"Not yet."

"I recovered the bullets. Both men were killed with a .38-calibre hand gun." MacMaster gave a small, secret smile. "Did—ah—you find cartridge cases?"

Puzzled, Thane shook his head.

"Then your killer must have taken them. You're looking for a .38 Walther automatic pistol—I think the magazine holds eight rounds."

Thane stared at him.

"You don't believe me?" Stooping a little, MacMaster carefully drew back just enough of the sheet to expose Inky Balfour's head and naked shoulders. "I'll try to explain."

"I'd like that," said Thane.

The blood had been cleaned away from Inky Balfour's head; his light brown hair had been shaved away from around the bullet wound near the base of the skull. Thane looked closer. A smudged tattooing of dark powder particles showed on the white skin around the puncture-like hole.

"Shot at close range?" He glanced up at MacMaster.

"Excellent—very close range," said MacMaster briskly. "Now let me show you it under infra-red light only."

He switched off the main lights, brought over a small hand lamp on a flexible cable, and held it close to the bullet wound. The infra-red glow settled on its target and suddenly the smudge had changed, had firmed, had become the clear outline of a pistol muzzle, a pistol muzzle with a distinctive foresight.

"Firearms aren't my field," murmured MacMaster. "But I have a certain basic knowledge. That foresight makes it a certainty, Thane—a Walther .38." He switched off the lamp, laid it aside, and covered Balfour's body again. "Have you seen anything similar before?"

"No." Thane moistened his lips. "Have you?"

"Only once when the result was quite so positive." MacMaster smiled benevolently. "It made a reasonable paper in the forensic journals of the time and this should make an interesting follow-up—I've taken photographs, of course."

"Of course." Thane drew a deep breath. "The gun was against his head?"

"In contact." MacMaster extended a bony forefinger and pressed it against Thane's temple. "Like this, otherwise the exhaust gases wouldn't have captured the muzzle pattern." He lowered his finger. "Coffee?"

They left the autopsy room and went along the corridor to a small office where Frank the attendant had left a tray with coffee and biscuits. MacMaster poured for them both, added sugar and cream to his own cup, and helped himself to a biscuit.

"Sit down, Superintendent." He waited until they were both settled. "Smoke if you want."

"I'm trying to stop," said Thane sadly. He leaned forward. "Professor—"

"What else can I tell you?" MacMaster sipped his coffee drawing-room fashion, little finger extended. "Well, I'll agree with your police surgeon that the approximate time of death for both men was roughly noon yesterday. I've seen his notes, I've seen the police photographs of the scene. Ah—would my opinion interest you?"

"That's why I'm here." Thane shook his head at the offer of a biscuit. "I need anything you've got."

"Even speculation?" MacMaster carefully set down his cup. "I'd presume both men knew and trusted your killer—"

"Trusted?"

"One hardly allows a potential enemy to stand close behind, close enough to suddenly put a gun against your neck." MacMaster chuckled. "At least, we wouldn't in the medical profession. So much for your man Balfour. His companion—"

"Jimmy Friend."

"Our friend Friend was probably out of the room, heard the shot, was surprised enough and foolish enough to run into the room, then tried to escape. He realised he couldn't, stopped, and turned in the hallway—perhaps to plead for mercy. Unfortunately, there was no dew falling from heaven at that moment." Pausing, MacMaster frowned. "That's as far as I think I can pursue the situation. I'd be happier dealing with fact."

Thane nodded and tested his coffee. It was worse than the Crime Squad blend.

"Were there any traces of powder burns on Jimmy Friend?"

"None. But space was restricted, the range could only have been a few feet at most. His murderer needn't have been an expert marksman." MacMaster stroked the rim of his cup. "When you make an arrest, I'd be interested in the clothing your prisoner was wearing—he or she, as the case may be. When the pistol was fired against Balfour's head there would be a pronounced leakage, a blow-back of powder residue and perhaps other material. Shirt cuff and jacket sleeve—we might even find some microscopic evidence of blood or human tissue."

"I'll remember." Thane took another token sip of coffee and got to his feet. "Thanks. I'll have to get back."

"Before you go"—MacMaster stopped him—"you'll recall the unfortunate matter of that first post-mortem report on Mary Dutton?"

"It's hard to forget."

"True." MacMaster clicked his dentures in acid agreement. "The individual concerned has now decided to withdraw from medicine. He agrees with me he might be better suited to a career in industry."

"Doing what?"

MacMaster shrugged. "Does it matter? His father owns the factory."

Thane said goodbye and left.

The same plump attendant was lurking in the corridor outside, ready to pounce.

"I've another good one for you, Mr. Thane," he said gleefully. "Have you heard about what happened when the Seven Dwarfs shared a bath?"

"Yes, Frank." It had been flogged around the duty room all the previous week. "Happy climbed out."

"That spoils it, Mr. Thane." The gnome-like face showed disgust. "Look, what you're supposed to say is—"

"I know," said Thane, cutting him short. "But I'm on Happy's side."

Feeling he'd won a small victory, he left the bewildered attendant and went back to his car.

The drizzle became a downpour on the drive out of the city, then suddenly died away. By the time the Ford turned in at the Police Training Area sign, there was blue sky overhead. When he left the Ford in the Crime Squad parking area, the puddled tarmac was beginning to steam in the sunlight.

Maggie Fyffe was lying in wait inside, with a summons from Jack Hart. Thane found the Squad commander at his desk, a tired man who hadn't had enough sleep.

"You." Hart gave him a jaundiced glare. "Colin, if you've any more little surprises ready, forget them. I'm two minutes in this morning and what happens?" He snorted. "I get Linda Belmont—that's what."

"She told you why?"

"Yes. This schoolteacher, Quanton." Hart leaned back in his chair and scowled. "You could have warned me."

"I meant to." But he'd forgotten. "I'm sorry."

"At least you were sensible passing it on—and I gave her the go-ahead. She's bringing him in." Hart sighed and thumbed at a chair. "Sit down. What did MacMaster have for us?"

Thane told him. Hart listened then swore softly and admiringly.

"The old devil—all right, it's a Walther .38. If he said it was a damned anti-tank gun I'd probably believe him. Do you buy the way he put the rest of it together?"

"Yes. Someone they knew and trusted—it fits."

"Someone." Hart nodded. "Have you spoken to Havergall at Northern Division?" He frowned to himself. "No, you haven't had a chance yet—and I can save you the trouble. I called Buddha Ilford. They've nothing fresh, Havergall and his troops are out knocking on doors, and Ilford says the next time you organise this kind of party do it outside his patch."

"I'll try," said Thane bitterly. "But the way I remember things I didn't volunteer. You handed me the Mary Dutton case."

"The Mary Dutton case—sir. I deserved that one." Hart's lined face twitched a slight grin, then it faded. "My real problem is we're stretched for manpower, Colin—really stretched. I've two target operations hanging fire, good ones, this morning the makings of a third has started to show." He sucked his lips. "If I'd sense, I'd ask Strathclyde to take over from you, totally."

Thane stared at him.

"Don't worry, I won't." Hart shook his head grimly. "She was Crime Squad, it stays personal." He straightened his back. "You still want to bring in Peter Crossley from the Peace Camp?"

"This morning, yes."

"Buddha Ilford's people can do it. We're extended enough." Hart made a note on his pad, then glanced up. "One other thing. There were two damned great dogs in the duty room a few minutes ago. I want them out, I want them kept out."

"I'll tell Dawson," said Thane neutrally. "What were they doing?"

"The dogs?" Hart scowled. "Eating somebody's damned doughnuts—just get them out. That's an order."

Thane went through to his office. It was already occupied. He found Francey Dunbar standing using the telephone and Alex Riney waiting in one of the chairs. Dunbar saw him, gave a grimace that could have meant anything, and kept on with the call. Riney, still wearing his rain-coat, greeted him with an embarrassed nod.

"I thought I'd come over." The plump, middle-aged Strathclyde fraud expert shaped an apologetic, lop-sided smile. "After last night—well, I've a vested interest. But if I'm in the way—"

"No. You're welcome." Thane flopped into his own chair. Dunbar was still using the phone, listening more than talking. "Anything new for us?"

Riney shook his head. "That's what I was going to ask you."

"If Friend or Balfour were holding anything that mattered, it was taken." Thane left it there as Dunbar put the phone down. His sergeant's face was a study in disbelief. "What's wrong, Francey?"

"We've lost the Thorntons—both of them," said Dunbar thickly.

Thane stared at him. "How? Wasn't that car—"

"We were there, sir." Dunbar swallowed. "Then along come the local vigilantes, a couple of stubborn, thick-headed farmers with shotguns, certain they'd caught themselves a couple of thieves on the prowl—they've had a spate of break-ins around there. So it was 'Out of the car, get your hands in the air'—" He leaned his hands on the desk and shook his head in despair. "By the time our people could make them see sense, the Thorntons had gone."

"Both cars—the white Jaguars?" asked Thane.

Dunbar nodded and tried to be optimistic. "Maybe they're just heading into town, to work."

"With our luck?" Thane mentally cursed all law-abiding citizens who owned shotguns. Alex Riney was diplomatically considering the view outside the window. "Put Joe Felix on it. Is Sandra in?"

"Yes."

"Send her through." Thane turned to Riney again as Dunbar went out. "You know we ran a check, to make sure there was no prison link between Peter Crossley and either Friend or Balfour?"

"I heard." Riney frowned. "I thought—"

"There wasn't. But I'm going to widen it." Thane brought out the Cheque and Credit Card collection of record photographs and spread them on the desk. "Friend and Balfour are out, but that still leaves eight."

"And it only needs one of them—yes, I'm with you." Riney scowled at his ample paunch then sucked his teeth. "We haven't stopped trying,

Superintendent. There was a moderately big kiting hit in Dublin last week, so we tried the Irish police. But they reckon it's a new home-grown team, we can't come up with anything else." Reaching across, he flicked the pictures of Balfour and Friend away and considered the rest. "Hell, I just don't know!"

"Who does?" asked Thane bitterly.

They sat in silence until Sandra Craig came into the room. She was wearing bleached-out denims and a laundry fresh cream shirt, her red hair had been brushed to its usual gleam, but she was another one who looked as though she hadn't had enough sleep.

"Good morning." She gave Alex Riney a slight, courtesy smile then glared at Thane. "If this is about Jock's dogs, sir—"

"No. Just keep them out of the commander's sight."

She subsided a little. "Then if it's last night—"

"When you were left howling at the moon?" Thane shook his head. "My fault, I've said sorry. Now I've a job for you—right?"

Sandra blinked. "Well—"

"These people." Thane swept the eight record pictures towards her. "These are yours. Check if any of the men could have served time with Peter Crossley."

"I always get the interesting work." Showing no particular enthusiasm, Sandra began to gather up the photographs. Then she stopped. They heard her give a stifled gasp.

"Something wrong?" asked Thane.

"I—yes." Twin spots of colour flared on her cheeks; she stood staring at one of the photographs. "This man. I saw him yesterday."

"Eh? Are you sure?" Alex Riney was up, peering over her shoulder. "Where was he?"

"At the airport." She bit her lip, glancing at Thane. "He was with Magnus Thornton. They—I thought he was just someone Thornton met on the flight down from Aberdeen."

Thane stiffened. "Alex?"

"We know him. He's one of the best." Riney shook his head and almost sighed. "John James Tannick, except everyone calls him The Major. He can act the ex-officer well enough to fool the real thing, he plays the credit card racket like it was set to music."

"Oh God," said Sandra miserably.

She handed Thane the photograph. The Major had lazy, mocking eyes and a fleshy face; he was looking at the camera with a studied, upper-class contempt.

"He was an army cook for a couple of years," said Riney. "They threw him out because too much food was leaving by the back door."

"Sandra?" Thane said her name quietly.

"I'm certain." She bit her lip. "They were together till they left the terminal building. Then Thornton collected his car."

"And Tannick?"

She shook her head. "I don't know. I think he took a taxi."

"Start at the beginning." A wild, barely possible notion stirred in Thane's mind. "You went out with Jock Dawson, you were there when the Aberdeen flight touched down. When did you first see Thornton— more important, where?"

"He was with Tannick, in the terminal lobby, leaving like the other passengers."

He frowned, thinking of the airport layout. "Did you actually see him come out at the main domestic gate?"

"No." She was puzzled. "That's too open, he knows me—he could have spotted me. I stayed farther back, where I could watch the exit doors."

"Where was Jock?"

"Outside the terminal, waiting in our car."

"Suppose Thornton wasn't on that flight, suppose Tannick was the passenger and Thornton met him?" He saw the protest forming on her lips and stopped her. "I mean it."

"There's a men's room almost opposite the main gate," murmured Riney, beginning to understand.

Thane nodded. "Well, Sandra?"

"It could have been that way, sir." She gestured miserably. "I'm sorry. But he was booked on the flight"—her eyes widened—"unless, you mean maybe Tannick travelled as Thornton?"

"Why not? Who asks for identification on a booked domestic flight?" He slid the photograph of John Tannick, otherwise the Major, across the desk towards her and wished they'd had one of Magnus Thornton to go with it. "On your wheels, Sandra. Get back out there, and if you find anyone who says Tannick was on yesterday morning's flight to Aberdeen, I'll buy the rest."

Hastily, she gathered the photographs, turned to leave, then hesitated.

"What about the check you wanted on the rest of them?"

"Dump that on someone else," he ordered. "You've got the part that matters most."

She nodded and almost ran from the room.

"I wouldn't particularly blame her," said Riney.

"I'm not," said Thane bitterly. "I fell for it."

"But"—Riney scraped a thumbnail across his chin, frowning—"yes, you're saying Thornton went to one hell of a lot of trouble to set up an alibi for yesterday? Down to meeting Tannick at the airport?"

"He had to do that." There had been Thornton's complaints about the Aberdeen weather, the casually dropped Aberdeen newspaper, the other small details he needed to polish his story."

But if Thornton hadn't been out of the city, if that alibi had been so important to him, then one immediate possibility shouted for a hearing—

He had to leave the thought as his telephone rang. When he answered it, Phil Moss's voice crackled over the line. He was using one of the Royal Infirmary pay phones.

"Why aren't you in bed?" demanded Thane.

"I'm on parole," said Moss. "And I've seen the morning papers—Friend and Balfour. You're having a rough time."

"It can only get better—I think." Thane managed a wry grin at the mouthpiece. "The first chance I get, I'll look in and tell you."

"Do that," said Moss eagerly. "But there's one thing I don't understand. What's this hint about a drugs angle? Did you find any?"

"No. That's Buddha Ilford's idea of a smokescreen."

"I wondered." Moss chuckled. "Hey, there's another reason I called. We've a new patient in the ward, brought in around midnight—you know him."

"Who?" Thane saw Alex Riney stirring, wanting to leave, but tried to be patient.

"Ratbag Monarch," said Moss happily. "He looks like someone hit him with a wall—several walls. He's a mess. One of yours, isn't he?"

"Yes." Rathbone Monarch had become Ratbag when he'd operated as a bogus charity fund-raiser, had switched to being a fence, had been one of Thane's regular, not totally trustworthy informers for years. Thane frowned, remembering something else. "What happened?"

"It seems he can't remember," said Moss sourly. "Isn't that sad? Somehow, I was thinking of your lady friend Brenda—"

Thane swore under his breath. It was regular gossip that Ratbag was left to fence stuff that Brenda had rejected, knew it, and didn't like it. Ratbag, like Brenda, had known he wanted any whisper that related to Mary Dutton's death.

If Ratbag had tried to score off Brenda by feeding her the story which had taken them to Jacko's Amusements, and if Brenda had found out—

Tank Mallard had been on his way to an "obligement" for Brenda.

"Colin?" Moss was waiting.

"Does it matter?" asked Thane wearily.

"Not to me," said Moss cheerfully, and hung up.

Thane replaced his own receiver.

"Phil Moss," he explained to Riney. "He's restless."

"They should tie him down." Riney got to his feet. "I'd better get back and do something useful."

"Wait." Thane stopped him without being totally certain why. "Are your people sure Jimmy Friend was on drugs?"

Riney blinked. "Yes. Heroin, but not in a big way. Though the word was his habit was growing."

"Then why didn't we find any?"

"Well—" Riney hesitated.

"Why?" Phil Moss's call had prompted the thought, and there was something wrong. "Would Jimmy Friend be likely to buy himself one fix at a time?"

"That's for kids in back-alleys," said Riney, dismissively. "He wasn't a needle freak, he 'chased the dragon'—you know, snorted. He'd have his stock, he'd keep it stashed, hidden—" He stopped and took a deep breath. "Hidden?"

Thane nodded and got to his feet. "Want to come along?"

Riney grinned.

They reached the duty room as Francey Dunbar was coming out.

"No luck with the Thorntons," he began. "Magnus hasn't showed at his office, Barbara told her staff yesterday that she'd take today off—"

"Leave it." Thane saw Jock Dawson loafing in the background, beside Joe Felix. Shoving Dunbar aside, he went straight over.

"Jock, I saw Goldie work on cocaine. How is she for heroin?"

"No problem," said the dog-handler confidently. "She did the full course."

"I'll give you a chance to prove it," Thane told him. "At Graduate Street."

CHAPTER EIGHT

They drove in a two-vehicle convoy to Graduate Street, Alex Riney travelling with Thane and Dunbar in one of the Crime Squad cars, Joe Felix using the passenger seat in Jock Dawson's Land-Rover with the dogs behind them giving an occasional excited bark.

The street outside the maisonette block was quiet. A solitary Northern Division car was parked outside; a constable in uniform stood like a doorman at the main entrance. Thane checked with the plain clothes man who was sitting alone in the Divisional car. Detective Superintendent Havergall had been called away; his men were working door-to-door farther along the street posing the usual questions and getting the usual answers.

He asked the Northern Division man to let Havergall know they were in his patch then went back to the others. Dawson had Goldie and Rajah out of the Land-Rover, each dog waiting patiently on a short leash.

"Both of them?" queried Thane.

"For company, sir." The lanky dog-handler eyed him seriously. "This is Goldie's line o' work, but she's young." He glanced up at the maisonette block. "A dog smells blood—senses atmosphere. I'd like Rajah with her."

"To hold her paw," suggested Francey Dunbar.

Dawson ignored him. "Then we cut down on distractions, sir. The dogs go in, I go in—you too, if you want. But anyone else waits on the landing till we're finished."

"Your dogs, your rules," agreed Thane. "Can we get on with it?"

They went in past the constable at the entrance. Thane and Riney took the elevator up first, then Dawson and Francey Dunbar followed with the two dogs. Another uniformed man was on duty at the broken door of the murder apartment and went through the routine of asking for identification. Then, eyeing the dogs with a puzzled interest, he stood back and was joined by Riney and Dunbar.

Thane pushed open the door and went in, switching on the light in the heavily shadowed lobby. A chalked outline and a dried stain of blood showed where they'd found Jimmy Friend's body. In the living room, another chalked outline and more dried bloodstains marked where Inky Balfour had been. The rest was a strange, unlived-in silence broken only by the soft clink of the metal in the dog's leashes as Dawson followed him.

"Need anything?" asked Thane.

"No. But I won't rush her." Stooping, Dawson unleashed both dogs. Goldie gave a slight whine. Her tail was down, and she began to back out towards the lobby.

"Easy, now." Dawson rubbed her coat, made soft clicking noises with his tongue, then glanced round as a low rumble began deep in Rajah's throat. "And you sit, you stupid devil. Stay with the boss."

The rumble became a grumble, but the giant black dog sat obediently beside Thane, watching. The yellow-haired Labrador bitch gave another short, almost questioning whine and Rajah gave a single, soft bark.

"Right." Dawson drew a deep breath, his manner changing. "Goldie —search."

The snapped command sent the Labrador forward, reluctantly at first, then showing a gathering enthusiasm. Dawson close behind, she began to prowl the room. She stopped occasionally, sniffing, then would move on again slowly and carefully. Completing the full circle, she totally ignored Thane and brushed past him.

"This room is clear. Will I move on?" asked Dawson.

Thane nodded. Snapping his fingers, the dog-handler led Goldie back out into the lobby and Rajah growled, shifting slightly. Without thinking, Thane reached down and scratched the German Shepherd reassuringly between the ears. The growl deepened then stopped. Suddenly a cold, damp nose briefly nuzzled his fingers.

"Nobody likes waiting," he agreed, looking down.

Minutes passed while he heard Dawson and the Labrador bitch continue their gradual progression. Suddenly there was an excited barking, a scraping, and Dawson shouted.

He found them in the kitchen. Goldie was standing on her hind legs, tail thrashing, front paws on a waist-high kitchen worktop, trying to get at a twin plug electric wall socket unit set flush into the tiles above. The fitment had been dusted with fingerprint powder; the lead for an electric kettle was plugged into one of the sockets.

"Move over, girl." Dawson shoved the Labrador aside, peered at the socket, then grinned at Thane. "I think she's right."

Never ignore the obvious—Thane watched while Dawson opened a drawer, took out a kitchen knife, and used it to poke between tiling and unit.

"The real thing too, not one of those fancy wall-safe units." Dawson levered with the kitchen knife then used his fingers. The entire socket unit, supply wires attached, came away from the wall and hung loose against the tiles. Reaching into the hole he'd exposed, the dog-handler drew out a small wooden cigar box. "Sir?"

"You found it, you open it."

Goldie began barking again. Rajah had padded through to join them. Setting down the box, Dawson produced a badly mashed chocolate bar from his pocket and gave each animal a piece. They settled, and he opened the cigar box. Glancing at Thane again, seeing no objection he took out a small, fold of paper, opened it, and touched a finger to the "fix" of white powder inside. He brought his finger up to his lips, tasted, and nodded.

"Heroin, sir. I'm no expert, but it's reasonable quality."

Thane tasted for himself. "Better than reasonable."

"He could probably afford it," said Dawson.

He took the two dogs out, back to the Land-Rover, and Francey Dunbar and Riney came in.

Thane had the cigar box unpacked. A dozen different credit cards, each with a fresh, still unsigned signature slip, had been held together by an elastic band. There were several of the paper-wrapped fixes and a small plastic bag with more white powder. Jimmy Friend had bought in bulk then made up his own requirements.

"The dreaded Dawson does it again?" asked Dunbar.

"Does it sweetly!" Alex Riney didn't hide his delight. "What else have we got, Superintendent?"

Thane laid two slim rolls of high-denomination banknotes on the worktop. Friend and Balfour had apparently believed in keeping an emergency fund handy. Frowning, he reached into the cigar box again and fished for the two small sheets of blue writing paper lying at the bottom.

It was one sheet, torn carefully in two, each half covered in a series of columns of closely written figures. Both had been written by the same neat, precise hand, both had roughly the same general shape, but the figures and the key letters beside them differed.

"Alex." He saw Riney hovering hopefully, gave him one of the sheets, then made another try at studying the one he'd kept.

It was no kind of arithmetic, didn't seem any kind of code. If it was anything, perhaps it was a timetable—but it was unlike any timetable he'd ever seen before. Numbers followed by letters, other letters followed by numbers, other numbers that could have been hours and minutes, or anything else.

"Oh God," said Alex Riney softly.

Thane stared at him. The Strathclyde fraud expert's round, good-natured face was pale; the pudgy hand holding his copy had developed a slight quiver.

"What's wrong?" asked Francey Dunbar.

"It's a crossfire," said Riney weakly. "A damned crossfire—nightmare size. They couldn't'"—he swallowed—"not on their own. But if this was just their share of it—"

Bewildered, Dunbar looked at Thane for help. But he felt as helplessly lost as his sergeant.

"What do you mean, a crossfire?" He caught Riney's arm. "What's happening?"

"What's happening?" Riney fumbled in his raincoat pocket, produced his cigarettes, and lit one. He drew on it deeply and let the smoke out in a sigh. "Ever play ring o' roses when you were a kid, or pass the parcel? Well, they're doing it with bank accounts and they could clear a fortune."

"They?"

"The rest of the team, whoever they are—wherever they are." Riney thumbed at his copy of the figures, now lying beside him. "That's one man's schedule. Your copy is different?"

Thane nodded.

"What's a fortune?" demanded Francey Dunbar.

The Strathclyde fraud expert gave a sour laugh.

"Make a guess, Sergeant. It could be a million, it could be less, it could be a damned sight more! And don't talk to me about bank computers. They only make it easier."

They stared at him in disbelief.

"Alex." Thane made it a plea. "Spell the thing out. A crossfire?"

"Let me sit down first." Riney left the kitchen. They followed him through to the living room, where he sagged down on the couch. Drawing on his cigarette again, he looked up. "This isn't easy."

"You try, we'll try," said Thane.

"Here's as simple as I can make it," Riney pursed his lips. "Your sergeant hasn't any money in his bank account—"

"True," agreed Dunbar.

Riney frowned. "He hasn't any money, but he gives you his personal cheque for one thousand pounds. You pay that cheque into your account in another bank and give me a cheque for a thousand pounds. I pay it into my account and give your sergeant my cheque for a thousand pounds—"

"Achieving what?" demanded Thane.

"Credit—money on paper, money that doesn't exist. Money we can play with for the two or three days it takes for each cheque to be cleared. Then nobody is out of pocket, the bank ledgers balance, the computers stay happy." The Strathclyde fraud expert shrugged. "A week later, we do it again. But I pay you, you pay your sergeant, your sergeant pays me —and so on."

"You're saying it happens?" asked Dunbar incredulously.

"Every hour of the day, Sergeant—in almost every country in the world," said Riney patiently. "Pass the parcel, keep it moving, and you're usually talking big money. Any time you want, I'll give you a list of firms that stay alive that way." He looked at Thane. "There's nothing illegal unless there's a deliberate intent to defraud."

"Suppose it breaks down?"

"Then some unhappy bank manager might as well jump out of a window." Riney paused. Most of his cigarette had burned away to ash and he tossed the stub into a handy vase then tapped the list beside him. "But if I'm right, this is different. You wanted a motive for murders, Superintendent? You've got it—a cash crossfire."

"It looks like a timetable," ventured Dunbar.

"It is, for one man. How many entries on your list, Superintendent?"

He counted. "Ten, then a break. Then another twenty-five. Spread over two days?"

"An afternoon and a full day," corrected Riney. "Thirty-five bank branches, one man. Seventy between them—go back to it being you and I and your sergeant. You hand his cheque across the counter, but you say you'd like half of it in cash, right now. They know you, you've done it before, there's been no problem. You walk out with the money. Thirty-five times, Superintendent—or say thirty, to be on the safe side. The odd bank manager could be awkward."

"How much?" demanded Dunbar.

Riney shrugged. "How big was the cheque, what size of account were you operating? You tell me, Sergeant—and even if these two are dead, how many more spokes are left in the damned wheel?" He turned to Thane. "Except maybe we can guess that now."

It was almost too big, too complex to grasp. Colin Thane felt his mind spinning as he tried to project Alex Riney's simple example, expand its complexities, accept its simplicities. He moistened his lips.

"The other eight on your list—could any of them have organised this?"

"No way. They're kiters, good front men, but this needed somebody with more brains than they've got put together, money-trained."

"We know someone," said Dunbar.

It had taken time; it had taken planning; it had meant gathering that team and a whole lot more—a hundred questions came flooding in behind that. Thane fought them back. They could wait.

"When?" he asked. "There's no day, no date—"

Riney picked up his list and shook his head. "The way things were between Friend and Balfour, they probably copied these from the original. So each would know what the other was doing, in case anything went wrong."

"When?"

"When?" Riney drew a deep breath. "Another guess, Superintendent? I think it started yesterday afternoon, I think today is the main effort, and I'll tell you why. Today is Friday, then you've the weekend."

"And Monday"—Francey Dunbar understood first—"it's a Public Holiday?"

Riney nodded. "The May Holiday. Every bank closed, it'll be Tuesday or Wednesday before yesterday's cheques get anywhere near being cleared through the system."

They heard footsteps, then Joe Felix came in. He glanced at Thane first, then at Dunbar, as if assessing the general mood.

"Something wrong, Joe?" Thane raised an eyebrow.

"Commander Hart called us." Felix trimmed his words to the minimum. "It's good and it's bad."

"That's our average," nodded Thane.

"He says Sandra struck lucky at the airport. One of the check-in girls identified The Major's photograph, says she's positive he was on yesterday's morning flight to Aberdeen."

Thane allowed himself a soft whistle of satisfaction.

"What's the rest of it?"

Felix shrugged. "We've lost Peter Crossley. The Strathclyde cops phoned from the Peace Camp. He upped and left in his car about nine this morning, no explanation to anyone."

"Anything else?" First the Thorntons, now Crossley—Thane was surprised at how calm his voice sounded.

Joe Felix shook his head. Very deliberately clearing his throat, Francey Dunbar thumbed towards the kitchen and Felix followed him out.

Going over to the window, Thane looked down at the traffic moving below. Good news, bad news—put them together and he still felt strangely relieved. Gradually, whatever the order, more pieces were beginning to fall together. There could still be surprises, but at least things were taking on a definite shape.

Riney had joined him.

"Clear thinking, discipline—you need both for a crossfire." Riney scowled with a grudging admiration. "Everything has to interlock. If this Thornton did the planning, Superintendent, it's quite an operation."

"Even without Friend and Balfour?" Thane kept his eyes on the view.

"He loses," admitted Riney. "You can't substitute faces on a crossfire —you need the personal touch at the bank counter." He shrugged. "Maybe he accepts that, maybe he'll boost some of the hits to compensate."

"Don't ask me to wish him luck," said Thane.

"No." There was something else on the Strathclyde man's mind. He sucked his lips. "When do you tell the banks?"

"The banks say, 'Thank you, but no, thank you.'" Commander Jack Hart sat secure and impassive behind his desk. "I've spoken to each head office, they've all got the same answer. They won't warn their branches, they'll let it happen."

"They're out of their tiny minds!" Thane was on his feet, unable to believe what he was hearing. It was almost an hour since he'd returned to the Crime Squad headquarters building. Every man and woman available had been drawn in to help—and now this. "You mean they don't care?"

"They care." Hart refused to be ruffled. "Sit down." He waited until Thane subsided. "Now listen, see it from their viewpoint."

"If they've got one."

Hart's lined face shaped a slight grin. "They have. Not just a viewpoint, a mutual code—it begins, no heroics and no hassle. You want to rob a bank? Go ahead. Bank rule number one is don't resist, give them the money."

"All right." Thane knew the code. Banks didn't like violence or shootouts, saw them as bad for business. They relied on close-circuit TV cameras, sophisticated alarms, and the police making arrests. "But this time—"

"This time, what have we got?" Hart leaned on his desk. It had been swept clear of paperwork, a sign of his own priorities. "Think of this city, Colin. It has more than three hundred bank branches inside its boundaries, then add another couple of hundred within an hour's travel by road. So we call it a million-pound crossfire—but where, when, are we sure of anything?"

Thane shrugged. "You know what we've got."

"I know—and you've tried," agreed Hart. "But they don't want panic, they don't want chaos, they don't want customers upset. I had to admit we couldn't rule out violence. What do you want them to do—shut their doors for the rest of the day?"

"You mean they want to keep their hides in one piece."

"Don't we all?" said Hart. "But that's how it is. Be glad. Do you think Strathclyde has a few hundred spare cops available to give them backup?" He gave a humourless chuckle at the thought. "So let's be practical. Work on what we've got."

There had been one new fact waiting when Thane had returned. The new Records check had paid off, they now knew that John Tannick, otherwise The Major, had served time beside Peter Crossley. It was another link, but where was Crossley, where were the Thorntons? That was the real effort, the search was on, but so far they had simply vanished.

"Those timetables." Hart was thinking aloud. "They're as dead as Friend and Balfour. But if there had been more detail—"

The kind of detail on the originals, originals that had to have been taken from Graduate Street by their killer—what they'd been left with was a skeleton outline, a code without a cypher.

Yet it still gave a pattern, based on how the two dead men had been intended to operate. The timings between hits indicated a lot of travel, that each of them would have worked several areas, not one localised group of banks.

"If it's Thornton, he's a damned good general," mused Hart. "He's making sure everything runs to schedule."

Thane nodded. That was one thing they could guess from the timetable. Every fourth or so timing was followed by the letter *B*. Return to base, check in at wherever Thornton was controlling the crossfire operation, maybe even unload the latest instalments in cash from the banks.

While more crossfire cheques flew around like snowflakes. . . .

"You know what I want to do," he said bluntly.

"Raid the Thornton cottage, raid their offices?" Hart sighed and half closed his eyes. "This isn't a Graduate Street situation, we're not talking active pursuit and known criminals. We need warrants, there's no way we'll get them."

"But—"

"I've tried," said Hart simply. "While you were still out."

"So what do we do?" asked Thane despairingly.

"Wait. Try punching a wall if you want—but not one of mine." Hart watched Thane get to his feet. "Did you know Linda Belmont and her Drug Squad pal brought in your schoolteacher? He—ah—appears to have been difficult."

"I heard." That, at least, was over.

"Resisting arrest." The Squad commander pursed his lips. "He denies it."

"They usually do," said Thane unemotionally. The schoolteacher had been brought in considerably the worse for wear, whatever had happened. "Any witnesses?"

"None," said Hart thankfully. "But for God's sake, I don't want it to become a habit."

Thane headed back towards his own room. Maggie Fyffe had left a note on his desk, in large capitals, YOUR WIFE PHONED. Which probably meant Mary had heard about the arrest on her clinic grapevine. Or maybe even from Katie direct.

He was reaching for the telephone when the door flew open and Sandra Craig grinned in at him.

"We've got Crossley," she said excitedly.

"Where?" He stiffened at the news.

"He stopped a beat cop in Central Division and gave himself up. He says he wants to see you—they're sending him out."

Delivered, Peter Crossley was taken straight to an interview room. He wore a wool shirt, corduroy trousers and a waterproof jacket, an outfit for the hills which made him look out of place in the city.

"Sit down," said Thane.

Awkwardly, Crossley took the chair on the other side of the narrow table. Jack Hart straddled another chair in the background, saying nothing, watching as the man nervously ran a hand through his thinning, sandy hair. A detective constable stood impassively at the door.

"We've got questions, you'd better have answers," said Thane curtly. "You understand me?"

"That's why I'm here," said Crossley in a shakily determined voice. "I"—he reached into one of the jacket's pockets—"well, Mrs. Thornton told me it was the only thing that made sense. I've got a letter for you."

"From her?" Thane stared at him.

Nodding, Crossley brought out an envelope. It was addressed to Thane in a bold hand, written in dark blue ink.

"Where is she?"

"Now?" Crossley shrugged. "I don't know. She said goodbye."

Thane glanced at Hart then grabbed the envelope and ripped it open. There was a single sheet of notepaper inside, in the same bold handwriting.

"Dear Superintendent Thane—to keep this formal . . ."

Forgetting Crossley, ignoring Hart waiting impatiently behind him, he read it through. Then again, more slowly.

"Peter will deliver this, I hope. Please believe that some part of his silence until now has been because I told him I wanted it that way.

"I think you know how things stand between Magnus and myself, that we haven't had a lived-in marriage for some time. But I have to set the record straight. I let you believe that Magnus and I were home together on the night Mary Dutton died. That was a lie because I didn't want to shout the truth—that I spent the night with someone else, somewhere else, that I don't know where Magnus was or what he did.

"Perhaps I had other reasons. They don't matter. Peter can explain some of them. Then I heard of the Graduate Street shootings on the radio and I know Magnus has a gun.

"Don't try looking for me. I sold my travel business yesterday, which is why we couldn't have lunch together. I have been thinking of leaving for some time, and part of the deal was a bundle of blank airline tickets.

"Wouldn't it have been good if we'd met a lot of years ago?"

It was signed "Barbara."

With a defiant flourish.

Silently, Thane passed the letter to Hart, let him read it, then eyed Crossley grimly.

"She says 'Peter can explain.' "

Crossley nodded.

"Start at the Peace Camp. She gave you your chance there, yet you were working behind her back for Thornton. Why?"

"Someone he knew recognised me, told him about me—"

"The Major?"

"Yes." Crossley's eyes widened.

"Then what?"

"I told Thornton his wife already knew about me. He—he said that didn't matter. That he could make things bad for me, frame me if necessary—and with my record, I'd be back in jail." Crossley moistened his lips. "I couldn't take that again, Superintendent. Not the way it was. But—but—I knew he could do it."

"Did you ever see him with a gun?"

"Yes." Crossley swallowed. "He stuck it under my nose once."

"What kind?"

"An automatic pistol. I think it was a Walther."

"Right." Thane paused as the interview room door opened. Francey Dunbar slipped in, closed the door, and signalled. Thane frowned and gave a quick headshake. "We know about the cabin, we know Thornton used it as a meeting place. Had you told Barbara Thornton what was going on?"

"Yes." Crossley nodded wearily. "I asked her to help me. But she said

I was to stay quiet, let things happen. That she'd make sure nothing happened to me."

"You believed her?" asked Hart.

Crossley spread his hands. "What kind of choice did I have?"

"Sir—" Francey Dunbar tried to break in.

"Wait," said Thane brutally. He glanced at Crossley. "Thornton's team—the people who met at that cabin. Did you know what they were planning?"

"I got a hint or two—from Thornton then from The Major." Crossley shifted uneasily. "It was some kind of bank fraud, according to Mrs. Thornton."

"How did she find out?"

"She went through Thornton's briefcase one night, found some papers—"

Thane stopped him. "Did Thornton's team have a meeting the night Mary Dutton was killed?"

"No." Crossley paled. "The only two at the Peace Camp were Friend and Balfour."

"So you did know them." Jack Hart leaned forward, puzzled. "What did they want?"

"A package I had for them."

"What kind of package?"

The man's shoulders slumped. "Friend used me like a post box, said it was a good arrangement because the Camp was so far out of town. He had this contact—"

"Drugs? His personal supply?" guessed Thane.

"Yes." Crossley's voice cracked. "But I meant what I told you from the start, Superintendent. I didn't know Mary Dutton was a policewoman, I didn't know she recognised them or anything else about that night—not even when I heard she was dead."

"But when you did find out, you kept quiet."

"Yes." Briefly, Crossley buried his head in his hands. "Damn them, damn them all. I cared, if that's what you want to know." He looked up. "But Mrs. Thornton—"

"Told you to wait," said Thane grimly. Francey Dunbar was getting more and more impatient, signalling frantically. "Do you know anything about the bank fraud, when it is, where it's happening?"

Crossley shook his head. "Mrs. Thornton phoned me this morning, told me to meet her in Glasgow. Then—" He shrugged, already lost in his own thoughts.

Thane glanced at Hart and saw the Squad commander had heard enough.

"Hold him," he told the detective constable at the door. The man tapped Crossley on the shoulder and led him out. Thane drew a deep breath as the door closed. "All right, Francey, what is it?"

"I didn't mind waiting—sir," said his sergeant with an indisciplined glare that didn't spare Jack Hart. "It's just an idea where you might find Magnus Thornton and his money-tree."

Hart's mouth fell open. Thane felt the same. They stared at Dunbar.

"What kind of an idea?" asked Hart dangerously.

"Sandra wanted to see the stuff we found at Graduate Street. For the first time, Thane noticed the small plastic evidence bag in Dunbar's hand. "She noticed it first—"

"Noticed what?"

"Exactly how Jimmy Friend had split some of his bulk heroin into fixes. The way he'd wrapped them in paper." Francey Dunbar enjoyed his moment. "Remember?"

Hart scowled. "Get to it."

"I'm trying." Dunbar's thin moustache twitched indignantly. "He'd done the usual, cut squares of paper to size, right? But they'd some kind of colouring, printing." He laid the evidence bag on the table. "We put them together."

There were half a dozen carefully flattened squares, placed like pieces of a jigsaw, with gaps to show where other squares were missing. But the result was part of a printed page and the reproduction of an old-fashioned portrait of a young, bushy-haired man dressed in black with a broad white ruffle at his throat and a floppy-brimmed black hat. It was strangely familiar, it teased at Thane's mind.

"Rembrandt van Rinj, a self-portrait. God knows how much the original is worth." Gently, Dunbar turned over the bag. The reverse of the page had another reproduction, a Virgin and Child. "That's your clincher—it's a Bellini."

Jack Hart chewed his lip. "Part of a catalogue?"

Dunbar nodded. "Go back to Graduate Street and we'd maybe find the rest."

"But you know." As he said it, Thane also understood.

"They're both in the Burrell Collection," said Dunbar very quietly. He turned to Hart. "We thought *B* in that timetable meant Base. But suppose base is also Burrell—the Burrell Museum?"

Hart looked dazed.

"Colin?" he asked. It was a plea.

"It could be," said Thane slowly.

The Burrell was within the city yet set in green fields. It had almost direct access to the city's motorway links, it had sprawling car parks, it had telephones and a restaurant, and thousands of visitors came and went every day. If Magnus Thornton had chosen it as his base . . . suddenly, and deciding it, he thought of the reproduction Tang horse in Barbara Thornton's office and the jibes Thornton had made about her father's collection.

"Could be?" Hart was waiting.

"Yes." Thane saw a grin split Francey Dunbar's face and was caught up in the same infectious conviction. "I'll buy it."

"It's yours." Hart straightened. "Crossley gave us the rest—you'll get your raids." He glared at them. "Don't just sit there grinning at each other. Do it. Or do you want some kind of a blessing?"

Sir William Burrell, a hard-nosed Glasgow-born shipping millionaire who died at the age of ninety-eight, had also been a magpie art collector. He'd bought anything he liked, anywhere in the world, if the price was right. That could have meant Islamic prayer rugs or Renaissance paintings, Etruscan craftsmanship or Japanese prints, stonework from a medieval chateau or a German drinking horn.

They had always been the best. He'd had them shipped home to Scotland in packing cases that might never be opened again.

There were eight thousand items in the collection he'd gifted to his native city, with typically hard-nosed conditions as to how they were to be housed. It took almost forty years for a bewildered Glasgow Town Council, elected politicians who knew more about football, to actually build the Burrell Museum. By that time, in 1983, the Burrell Collection was conservatively valued at £50 million—and there were still packing cases that hadn't been opened.

Within a year it had become Scotland's top tourist attraction. Package tours from North America, Europe and the Far East were and are an accepted part of the normal pattern. They came and they come to be bewitched by the majesty of the giant Warwick Vase from Hadrian's Villa at Tivoli, by stained glass which stands comparison with the Cloisters in New York, by tapestries rated next to the Victoria and Albert in London, by the unique and the beautiful from all cultures and all ages.

The Burrell is in the middle of Pollok Park, a sprawling estate of tree-lined drives, walks, fields and ornamental gardens located only five miles out from the centre of Glasgow. Its permanent residents include a herd of shaggy, long-horned Highland cattle, and its boundary walls hold at bay everything from high-rise housing to commercial developments and a railway line.

Any day it is a green, pleasant area of clean air which attracts its own visitors, quite apart from the steady flow heading for that new centrepiece, the long, proud building of red stone, stainless steel and glass with a main door which once belonged to an English castle.

The last hints of cloud had gone from the sky and the day was warm and sunny when the Crime Squad task force began to arrive. They'd drawn a deliberately motley assortment of vehicles from the Squad pool, including a minibus covered in stickers, a taxi, and an open sports car. They were "tooled up"—Francey Dunbar's phrase. When Jack Hart knew the opposition could be armed, he didn't hesitate to authorise weapons.

The Squad force, carrying .38 Smith and Wessons and concealed pump-action Savage shotguns, drove past the other world of people pushing prams or jogging. A school party picnicked in a field; a tennis court was busy; a group of old men were leaning on a fence. One of them waved.

They reached the Burrell Museum. The parking areas were filled with coaches and cars, and another area of ground had been opened to take the overflow. The Squad vehicles found spaces and then the crews climbed out. They spread out. On his own, Francey Dunbar headed through the castle archway into the modern complex beyond.

Colin Thane wasn't with them. His car turned off at a service road, travelled between trees and shrubbery, and stopped at a rear delivery door. His passengers, Joe Felix and Sandra Craig, got out and followed him.

The man waiting at the delivery door was willow slim and had long fair hair. His name was John Dempster, he was an Assistant Curator, and looks could be deceptive. He had a firm handshake and wore a tie which told the initiated he was a Royal Marines reserve volunteer.

"Superintendent Thane? Thanks for your telephone call. My boss and his boss are at a conference, I'm running the shop—which is my bad luck."

They went with him along a basement corridor to an elevator. It carried them up to the museum's administrative area and security room.

"We've a reasonable set-up." Dempster indicated a bank of television monitor screens with an operator sitting at a console. "Closed circuit cameras cover most of the galleries, then we've our own security guards, with personal radios. So how can we help?"

"Suffer us for a spell," said Thane. Joe Felix was setting up their own two-way radio, crystalled to the Squad frequencies. "We'll play it quietly."

"Good." Dempster grinned in relief. "Cops in a museum can be like bulls in a china shop—which isn't a very good joke." Sandra Craig was studying the monitor screens as they scanned the building and the Assistant Curator considered her with equal interest. "You said this was a 'maybe' situation. How soon will you know?"

"Very soon." Thane glanced at the clock above the monitor screens. The hands showed twelve-thirty. "Any time now."

Dempster raised a polite, puzzled eyebrow.

"Most banks close for an hour now, for lunch."

"And your little friends can also take a break?" Dempster sighed. "I hope they like our restaurant menu."

"They've had a hard morning's work—if we're right," said Thane grimly.

"Having to carry all that money—tiring," murmured Dempster. "Let me know when you're sure, then I can find some place to hide."

The console operator chuckled. At the far end of the room, Joe Felix was still fiddling with his radio and swearing under his breath.

"Trouble?" asked Thane.

Felix nodded and kept working.

The next few minutes dragged past. Briefly, laconically, Dempster gave them an outline of the building's other security systems. They were impressive, from the intricacy of sensors which guarded individual exhibits to the solid steel walls, sunk to floor-level by day, which could be powered up at a flick of a switch to protect the Burrell's full-length windows.

"But we don't carry your kind of back-up." He frowned towards Joe Felix, still working frantically at the radio. Felix's jacket hung loose; the butt of his holstered .38 was plainly visible. "Smith and Wesson?" Thane nodded.

"Reliable enough." Dempster wasn't impressed. "Not exactly new technology, though. Get your people to try the new F.N. nine-millimetre —thirteen-round magazine, nice grip."

"We're traditionalists," said Thane sarcastically. "What's your museum speciality—arms and armour?"

"No, ceramics and glass." The Assistant Curator gave a mock grimace. "But it's a long haul, Superintendent. In my field, to be any kind of authority you've got to be old or dead. I'm in no rush."

He stopped. The door had opened. One of the blue-uniformed Burrell guards ushered in Francey Dunbar then left again. For a moment Dunbar looked at them, his tanned, lean face impassive. Then he gave a slight grin and nodded.

"They've arrived."

"You're sure?" asked Thane softly.

"I've seen faces." Dunbar thumbed at their radio. "Haven't you heard?"

"Not on this," grunted Felix. "There's a problem."

"Kick it," suggested Dunbar. He looked at Thane. "It's certain. Magnus Thornton's car is at the back of one of the overflow parking areas. His white Jaguar—we couldn't raise you from outside."

"What about Thornton?"

"Jock Dawson knew him from the airport. He's here."

"But where?" Sandra Craig frowned at the monitor screens. "I haven't seen him."

"He went into the men's room," soothed Dunbar. He gave an amused glance at the monitors then asked Dempster, "You don't—uh—?"

"No," admitted Dempster. He turned to Sandra. "And of course, not in—ah—"

"I'm glad," she said, then tensed and beckoned Thane. "Sir—"

They had Magnus Thornton in vision, just walking into the view of the security camera covering the museum's main courtyard. He strolled towards the lens, a small attache case under one arm, talking to a plump, middle-aged woman wearing a tweed jacket and skirt.

"She's on the list," said Sandra, watching Thornton's narrow face shape a smile as the couple talked. "She does a farmer's wife routine—and she gets top marks."

Thornton and the woman moved out of the camera's range. Dempster nodded to the console operator, the monitor screen blinked, and another camera took over. The couple were walking down the length of a long, busy gallery.

"Oriental art," said Dempster. He winced as a security guard stepped aside to let them pass. "You're right, Superintendent—they're using the facilities, heading for the restaurant."

"Ever seen them before?"

"Here?" Dempster shook his head. "People come through in droves. If we remember anyone, there's a reason. Hell, it's not even as if we made an admission charge."

A sudden crackle then a muttered voice from the radio showed that Joe Felix had triumphed. He spoke to the voice, received a reply, and looked happier.

"Two more of them," reported Dunbar. "No, three now—" He pointed to another screen. "Where's that?"

"Medieval arts," said Dempster. He followed Dunbar's pointing finger, saw the three men he meant, and ran a puzzled hand over his long, fair hair. "They look—ordinary."

"They work at it." Thane beckoned Sandra to take over. "Any loose ends, Francey?"

"None." Dunbar shook his head. "Everything the way you wanted, and I did a head count on Thornton's team. You reckoned he could have eight—D.I. Riney's list. We've got seven of them, plus a couple of outsiders tagging along."

They watched the monitor screens, Sandra and Francey Dunbar quietly identifying more of Thornton's group, following them as they gathered in the museum restaurant. Another woman joined the farmer's wife at a table with Thornton then The Major appeared at the next table. Within minutes the crossfire gang were all present, scattered at different tables in twos and threes, having lunch, blending totally with the other customers.

"Joe." Thane had waited long enough. His hands were sweating and he rubbed them together. "It's a 'go' for outside."

Felix spoke briefly into his radio and a murmur came back. It meant the vehicle exits from Pollok Park were sealed, that the Crime Squad force outside were concentrating on the main entrance or filtering into the lobby area.

"Superintendent, how much trouble are you expecting?" asked John Dempster suddenly. He had lost his laconic air, his face was worried. "You haven't said, I'm trying to guess."

"That makes two of us," said Thane simply.

"How many ordinary, innocent people do you think are in this building?"

Thane could almost have told him. Every gallery section was busy with visitors. As he glanced at the monitors, a disabled woman in a wheelchair came into view in one screen. On another, a group of school-children were being herded along by a teacher.

"That's where you come in," he told Dempster.

"How?" Dempster stared at him.

"A small fire somewhere."

Dempster's mouth fell open. Then he understood.

"Very small?"

Thane nodded. "And we do the rest my way. Minimum risk, minimum damage."

"Damage?" The Assistant Curator forced a brave smile. "What's the odd Ming vase between friends?"

The museum's blue uniformed security guards had to be warned first, told to forget their usual emergency drill. Even with their personal radios, that took time. Thane sent Dunbar and Sandra Craig down to the lobby, to reinforce the Crime Squad detail, then watched with Felix as John Dempster and his console operator set to work.

"Here we go," said Dempster. "I'm breaking every rule in the book."

First the Burrell's fire alarm bells began ringing then, at a signal from Dempster, they stopped. Taking a deep breath, he used the Public Address system.

"This is a special announcement." His voice was cheerfully apologetic. "Sorry, everybody. This is not—I repeat, not—an emergency. But we have a possible small fire in one of the basement storerooms."

He paused. On the monitor screens, everyone had come to an indecisive halt, listening. Glancing at Thane, crossing his fingers for luck, Dempster launched on.

"For your safety, we ask you to leave. Take your time, don't worry. It could all be a false alarm. Don't be concerned as we take some routine precautions and please leave in the usual way, by the main door. Our staff will assist. I repeat, this is not an emergency. But please leave now."

He switched off the Public Address, nodded to the console operator, and the alarm bells started ringing again. A soft rumble sounded beneath them then as people began moving on the screens, the giant steel shutters emerged from the floors.

"Lights," ordered Dempster as the galleries began to darken.

The museum's overhead lights blazed to life. Anxiously, Dempster stared at the monitors.

"Any panic?"

Thane shook his head. But people were leaving, heading along the galleries and corridors towards the lobby and main door. Here and there a museum attendant was helping someone along, lips moving in a cheerful encouragement.

Even the restaurant tables were emptying. Some of Thornton's people had gone, including the two women who had been sharing his table.

"And your people are ready?" Dempster touched Thane's arm. "That lobby is going to be crowded, then when they spill outside—"

"They'll cope." Making some arrests from an emptying museum, even with the Burrell's popularity, was child's play compared with any cop's frequent Saturday afternoon problems in a football crowd. Thane's unspoken worry was different, the outside chance that there might be a struggle, that some outsider might be hurt. But compared with the alternatives, it was an acceptable risk. Out of the corner of his eye he saw the steel shutters begin to slot into their overhead locks. "How long to get them out?"

"This way, not using the emergency doors?" Dempster frowned and fingered his Royal Marines tie. "Five minutes should be enough."

People were beginning to appear in growing numbers on the screen covering the lobby. As they began to stream out, Thane saw Jock Dawson and the Animal ease from beside a kiosk. Nothing seemed to happen, but suddenly they were heading out through the main door with a figure sandwiched between them.

"We've started." He glanced along at the restaurant monitor, then frowned. Thornton's table was empty. But he was still in the area, that attache case clutched in his long thin hands. He was talking to The Major and they were the last people remaining. Suddenly Thornton turned and seemed to stare straight at the camera lens.

The two men moved, and they vanished from the monitor screens.

"We've some blind spots," said Dempster apologetically as the console operator punched buttons.

Both women had been picked up in the lobby. They were the only ones who struggled. Then the radio murmured again and Felix listened then grinned.

"Sandra says that's it—more or less. They're only short of Thornton and The Major."

"I'll go down with you," volunteered Dempster as Thane headed for the door. "I've a vested interest—my job."

The fire bells had stopped ringing. They went down a stairway which took them into the glass-roofed central courtyard, where young trees and greenery formed a background frame for the cracked marble glory of the Warwick Vase, almost nine tons of Roman craftsmanship which towered above their heads.

The courtyard was empty of life. Beyond it, the lobby was deserted apart from police and a handful of the museum's guards. They went over, and Sandra Craig came forward to meet them.

"Where's Francey?" asked Thane.

"Sorting out what we've got." She chuckled, the overhead lights glinting on her red hair. "They hardly knew what hit them."

"Anyone hurt?" asked Dempster anxiously.

"No visitors. One of Thornton's men tried to pull a knife outside. He got bruised a little." She smiled at him then turned to Thane. "Thornton and The Major, sir?"

"We'll have to flush them." He glanced at Dempster.

"The system was built to keep thieves out, Superintendent." Dempster shook his head. "It'll be just as good at keeping them in." He was still worried. "All the people who had to leave—"

"We've told them you've closed for the day. Most of them are heading home," Sandra soothed him. "Everything's fine."

Thane grunted. He wasn't so sure.

They heard a brief, high-pitched tone, then one of the museum guards answered his personal radio. He came over and spoke quickly to Dempster. The Assistant Curator brightened.

"Detective Felix says they've spotted someone on a monitor. He's in the Elizabethan room." He eyed Thane hopefully. "You'll need a guide."

"And you've still a vested interest." Thane nodded. "Sandra, you and a couple more."

There could be confusion in numbers. They waited until two of the Crime Squad men in the lobby joined them, then set off. Sandra had drawn her .38; Dempster stayed close to her. It wasn't too clear who was protecting whom.

It was strange, almost eerie going along the empty galleries with their paintings and portraits, their busts and hanging tapestries. Turning one corner, one of the plain clothes men gave a surprised gulp as he walked head-on into the full-scale figure of a knight in German armour.

The Elizabethan room was one of a series of period rooms, the last in line. They reached it, stopped, and suddenly Joe Felix's voice boomed from the public address system.

"Behind that old chest. The one to your left."

"It's Tudor," said Dempster absently.

They heard a feeble curse then a revolver clattered out across the floor.

"I'm coming out," said The Major urgently.

He rose, came forward with his hands in the air, and was quickly handcuffed.

"Where's Thornton?" demanded Thane.

He got no answer. Collecting the man's revolver, one of the Crime Squad men took The Major back the way they'd come.

The Public Address came to life again.

"No sign of the other one, boss," apologised Felix.

Thane waved an acknowledgement at the camera then faced Dempster.

"You said there were blind spots. You know them?"

Dempster hesitated. "Roughly."

"Roughly is good enough. Let's try them."

They set off on another lonely journey past the steel shutters, through an area of stained glass and showcased silver, their footsteps echoing on the stone floor. Wooden sculptures of angels smiled at them from a wall; a warrior's bronze helmet glared at them like a skull.

"Around here." Dempster slowed. "The Oriental section—this part, anyway."

They were surrounded by pottery and porcelain, elaborately carved figures and gleaming jade. A movement beside a large figure of Buddha caught Thane's eye and the glint of metal. He shouldered Dempster behind a pillar and dropped down as two shots rang out, their harsh reports echoing. A glass showcase splintered; the remaining plain clothes man with them gave a shocked yelp and fell, clutching his leg.

"Sandra—" Thane rolled round anxiously.

A hand gave a quick wave. She was on her stomach, sheltering behind a stone statue of some kind of animal. Magnus Thornton showed himself briefly, fired again, and a bullet whined off the steel shutter behind her. She fired back and Thornton dived away. Then there was silence for a moment, broken only by the grunting of the wounded plain clothes man as he dragged himself along the floor into cover, leaving a trail of blood.

Dry-lipped, Thane realised Dempster had vanished. He had his revolver out, rose to a crouch, waited until Sandra Craig had done the same, then signalled.

They started forward, slowly, carefully.

"I've got him," Felix's voice bellowed from the public address. "I don't know where you are, but there's a thing that looks like a coffin—"

A shot blasted. The security camera on a wall to their right disintegrated, but the gun had fired from their left. Another shot came from the same direction and grazed a great bronze bell with an awesome boom. Darting forward, Thane saw his quarry for a moment, triggered his revolver, and saw Magnus Thornton jerk as the bullet hit him in the shoulder.

But Thornton's Walther was pointing again and Sandra Craig was out in the open. Thane aimed.

Before he could shoot, something long and sharp-tipped flew across the gallery from a nearby doorway. Thornton screamed, staggered back with both hands clutching at the spear buried deep in his chest, then crashed down. His legs kicked once, then he was still, and a pale-faced John Dempster emerged from the doorway.

He was standing over Thornton's body when Thane and Sandra Craig joined him. The Assistant Curator gave them a weak twist of a smile.

"Thanks," said Sandra. She looked down at Thornton then turned quickly away. "My God. Where did you get that thing?"

"It's called a Partisan, sixteenth century, we've a collection—" Dempster saw she was shaking, stopped, and laid a hand experimentally on her shoulder. She didn't object. He looked at Thane and managed the same twist of a smile. "I had to do something. This could be one hell of an expensive shooting gallery. But—it's over?"

Thane took a deep breath and nodded.

He was wrong. But several things had to happen before he was told. First there was a rush of footsteps as Francey Dunbar led a would-be rescue party storming in on them. Then there was the necessary mopping up, the wounded plain clothes man to be carried to an ambulance, Magnus Thornton's body to be taken out—John Dempster making worried noises about the museum's spears then being led away by Sandra Craig.

Outside the museum, the rest of the crossfire team were waiting in a patrol van. The doors were open; Jock Dawson's two dogs sat on the grass watching them hopefully. Jack Hart had arrived with more reinforcements. But there was a strange scowl on the Squad commander's face.

"You've heard?" he asked.

Thane glanced at Francey Dunbar. His sergeant gave a wary shrug.

"I haven't had a chance yet, sir." He eyed Thane awkwardly. "You know we had Thornton's car?"

"Had?" Thane stared at them.

"Had," snapped Hart. "Except it was magicked out of the parking lot while you were doing that re-run of Exodus."

"There were problems," said Dunbar in a chastened voice. "We did find it—"

"Yes." Hart beckoned. Carefully avoiding Rajah and Goldie, he led them to his car and thumbed them aboard.

It was a short drive, to a quiet corner of the parkland around the museum. As the car stopped, Thane swallowed.

Two white Jaguars were lying on the verge of the path just ahead. One was Magnus Thornton's. The other—he swore softly as he saw the registration plate.

"Wife," agreed Hart.

They got out and walked over.

"She would have keys," said Hart on a tightly controlled voice. "She took her chance." His mouth tightened as Thane moved nearer to

Magnus Thornton's car. "Don't bother. She cleaned it out. Like—like emptying a damned bank. That's what it was—the whole crossfire take from this morning's little effort."

"Do we know how much?" asked Thane wearily.

Hart glared at Francey Dunbar in a way that would have shrivelled anyone else.

"Maybe three hundred thousand, in hundreds and fifties—that's what that bunch back in the patrol van reckon." He drew a deep breath. "We found yesterday's take in his office, just short of a quarter of a million. He used a blasted home computer to do his sums. They'd have gone for another quarter of a million this afternoon."

"We had the exits sealed." Thane leaned against Magnus Thornton's car, feeling suddenly weak.

"Sealed to vehicle traffic, with a string of complaints from here to hell and back," snapped Hart. "But who checked on people on foot?"

Francey Dunbar sighed but said nothing.

"So she back-packed it out?"

"And probably caught a bloody bus," agreed Hart sourly. "Well, you know her. Where do we start? The airports, of course. But—"

Thane didn't answer for a long moment. He was thinking of Barbara Thornton, hearing her determined voice, seeing her face, remembering the way she smiled. She had those airline tickets; she knew the travel world; she had been prepared to risk a lot more than he'd realised.

"I wouldn't know," he said truthfully.

He was almost glad. Maybe she'd be found; maybe she wouldn't. They could close the file on Detective Sergeant Mary Dutton's death; the banks could sort out how much they'd really lost in the crossfire plan and probably reckon they'd still been right to let it happen.

"Damn the woman," growled Hart, and turned away.

"Sir—" Francey Dunbar made an unhappy noise.

"Shut up, Francey," said Thane, and gave him a fractional wink.

"Yes, sir," said Dunbar dutifully.

There was a first time for everything.

About the author

The author of numerous novels and television scripts, Bill Knox is a popular and prolific mystery writer. His recent Crime Club selections include *Wavecrest, The Hanging Tree* and *Bloodtide*. A native of Scotland, Mr. Knox lives in Glasgow with his wife and three children.